MURDER
DURNOVARIA

Paula Harmon

January Press

Dedication

*This book is dedicated to my mother Christine with lots
of love and immense gratitude for all your help and
support especially when accompanying me as I
followed the Cohors I Durotriges round Dorchester one
very hot summer in the name of research.*

Dramatis Personae and Place Names

Dun & Gris	Grave-robbers
Lucretia	Rich woman
Tryssa	Wise-woman
Olivarius	Secretary
Amicus	Duovir
Max Hygarix Agricola	Prominent Durnovarian
Eira	Lucretia's first cousin
Deryn	Eira's brother
Berenice	Eira's daughter
Ieuan	Berenice's fiancé
Nia & Riona	Eira's slaves
Favorix	Augur
Contractes	Maker of magic!

Aquae Sulis	Bath
Armorica	Brittany
Durnovaria	Dorchester
Durocornovium	Swindon/Wanborough
Isca Dumnoniorum	Exeter
Isca Silurum	Caerleon
Lindinis	Ilchester
Moriconium	Poole
Pecunia	*Imaginary North Cardiff*
Sorviodunum	Salisbury
Vademlutra	*Imaginary Blandford area*
Venta Belgarum	Winchester
Vindoclavia	Shapwick/Wimborne

5

Durnovaria
South Britain
1st October 191 A.D.
Chapter 1: Diggers

The hand gestured in an unmistakable manner.

'Well that's nice,' said Gris. 'Charming.'

Dun leaned on his shovel and shrugged. 'Don't take it personal. He's bound to be annoyed.'

'Ain't my fault. I never put him there,' said Gris.

'If it is a him…'

'Of course it's a him. What sort of lady makes that sort of gesture?'

The hand remained rigid in obscenity, one protruding bony digit stabbing upwards while the remainder curled, half obscured by earth.

'Reckon we should tell the guard?' asked Gris.

'What's the guard gonna do about it? Be fair —' Dun nodded at the offensive hand, 'it's not like anything's gonna change his opinion on life … or, let's face it, death.'

'True,' said Gris. 'Wot you reckon? Bury him again?'

'Yeah,' said Dun. 'Save a lot of bother. The guard don't need to be bothered with a skellington. Probably bin dead an 'undred years anyway. Not like anyone will care.'

Gris dug up a shovel full of earth and prepared to tip it over the hand.

'Hang on a mo,' said Dun. 'Don't be too hasty.'

He peered across the field. Apart from a herd of cows, they were alone. To anyone watching from the ramparts of Durnovaria, they would just be muddy blobs in the distance.

'Wot?' said Gris. 'Wot you thinking? We oughta cover him up really. 'Snot respectful leaving a skellington in the open. His spirit might walk.'

'Yeah we will,' said Dun. 'But first, let's have a quick look-see. I think there's a gold ring on his pinky. Let's just check him over for things he don't need no more, then we'll bury him nicely. He won't haunt us then. We'll have some readies, he'll be back at rest and no-one need ever know. What could possibly go wrong?'

3rd October
Chapter 2: Lucretia

A lot had changed in forty years, but the journey to Durnovaria, if tortuous, was still beautiful. Probably.

By the end of the fourth day, Lucretia wouldn't waste the energy to peer out of the wagon. She burrowed into cushions as far as possible without messing up her hair, trying to work out which irritated her more; the incessant rain on the canvas roof, interspersed with heavier downpours as they brushed against low-hanging branches, or her companion.

Tryssa sat opposite. It was impossible to see properly now, but Lucretia knew that despite the dark, she was still sewing the same something she'd been fiddling with since they left the tiny town of Pecunia where Lucretia was the richest woman for miles and locals made out that Tryssa was the wisest.

Lucretia snapped for the four-hundredth time, 'If I'd known you were going to fidget all the way here I wouldn't have brought you.'

For the four-hundredth time, Tryssa replied without rancour. 'I would have been happy to come alone. You're the one who offered me a ride.'

'It would have been unneighbourly not to.'

'I'm paying you.'

Lucretia shrugged. 'Of course, it wasn't raining when I came this way last.'

'Ah yes,' said Tryssa. 'When you were in the first flush rather than a hot flush.'

'I'm still in my first flush, thank you,' said Lucretia. 'I'm just improved a little with time.'

'You mean you're more piquant. Or do I mean acidic?'

'Really Tryssa, I preferred it when you were silent.'

'No you didn't.'

9

Now their journey was nearly at an end, Tryssa finally put her handiwork down and gave Lucretia the attention she deserved.

Lucretia took care to look much younger than fifty-something. In her opinion Tryssa, who was the same age, took none. She wore the dullest of gowns, its only ornament an embroidered garland of ivy round the neckline. Greying hair framed her unpainted face with a wreath of braids from which curls escaped here and there, particularly over small ears from which dangled simple jasper earrings.

Lucretia, on the other hand, wore plenty of cosmetics and a fashionable wig. Her cheeks blushed with rouge, her eyes were smoky with kohl. She would have offered to improve Tryssa, but Tryssa would have smirked in her annoying way and cosmetics were too expensive to waste on someone who'd crack them by smirking.

It seemed Tryssa was about to unstopper her thoughts. 'I'm grateful for the lift, Lucretia. It would have been a trying journey in this weather without the wagon. But you still haven't told me why you're travelling to a town you once said you never wanted to see again.'

Lucretia cleared her throat. The top of the wagon brushed against a branch and what sounded like a cauldron of rainwater tipped and bounced on the canvas above them. Tryssa's stare remained steady. Lucretia felt like a winkle being contemplated by someone with a pin, and fidgeted until she recalled that the inside of a shell has a lot of hiding places.

'If you must know,' she said, when she felt the pause had been long enough, 'I had a letter from a friend of my cousin Deryn. Or at least, Favorix who ran in the same crowd when I was sent to marry him. Deryn, I mean.' Lucretia told herself to calm down. It didn't pay to lose composure in Tryssa's presence. 'You remember I was supposed to marry Deryn.'

'But didn't. And that's why you never wanted to go back.'

Lucretia squirmed. 'This seat is abominably hard. These cushions are no good.'

'It must have been a surprise to get the letter after forty years.'

'Favorix was a nice boy,' Lucretia answered, glad Tryssa couldn't see her screw up her face as she tried to recall what he'd looked like. Or been like. 'He wanted me to know my aunt had left me something substantial, and was afraid my cousins' letters might have gone astray.'

'Had they?'

'It seems so. I wrote to them immediately saying that I would visit the town to see Aunt Ursula and reminisce.'

'Instead of saying you knew she was dead?'

'Tsk.' Lucretia had never worked out why Tryssa never understood the benefits of being indirect. Perhaps there was a Roman in her ancestry. 'Eira was very apologetic. She was surprised I hadn't received their letter saying that Aunt Ursula had died and left me some coins, having heard - Minerva knows how - that I am but a poor widow -'

'Hardly poor. Couldn't you just have asked Deryn and Eira to send it?'

Lucretia rolled her shoulders. 'Favorix implied the legacy wasn't portable. Eira said it was just money. *Just* money. Ha. But she invited me to stay anyway. Perhaps she just wants *me* to take the risk of carrying it home on the road rather than them sending it, but somehow I think she and Deryn are trying to trick me.'

'What did she say about Favorix writing to you?'

'Why should I tell her?'

Tryssa shook her head. 'Ah.' She slid up the bench to peek through the opening at the front of the wagon. Lucretia could just make out her groom Ondi, huddled on the driving seat, discernible as a lump of leather trickling with water. He was conversing in low tones with their escort Olivarius, whose pony plodded alongside.

'How far away, do you think?' Tryssa called.

'Half an hour maybe, Mistress Tryssa,' came Ondi's voice. 'Tell my lady we're just coming up to some sort of *old place* and we can make out the ramparts up yonder despite the rain. Can you see them?'

Tryssa leaned forward and Lucretia heard her gasp before she came back into the body of the wagon and settled back against the cushions. 'It's so exciting. I've never been further afield than Isca Silurum before this week. Did you hear what he said?'

'I'm not deaf,' snapped Lucretia then shouted 'Hurry up Ondi!'

'Yes Madam.' The wagon jolted forwards and the clopping increased tempo. Ondi's voice could just be made out. 'That grove looks like it's watching us.'

A chuckle came from Olivarius. 'There's a beggar under the trees, that's all,' he said.

'I can't see one,' muttered Ondi. 'It's the *stones* watching. Or a spirit.'

Olivarius's voice called out. 'It's too wet to stay here. Have a *sestertius* and get on to the town.'

Maybe another voice called its thanks. Maybe it didn't. Lucretia shivered. It was getting cold.

'I hope that's his own money he's using,' said Lucretia. 'And not from the purse I gave him.'

Tryssa tutted, but as the wagon sped up she spoke. 'Durnovaria looks very impressive, and half the world seems to be trying to get in too. Can you imagine Pecunia like that?'

The thought of hordes of paying visitors arriving to gain the blessings of the spring on her land warmed Lucretia a little, and she smiled. Once her Aquae Diffis baths were bringing in outsiders, perhaps they'd put a stockade up and charge people to enter out of hours. Or in bad weather. Or in October. Or just anyway.

The idea made her relax a little. 'As I say, Tryssa, a lot of water has passed along the aqueduct. My cousins are *longing* to see me again. You wouldn't understand, perhaps, since the only relations you have are Corryx who travelled the empire rather than stay in Pecunia, and his wife whom you've never met. And they've now settled among the Durotriges despite knowing what they're like.'

'What are they like?'

'They suck up to the Romans, for a start.'

'You're engaged to Anguis and *he's* a Roman.'

'He's engaged to me,' said Lucretia. 'Different thing altogether.'

'Well,' said Tryssa, shrugging, 'should it turn out that your relations aren't clamouring after all, I'm sure mine can put you up.'

Lucretia found her beyond annoying, but the journey must be nearly over now. The road's incline changed and the two women found themselves sliding towards the back of the wagon. One of the wheels stumbled over some small obstruction and jolted Lucretia's head against an upright.

'In the name of Neptune and all things wet!' she bellowed, 'where did they teach you to drive?'

There was no response. She could make out the sounds of other wheels, other horses, greetings and curses.

'We must be entering the town,' said Tryssa.

'Not a moment too soon,' grumbled Lucretia.

The wagon lurched to a halt. Lucretia moved to the front, unlaced the cover and looked out. 'Ondi! Hurry up!' she snapped. 'Use a whip or something.'

Her slave took a deep breath before turning. 'Use a whip on whom, Mistress?'

They were wedged in a line of wet conveyances, riders and people on foot, trying to avoid treading on the muddy verge as they squeezed into the town. Worsening the rainy gloom, evening was descending, and everything had merged into a grey sludge of sodden creatures and muddy vehicles. Two men, one small and bent, his aged face creased like crunched-up parchment, and the other in his prime, his tunic bulging with muscle, appeared to be in their way.

'Nonsense.' Lucretia grabbed the whip from beside Ondi and flicked it. The horses jolted forward and reared, nearly knocking over the old man.

'Here,' said the younger one, 'what's the big rush, chaps? Still plenty of time before nightfall. I know it's a bit wet, but pushing won't help. Take things easy, and you'll be tucked up in the dry in no time. Where you bound, anyway?'

'Somewhere stationary with no fools,' said Lucretia. 'Ondi, do your job and get us through. Don't any of these people know who I am?'

'Important, is she?' said the young man in a stage whisper to Ondi. 'You gonna tell me who she is in a few simple words?'

'I can think of more than a few,' muttered Ondi.

'This is Lucretia Siluriensis and her ... friend Tryssa Doethion from Pecunia,' Olivarius declaimed over the top of the hubbub. 'She has come to visit her kinswoman Eira Junia, wife of Maximilian Hygarix Agricola.'

The old man approached the wagon and stared up with rheumy blue eyes. 'Lucretia Siluriensis, eh?'

'What of it?' sneered Lucretia. 'My cousin is waiting and we are late. Let us through or I'll report you both.'

'I remember you,' said the old man. 'A good many summers have passed since you were last here. You look older, but you still look like trouble. So ... come on through.' He slapped the horse's rump and stepped back. 'Things are a bit boring round here these days. Let's see if you can stir them up again.'

Chapter 3: Amicus

Amicus was ushered into his friend Maximilian's study.

Max was perusing himself with difficulty in a mirror. The rain and dusk outside meant little light was cast into the room and the lamp was guttering.

He was clearly proud of how he looked, with good cause. Both men, though now in their fifties, trained together in the gymnasium at the baths, their muscles firm, their stomachs flat and taut.

Max ran his hand over his face and head and sighed.

'Whyever did you agree to Lucretia's visit?' said Amicus. 'Haven't you enough to do, campaigning to be made duovir?'

'Then she'd probably have pestered to stay with Deryn. I dread to think what he'd do if he had to put up with her alone.'

'So why are you worrying about what you look like?'

'I'm getting old.'

'So what? It doesn't stop women looking at you. Are you wondering if your guest will find you attractive?'

Max pulled a face and dropped his voice. 'She *was* rather captivating.'

'Beautiful.'

Max hesitated. 'Captivating,' he repeated. 'I've often wondered … whether *she* wondered … oh never mind.' He picked up a hand mirror and tried to make out his features.

'Why does it matter what she thinks?' argued Amicus. 'You're a man of significance and power now. A god in your own home.'

'Whatever are you doing?' Max's wife Eira had slipped into the room. 'If your nostril hairs need plucking again, send for a slave. I'm not doing it.' The small dog clasped to her bosom yapped in agreement and smirked. 'Stop fussing, Max,' Eira continued. 'Lucretia won't notice. Will she, Nux?' She kissed the dog's head and noticed the other man. 'Oh good evening, Amicus. Can't you tell him there's no point in trying to look younger than he is.'

'I don't know what you mean,' said Max indistinctly as he attempted to investigate the inside of his nose. 'A man should be proud of his appearance at all times. I don't ask why you're wearing that dress.'

Eira's embroidered linen robe skimmed over a body slender as a willow. She was as lovely as she'd ever been. The few threads of silver in her dark braids seemed part of a hairstyle which incorporated small pearls. Her face was somehow more statue-smooth in her middle years than it had been in her girlhood. Barely a line creased around those unreadable eyes, blue as a still pool under calm skies. Amicus had known her since their youth, but had never been quite sure if her cool exterior hid a passion that she kept only for Max, or whether she was like ice all the way through. Whichever way, he was certain she'd have picked her dress for no reason other than because the fancy took her.

Without changing expression, Eira said, 'There's no point, Max. Lucretia is all but engaged to the decurion at Pecunia, who's at least ten years younger than you. And as I say, she'll never notice anyone she can't see in a mirror. She was never interested in anything but Lucretia and what benefited Lucretia. I don't believe for one moment she's changed.'

Max put down the mirror and cleared his throat. The glance he gave his wife appeared to suggest she should keep quiet in company, but she gave no indication of caring what he thought. The rain still poured outside and the sky through the high windows was dark. The lamp faltered and stuttered and its flickering light made the frescos on the walls come alive. Lovers romped and cavorted through trees and on river banks, or lay encoiled in each others' arms, their faces suffused with pleasure. They had presumably been painted to resemble Max and Eira in their youth. But if Eira's cold indifference was what happened when you'd been married for a long time, Amicus was glad he'd never found a woman he'd wanted to wed.

Now Max put his arm around his wife's shoulder and sighed. Nux growled a little and yapped.

'I chose *you*, didn't I?' he said. 'All those years ago, it was you I married.'

'Yes.'

'I didn't want anyone else to have you. You were the loveliest thing and you still are. But it's natural to think, "I wonder what Lucretia will make of me." I'd think that of anyone I hadn't seen for nearly forty years. Wouldn't you?'

'I'm not interested in the past and Lucretia won't notice me,' said Eira. 'She never did. I doubt she could describe me or tell you anything about me. All she wants is to argue about Mother. Anyway -' She slipped out of his embrace and kissed the top of Nux's head, 'she is very late. If she doesn't arrive soon there will be no time to bathe before dinner. Cook is becoming anxious.'

'The weather is atrocious,' Amicus pointed out. 'I imagine her journey has been appalling.'

'Precisely,' said Max. 'Cook can boil his head. Did you remember that Lucretia said she has no body slave accompanying her?'

'Of course. I wonder what the story is behind that. But no matter, I was thinking of selling Nia, so Lucretia may have her as a gift if she finds her pleasing during her stay.'

18

'I thought you found Nia pleasing.'

Eira shrugged. 'She chatters too much.'

The outer door banged and someone shouted down the hallway. A slave ushered in a man wrapped in a leather cloak, who stormed past and slammed the door behind him, almost severing the slave's hand.

'Max! Eira! Is that damned woman here yet?'

'Not yet, Deryn,' said Max. 'I expect she's been held up by the weather. Have some wine.'

'That won't help.' Deryn thrust his hood back to reveal short grey hair and piercing blue eyes under scowling brows. His tall frame was slender but wiry, as full of ambiguous potential as a coiled snake. He glared round at Amicus. 'What are *you* doing here?'

'I'm waiting to collect Lady Lucretia's escort Olivarius,' said Amicus. 'He's looking for a new position and I need a secretary so I'm putting him up. It's a chance to see if we're suited.'

'If he works for *her*, he'll be no good.'

'He doesn't work for her. But I'd give any man a chance to prove himself.'

Deryn grunted. 'I apologise. You're capable of making up your own mind about these things. But I'm still furious that Max let her invite herself here.' He accepted a cup of wine from Eira. There was no doubting they were siblings. Their features were so similar they might have been twins. And while on the surface their temperaments seemed different, Amicus suspected tributaries of the same secret river ran through both their souls.

'It was *my* decision to let Lucretia stay,' said Eira. Amicus saw a flicker of a glance between her and Max. 'Though I don't understand how she received word of Mother's intentions so soon. Who'd have thought news could travel to that bog-infested bit of nowhere so quickly? But somehow it did, so she'd have come

19

anyway. Better here where we can keep an eye on her than somewhere else. She *is* our cousin. What would people think if I turned her away?'

'If she spent two days with them, they'd help pack her bags and pay her to leave,' snapped Deryn. 'Mother's ashes are barely cold and here comes Lucretia to see what her inheritance might be. I'm telling you, she won't come here without expecting something more than she's due.'

'I thought your mother left her that grove,' said Amicus. 'I understood it was a bit of an insult.'

This time the exchanged glances were more obvious while at the same time, excluding.

'You can't just give away the old places, Amicus,' said Max. 'You've spent too much time with Romans if you don't understand that. If you don't want trouble, you leave sacred groves undisturbed. We were going to send some money to her instead. She'd needn't have known if some … someone hadn't -'

Deryn grunted again, the anger softened a little. 'I used to take Lucretia to that grove. She liked it very much, despite everyone saying it was haunted.'

'She probably felt right at home with the ghouls,' said Eira. 'But she won't want it now, you watch. She'll try to get us to give her something else.'

Deryn's face darkened again. 'If she'd desired our land so badly she could have married me like she was supposed to,' he said, decapitating a painted dryad on the fresco as his fist slammed into the wall. 'It's no good. I can't stomach meeting her today, but you can tell Lucretia from me - she missed her chance all those years ago and she'll get nothing more than Mother thought she should have.'

'Oh I shall,' said Eira, the tiniest of smiles curving her mouth. 'But I shall have fun first.'

Chapter 4: Lucretia

'Of course,' said Lucretia, selecting another olive and dipping it in garum, 'I can't pretend that Pecunia is ready to compete with Durnovaria, but Anguis Superbus and I are trying our best to put it on the map.'

'Isn't it on a map already?' said Max's daughter Berenice. A slight shiver ran through Lucretia, remembering the events which had unfolded when her niece said something similar a few months before, and then she shook her head before popping the olive in and munching. Adolescent girls were all idiots, it was as simple as that. No ghosts would dare to bother her.

Berenice was dimmer than Camilla by a long way, although of course she was a little younger, and a dumpling of a thing, curvaceous and trusting. Her eyes were as blue as Eira's, but nothing hid in their depths. Every passing mood was reflected in them. At the moment she was simply curious, and ignored her meal as she absorbed Lucretia's every word. It was very gratifying.

'Pecunia may be little more than a dot on the map at present,' Lucretia answered. 'It may be tucked into a depiction of forests, mountains and dragons along the road from Isca to Moridonium, but one day... one day Pecunia will rival Aquae Sulis.'

'Is there enough flat land that isn't a bog?' asked Eira, with a guileless smile. Lucretia slurped an oyster and observed her cousin. On the journey south she had tried to recall Eira from all those years ago when Lucretia had been sent to meet Deryn. But she simply had an image of a boring girl with unusual eyes who hid in corners behind a lot of messy hair. She seemed to have aged well. Perhaps that was the effect of sulking.

'There is sufficient, thank you,' she said. 'We may build a better temple elsewhere in the town.'

'I see,' said Eira, feeding a tidbit to the small brown unidentifiable dog who reclined between them. Lucretia had yet to see her cousin eat anything herself.

'I don't recall you having a fondness for rats,' she said.

Eira's lips narrowed very slightly and then something like a smile returned. 'Nux is almost a terrier. He was the tiniest of the litter. They would have drowned him, but I took him for my very own, didn't I Nuxikin?'

'Nux?'

'He's brown as a nut.' Eira kissed the animal's small misshapen head and Nux turned towards Lucretia and yapped. A slight odour emanated from him.

'He's brown as something,' muttered Lucretia.

'Are there really dragons?' Berenice interrupted. 'Have you seen one?'

'Not for a little while,' said Lucretia.

'I can lend you a mirror,' Eira offered, her face still neutral.

'I expect the wolves eat them,' said Berenice and took a sip of wine.

Lucretia wondered what would happen if Berenice met her cynical nephew Fabio. Perhaps she might suggest a match.

'I'm getting married,' said Berenice, as if reading her mind. 'Ieuan's very lovely. His family's land runs between ours and Uncle Deryn's. It's a shame Uncle Deryn couldn't come tonight but then he doesn't socialise a lot.'

That was one of the reasons he and Lucretia hadn't been suited, of course. She could recall him clearly: darker than Eira but with the same slim frame. He had been strong and wiry. Not a man to cross, they said. But he spoke so little, plodding along, hanging on her every word, clasping her hand, gazing into her face; and then

22

crying when she rejected him. Was that Deryn? Or was that Max? It was someone. Someone had cried like a baby when she'd spurned him. It had been both irritating and satisfying. Lucretia smiled, imagining herself standing on their fallen, weeping bodies like a mighty huntress.

'This wine you've brought is delicious,' said Max, breaking into her thoughts and raising his goblet to her. 'What a wonderful richness grows in your neck of the woods.'

'Full-bodied,' said Eira, taking a tiny sip and running her eyes along Lucretia's figure.

'Better full-bodied than insipid and thin,' said Lucretia, returning the gaze.

'You won't be disappointed in our wines,' Max assured her. 'We have a selection from vineyards right across southern Britain, as far afield as Cantabrigia and even fine examples from Gaul and Iberia. It's a hobby of mine. I believe your late husband was a keen disciple of Bacchus.'

'He worshipped a great deal in private,' said Lucretia. 'I had to hide the key to the wine-cellar in the end.'

'Oh dear,' said Berenice, 'is that what killed him?'

'No, but not for want of his trying.' Lucretia shuddered.

'Did a dragon from the forest get him?'

Dear heavens, the girl was fixated. Lucretia fixed her cousin's daughter with a blank stare and finally said, 'Not precisely.'

'You must be heartbroken without your husband,' Berenice continued, her blue eyes wide. 'I know I would be if I were separated from Ieuan. I hope I die first so that I don't have to be bereaved. Is that how you feel?'

'Oh, I miss him like I miss the sun when it sets in the east, like I miss the swallows as they head north for winter, as I miss the singing of my favourite pig at slaughtering time,' said Lucretia, wiping an imaginary tear and watching Berenice's lips move as she tried to work out what she'd heard. 'But I have better things to do than die.' How could she be related to this nitwit?

Lucretia pondered Max. Now in his middle years, he was definitely a handsome man. Tall and powerful, yet watching her from his couch with a puzzled smile. Well, no wonder. If one marries someone as passionless as Eira, one will be overwhelmed by the sight of a real woman. She smiled back and licked a little wine from her upper lip. It was good to be appreciated. Eira shifted a little next to her and Nux broke wind.

'I am glad that you are sufficiently recovered from your grief to be marrying again,' said Eira. 'When should we expect the happy event to take place?'

Lucretia summoned a slave and took a proffered pastry. 'We haven't set a date yet. There is no particular rush, and I would really like the new mosaic to be laid before I consider it. After all, that's partly why I'm here: to commission the finest design from the best makers in the Empire.'

'You had one for your last wedding, didn't you?' said Eira.

'Yes. But I always wanted another. A better one.'

'I'd like a mosaic for my house,' said Berenice.

'Berry, you'll be living with Ieuan's family for a while,' said Max. 'It will be some time before you have a house of your own.'

'But I want one.' Berenice's eyes sparked and she pouted. Nux yapped.

'Well, one day,' coaxed Max. 'I am sure Ieuan will have one built for you.'

'I want it outside in the countryside, outside the town. I want it on that piece of land you promised me.' It was disconcerting how the girl's mood had switched from amiable to sulky. 'Cousin Lucretia, you understand: a bride should get what she wants, shouldn't she?'

'It's not for discussion, daughter,' said Eira. 'You will get a house one day, but not yet. You are merely a girl and you don't understand about land.'

'I don't understand the fuss about it!' snapped Berenice. 'It's not a large piece. You can manage without it. It could be my dowry. It's just so pretty.'

'Well, it has a sentimental meaning for your father,' said Eira. 'And he will not be parted with it.'

Lucretia looked at Max with even more respect. There was nothing as important as land. The girl could have money instead.

'It's just a strip of land, Berry,' said Max. 'I can give you another. It's unworkable really, too many roots and rocks.'

'But it's so pretty.'

'Yes it is, but pretty land isn't always best for building on.'

'It's not fair.' Berenice flung her half-full platter across the floor. Nux leapt from Eira's arms and went to nibble the tumbled morsels.

'Maybe when you've been married a few years and have some children, I will reconsider,' said Max. 'But for now, I won't have your mother upset about this any more.'

'Everyone hates me!' Berenice rose and, nearly tripping over Nux, stumbled from the room.

'I apologise,' said Max. 'We shouldn't be arguing in front of our honoured guest.'

'Don't mind me,' said Lucretia. 'I've had a mind-numbing few days travelling here.'

'You had a companion though, didn't you?' said Eira. 'A friend. Where is she now?' There was something about the way Eira said the word 'friend' that suggested surprise. 'Tryssa, isn't it? She could have stayed here.'

'There was no need. Tryssa is visiting her brother Corryx and his wife.'

'Ah,' said Max. 'I had no idea they had a connection with Pecunia. I believe Corryx has to sail to Armorica shortly, so you may miss him during your stay. Not a time of year I'd pick to sail, but business is business. Galyna will be company for her, of course.'

'Galyna's an *interesting* woman,' said Eira. 'We must invite her and Tryssa here for dinner.'

'Don't feel you have to,' said Lucretia.

Eira glanced at her, and Lucretia felt the best option was to change tack. 'Going back to Berenice, I'm curious…' She was aware of Eira tensing beside her, but when she glanced sideways, her cousin was summoning a slave to lift Nux onto the couch since either the dog's legs were too short or the dog was too stupid to manage on his own. There was something in her face, however, a flicker in her eyes.

'You'll meet Ieuan soon,' said Max. 'But the wedding itself is two months away. I'm afraid you are likely to miss it.'

'That's a shame,' lied Lucretia. 'I'll be sure to leave a gift. However, I was actually curious about the land.' Eira rolled her shoulders and fed Nux an oyster. It was hard to imagine what would happen to his insides later. 'I'm not wondering why you don't want to give it away, that's quite understandable. I just wondered which piece of land it is. I'm trying to picture everything as it was and it's slowly coming back to me.'

'Oh, you must remember,' said Eira, taking another tiny sip of wine. 'It's a copse. Oak trees and rocks set in a circle. One or two are tumbled very slightly but the circle is almost intact. Just a gap for someone to go in - or something to come out. Who knows what would happen if they were disturbed? One doesn't mess with that sort of land, does one?'

Lucretia felt a chill run through her. Yes, she remembered. She remembered far too well.

'No,' she said. 'One doesn't.'

Chapter 5: Tryssa

'Lucretia still obnoxious?' Corryx stoked up the fire and returned to recline by his sister.

He'd left Pecunia to join the army as a boy and returned to Britannia as a citizen to trade in Durotrigan pottery. In the intervening years, he had come home when their parents died, and after that sent annual letters to the town scribe from wherever he happened to be in the empire.

'She's Lucretia,' she said with a shrug. 'Everyone else is a fool.'

Corryx grunted. 'The only good thing about Rhys dying was that you didn't have to put up with being related to her.'

'Darling,' murmured Galyna, placing a hand on Tryssa's. 'That's not a kind thing to say.' She was tall with a rich, melodic accent. Her hair was black, her skin light-brown, and her dark eyes were warm and friendly. Tryssa already felt as if they'd been friends for years.

'I'm sorry,' said Corryx. 'Rhys was a fine man. He should have joined up with me. And you should have come to live with us when I retired. It's not like I didn't ask enough times. You're wasted in a town run by a woman like Lucretia.'

'Technically...'

'Huh,' said Corryx, dipping bread into his stew, 'technicalities are nothing to a woman like her. If you took her to Rome, I daresay she'd run that too.'

'Couldn't do worse than our dear Emperor,' muttered Galyna.

'Well, she's presumably a little more -' Corryx glanced round the room to check there was no-one to overhear, 'sane.'

'It's true then,' said Tryssa. 'I'm always afraid the news has been mangled by retelling when we get it.'

Corryx pulled a wry smile. 'These are unsettled times. I need to trade while it seems calm. I'm sorry I need to leave you so soon, but I've a consignment of pots to take to Armorica and the weather is finally clearing. I'll have to go down tomorrow and oversee storage. Pottery and choppy seas are not good companions. I'm sure you can get acquainted while Galyna shows you the town. Besides, there's going to be a show in the amphitheatre, you can see that too.'

'Tell me about Durnovaria,' said Tryssa.

Galyna shrugged. 'I don't know that we can tell you much. We've only been here a few months. The forum is good. People are friendly. The worst thing is that Sila the wise-woman is very young and inexperienced. Her predecessor didn't train her very well.'

'If you don't think she'd mind, I could help.'

'I'm sure she'd be very grateful.'

'Apart from the women's stuff,' said Corryx, 'Durnovaria is peaceful and in a good location for trade. A few prominent families have the main roles on the Ordo, of course. There's a vacancy for duovir - Amicus Sonticus is the only one administering justice at the moment. He's fair - not the bribable sort. Our son Petros works for him as a senior guard. It's a good position. Not that there's anything in the way of crime here apart from the usual petty stuff. Your young friend Olivarius should do well.'

'What happened to the other duovir?'

'Fell off a horse and broke his neck during a race,' said Corryx. He looked up from his food and, catching sight of Tryssa's face, chuckled. 'Half the town saw it, including me. It wasn't remotely suspicious. Don't worry, you're quite safe here. No-one's going to drag you into a murder again. You can relax.'

Chapter 6: Lucretia

The low autumn sun seemed apologetic, slipping over the ramparts to lurk above roofs and warm the town.

It was going to take more than a day to dry everything out, but laundresses rushed to air clothes, street slaves grumbled as they swept mud and excess water along the gutters, cats slinked through the vapour rising from damp tiles to find the warmest to sleep on, and the forum thronged with people who had been trapped inside for days by rain.

Lucretia walked alongside Eira in relative silence, eyeing the loathsome Nux out of the corner of her eye. She had slept like a log, safe in the knowledge that there would be no travelling for at least a week. Now she was ready to see what Durnovaria had to offer.

Ondi followed, ready to carry purchases. He was having a conversation with Nia. Or rather he was listening to her. Lucretia had yet to hear him manage to finish a whole sentence.

'And I turned to him,' chattered Nia. 'I turned to him and I said, "well I'm not putting up with that. I may be a mere slave but then who do you think you are? The Emperor?" - Which emperor are we on? Caesar someone innit? I mean they're all called Caesar. Stupid, I call it. What if *we* all had the same name? - Anyway, so he turns to me and says, "Mind your lip, girl," just like that. I mean, how rude. Who did he think he was? Jupiter? I mean just cos he's the groom don't make him a god, does it? I mean, you're a groom, aren't you? Or are you a butler? You ought to be the butler. You've got the right look for one. Very smart. You talk funny, though. Are you from up north? I mean norther than where you live now. I mean really north. Not Hibernia though. You're not blue. I bet you

30

wouldn't talk to a girl like he did, would you? I bet you'd be really nice. Have you got a girl back in - where is it you're from again? No? Well, that's just a crying shame. A nice lad like you. You ought to have a girl. Haven't you any girl slaves in your place?'

'Well there's Blod, but well...' said Ondi.

Lucretia stopped in her tracks and turned. 'Ondi, perhaps you could go ahead and find ... something. I don't really care what. Just see what there is and come back and tell me.'

Ondi slipped into the crowds. The expression on his face was one unfamiliar to Lucretia. She suspected it might be gratitude.

Under Lucretia's glare, Nia dropped her eyes and made a small curtsey. 'Sorry, Mistress.'

'I should think so,' said Lucretia, turning her back and continuing the walk.

'Nia's a very good body slave,' said Eira, indicating the way forward. 'Aren't you Nia? After a while, one lets the wittering pass over one's head. She tends to stop when she's concentrating on something like hairdressing. Although then she chews her tongue, which is disconcerting. I am always a little worried she'll bite it off.'

'That wouldn't be such a bad thing,' muttered Lucretia.

'Aren't you worried your slave will run away?' said Eira. 'After all, he's a stranger here and he may not be looking forward to your return as much as we are, I mean you are.'

'Of course there's a risk,' said Lucretia. 'But if nothing else, his accent would give him away. He is after all, as Nia so rightly observes, from "up norther" than Pecunia.'

'Or perhaps it wouldn't. After all ...' Eira's voice trailed off. Now that Lucretia listened, she became aware that the streets buzzed with myriad accents as soldiers, traders, householders and slaves mingled in the sunshine. 'After all, this is a major town.'

'Ondi has been with me through thick and thin.'

'Alms, ladies?' They smelled the beggar sidling up before they noticed him. His frame was large-boned and wrapped in a ragged cloak so bulky he might have appeared fat, but for the scrawny arms that held out a bowl. His skin was both tanned and dirty, his fingernails black. He hobbled on feet wrapped in filthy cloth, but smiled at them as if they were old friends. Rheumy as it was, his right eye was the bluest Lucretia had ever seen, while his left was obscured by a deep purple scar running from his bald scalp to his cheek.

He thrust his begging bowl in her face and she recoiled. 'How revolting.'

The beggar focussed on her briefly and then on Eira. A frown flickered and was replaced by a wheedling smile. 'I bin sheltering up by them stones. Cold for the bones it is, but they talks to me, don't they? The gods will bless you if you bless me - see if they don't. Ask the priests -' He nodded towards the temple. 'They'll say so.'

'Away with you!' exclaimed Eira and stalked ahead, her twig-like shadow stark black on the pavement. As Lucretia rushed to catch up, she wished they had come on a litter after all, although there was very little room in the forum for such an item.

'It's disgraceful,' muttered Eira. 'Ladies shouldn't have to put up with such riff-raff. They shouldn't be allowed entry into the town.'

'Winter's coming, Mistress,' said Nia.

'No-one asked your opinion,' snapped Eira. 'And if you insist on giving it, I can ensure you join him. Would you like that?'

'No madam.'

Lucretia put up her chin and straightened her back. 'Beggars are something we don't have to put up with in Pecunia,' she said. 'It's a very ordered community.'

'If you say so,' conceded Eira. 'There must be some advantages to living in a backwater. Talking of which, is that your escort?' Eira pointed along the road. Olivarius was striding towards the forum at pace.

'Yes, it is.'

'He's very handsome,' said Eira. 'But I suppose he's poor and very young. You always preferred mature men, didn't you? How old was Porcius when you married him? Thirty? Forty?'

'Twenty-three.'

'But you weren't even twenty,' persisted Eira. 'Barely more than a child. You could have married Deryn who's only a year older than you.'

'Well I didn't,' snapped Lucretia. 'Perhaps, unlike you, I wanted to marry someone who had seen the world.'

'Did you ever find out how much Porcius had actually seen? It was his brother who introduced you, wasn't it?' Lucretia looked at Eira steadily, and after a pause, Eira cleared her throat. 'I'm sorry, Lucretia. I imagine you prefer not to think of his family now.'

'No.'

'Let's not discuss Porcius any longer.'

'I wasn't.'

Eira pulled a tiny moue and brought Nux up to kiss him. 'I apologise, Lucretia. Tell me about Anguis Superbus instead. Is he an older man too? Oh no of course, I recall now, he's a little younger, isn't he? And a Roman. Is it true that they all like things which have been preserved for some time? Like garum?'

Lucretia stopped at a stall selling carvings and picked out an ivory hairpin which seemed to represent a tall undernourished goddess. It looked remarkably like

33

her cousin. She wondered if snapping its head off would be considered sacrilegious.

She opened her mouth to say so and then thought better of it. She would be staying with Eira for at least ten days, and her cousin was confident in her own town and could help or hinder as she chose. It would be expedient to bury the hatchet, even if it might be necessary to imagine it buried in Eira's skull. Lucretia put the effigy down and smiled.

'We seem to have got off to the wrong start,' she said, tucking her arm into Eira's and only very slightly dislodging Nux. 'Perhaps I should confess now that I don't recall having a great deal to do with you when I was here all those years ago. Forgive me. I was just a girl, sent to marry Deryn and although we were the same age, you seemed younger. I fear I considered you nothing but a child, but you were an observant one, weren't you?'

Eira, eyes narrowed, but she dipped her head.

Lucretia bit her lip before continuing. 'I imagine when I refused Deryn, you were aware that he was … perhaps … upset.'

'He was heartbroken.'

'He was just a boy, Eira,' said Lucretia. 'And a few years later he found a wife, didn't he? Someone who was good to him.'

'Elli. Yes. She was a thousand times better than…'

'Perhaps,' interrupted Lucretia. 'But I was a just a girl myself, remember. I had no mother, no brother, a little sister to care for and my father was ailing. The family land would be mine to take care of. People in the town looked up to our family. No-one understood how hard that was for me. I sacrificed myself for the land. Everyone is always thinking of themselves. No-one ever considers whether *my* heart was broken.' She withdrew her arm from Eira's and hid her face in her veil. Through her fingers, she watched her cousin's face. It was as neutral as ever. Only the possible clenching of her jaw suggested Eira might be uncertain.

'As you say,' Eira murmured after a pause, 'we've got off to the wrong start. Let's leave the past in the past. Perhaps you're right to say that what Deryn felt for you was just calf love. He got over you - they all got over you - and as you say Deryn did marry. But then Elli and their baby died. He's never been the same since then.'

'So it wasn't my fault really.'

'Perhaps not.' Eira appeared to make a decision and a grimace that was as friendly a grin as Nux's bared teeth flitted across her face. 'Let's begin again. I'll show you round the forum and this afternoon Max will take us to see the mosaic maker. I'm sure after all this time you've forgotten everything about Durnovaria, and much of it has changed. Everything will be new to you, I'm sure.'

There was a great deal of truth in that. Lucretia scanned the forum, trying to recall how it had altered. There were people of all sorts from high-born to beggars, from ladies to louts. The best thing she could say about the low-born was that at least their dogs were proper dogs. She sneered at Nux just as Olivarius, approaching at speed, collided with Berenice who had wafted up with her slave Riona in tow. There was a flurry of apology and introductions and Olivarius bowed deep, kissing Berenice's fragrant hand as she giggled and simpered. Olivarius twinkled his ridiculous elf eyes at her. It was nauseating.

Lucretia opened her mouth to speak and then, looking over Eira's shoulder, her eyes widened. Coming alongside were a small neat man and two enormous slaves.

'How do Lady Lucretia, fancy meeting you here.' The man moved a straw around his mouth as he spoke and the bodyguard grunted something which might possibly have been a greeting.

Eira blinked. 'Good morning Contractes. Lucretia, I didn't realise you were acquainted with this, er… circus owner.'

'You're still making it sound flat, lady,' said Contractes, pulling a face of woe. He made a bow. 'I am conjuror of magic, spinner of dreams, weaver of tales! I'm bringing Durnovaria a show such as it has never seen! It will have songs, it will have dances, it will have tears of joy and sorrow!'

'It had better,' said Eira, 'given that my husband is paying for it.' She turned and stalked towards Berenice.

Lucretia hesitated, frowning. Why was Max going to the expense of putting on a show?

'Nly vnt gt no pssss,' muttered one of the bodyguards.

'Vnt gt no plt,' grunted the other.

'Minor problems,' said Contractes, waving his arm. 'Hope we'll see you there, madam. Only this time, can we keep the drama in the arena? Right lads! You know what we're after, let's go.' He marched off across the forum between his minders like a cat escorted by bears.

'Ooh mistress,' said Nia, 'if you go, can I go? I'd love to see the show. I don't mind if I have to sit on the top row. It'd be such a treat. Can I - ooh look who's coming!'

Lucretia turned to see Ondi heading back towards her. He was accompanied by someone in priestly garb who approached and bowed before raising her hand to his lips.

'Lucretia,' the priest breathed. 'You've barely changed. Your slave here came to the temple petitioning for a safe journey back to Pecunia, so I asked him to take me to you. Not returning too soon, I hope. I imagine an *unexpected* letter brought you here.'

Something about him dragged at Lucretia's memory. A lanky boy with an eager face full of freckles. Here was a tall man with a bald head and an expression like a dog who'd caught a rabbit.

'Favorix!' she exclaimed. 'You're greatly honoured in office, I see.'

'Indeed. I'm an augur.'

'I don't recall you foreseeing that as a young man. Does the knack for prediction grow as hair recedes?'

Favorix blinked, then chuckled. 'How wonderful that you're still as droll, my dear Lucretia.' He glanced towards Eira, who was making her way back with Berenice and Riona in tow, and dropped his voice. 'Meet me at the temple tomorrow,' he said. 'I need to speak with you urgently.'

5th October
Chapter 7: Lucretia

It felt like the old days when Lucretia slipped out of the house unaccompanied and unnoticed. Admittedly she wasn't doing it quite as early. Nowadays dawn was for other people and besides, in October sunrise is virtually lunch-time anyway. She felt somewhat naked without a slave at her heels and at the same time, somewhat liberated. The only beggar she could see was at some distance, making shuffling rounds of the forum and she climbed up to the portico without interference.

Favorix was lurked behind a statue biting his fingernails, his face blurred by the smoke of incense as he peered past her. A man being standoffish is alluring when he's twenty and vigorous. It really wasn't the same when he was sixty and balding. Not that she could recall finding him particularly alluring forty years ago. Just useful.

'I don't recall you visiting the temple when you were a girl,' he said as she approached. 'Perhaps you've developed an awareness of the infinite, a desire for the gods' favour, the...' His nonsense withered under her glare.

'I can't imagine there will ever be a day when the infinite, whatever that is, will concern me,' said Lucretia swallowing a pithier retort. 'The gods' favour however is another matter.'

She glanced beyond him. Another priest in a cloak, deeper in the temple, was peering about in the gloom. Lucretia stood a little straighter and returned her gaze to Favorix, putting her head on one side and fluttering her eyelashes. However, he'd slipped behind the statue again so the effect was wasted.

'Have you brought a sacrifice?' he whispered. 'Or merely yourself.' His voice seemed husky from the smoke.

Lucretia blinked a little. It was hard to make out his expression in the shadow of some lumping great god through a smoke of oil, incense and tallow candles. Was he making some sort of joke? A sort of huffing noise suggested he might be.

'I've brought a prayer,' she said.

'For safety, no doubt.' The augur's voice was solemn again. 'You seek to propitiate Justicia or perhaps Tranquillitas.'

'Who? Why?' Lucretia was startled.

'It's why you're here isn't it? To find justice and peace.' His words came out in priestly liturgical tones and she half-expected the priest in the shadows to make an answering chant.

'Really,' snapped Lucretia. 'You needn't try casting a spell on me, Favorix, I'm not giving the temple any extra money, and if other people do so on the basis of a stupid rumour then they're superstitious fools.'

Favorix cleared his throat. 'From what I've heard,' he said, his voice oily, 'you're banking on superstitious fools with your own endeavours back in Pecunia.'

'Diffis is an ancient goddess who had been neglected. I'm merely assisting her to receive the worship she deserves. This incurs significant expenditure for which she naturally considers I should be reimbursed. I thought in your position you'd appreciate that.'

'Of course, of course. How silly of me not to realise.'

She took a breath and composed herself. 'All that aside, here I am with money for a prayer to Juno - goddess of marriage.' She peered into the temple, willing the statues to identify themselves.

'Ah -' Favorix's hand was on hers. 'Come to the side a little and you can see inside the temple.' His arm slipped round her waist as they peered deeper into the gloom. 'There she stands imperious.'

Back in Pecunia, what they liked to think of as the temple was a small building in which lurked some local weather-beaten stone effigies of such antiquity that no-one was entirely sure whether they were supposed to represent humans, animals, or indeed gods, together with two Roman statues - one male, one female - which were expected to deputise for the whole of the pantheon in exchange for doves and small change. Durnovaria, as befitted a significant modern town with prospects, tried harder. In the half-light, idols looked down their noses with smooth orbs. Two of the females had spears, which narrowed it down a little. The bigger of the two had something draped over her shoulders less delicate than a stola. Didn't Juno, despite her seniority, wear a goatskin?

Lucretia's face struggled to stop her lip curling as she stared the goddess directly in her blind eyes. She wondered whether to shift out of Favorix's embrace, yet it was pleasant having an arm around her, even the wrong arm. Being steered was aggravating, but at least it meant she was unlikely to trip under the smirk of some bloodless deity.

'I'll take your coin for later,' said Favorix. 'Now, we must talk and we cannot do it here. Let me take you to Mother's - I mean, mine. Where's your slave?'

'I didn't bring one.'

'Quite like the old days eh?' Favorix's arm squeezed harder before releasing her. 'Can you keep up if I go ahead? We need to be at a slight distance.'

'If you think I'm following like an inferior you have another think coming. No-one will notice us. It's very

40

busy and the light is dull. I shall put up my veil and walk alongside with a decent space in between.'

***

Favorix's house was just as she remembered, although it had perhaps more glass windows and a different door. Lucretia felt anonymous. Without a slave she must look humble and less worth looking at. Any remorse was overlaid with a tremor of illicit excitement she hadn't felt for years.

Slipping inside the front door, she waited for that imperious harridan's voice that had once demanded from the main room: 'Where have you been, Favorix? Is that Deryn's country girl I hear? What's she doing? How could you leave your poor mother? You and your father - just the same!' Miserable old bat. But all she could hear now was a less than delicate snoring.

'You needn't worry,' murmured Favorix, leading her into a small study with a couch pulled close to a blazing fire. 'Mother is quite deaf nowadays and sleeps a great deal. We have the place to ourselves, to all intents and purposes.' He summoned a slave and demanded refreshments, then sat close to Lucretia on the couch. His mouth was so close to her ear his lips brushed it. 'You're still so wonderful. I'm so glad you understood the import of my letter. Together we could be rich - but we need to be careful.' His voice faded into a soft moan. Despite her better judgment Lucretia considered turning into his arms. A kiss, after all, is a kiss. She wondered how much an augur was paid by the state, and whether the stench of animal fat ever came off a priest's clothes or from his skin. At least Favorix hadn't enough hair to absorb it.

'Be calm,' she murmured, twisting just enough to touch his cheek. The candle grease on it must surely be imaginary.

'But -' His voice was still hoarse.

41

With a flutter of eyelashes, Lucretia squirmed out of his arms and moved to the far end of the couch. Men never did understand priorities: you need to scheme first and *then* get frisky.

'What is it you need to tell me, Favorix?' she said. 'I'm grateful for you writing to say I'd been left something. I'm still convinced Deryn and Eira had conveniently forgotten to write themselves. What is it you think is more worthwhile than the money they offered when I exposed their deceit?'

Favorix smirked. 'Land.'

'Land?' Lucretia pondered. 'That's odd. So they *are* trying to cheat me. Are you saying the money they're offering isn't to the same value?'

'What money?'

'What do you mean "what money"?'

'Who's offered you money? Deryn or Eira?'

Lucretia raised her eyebrows. 'It's immaterial, surely.'

'Is it?'

'Well, Deryn is rich and doesn't spend anything as far as I can gather, and Max is rich enough to finance a show in the amphitheatre to bolster his election chances. That's hardly cheap. The one in Pecunia last year cost the decurion a small fortune.'

'Has he paid, though?'

'Who? Anguis?'

'Max.' Favorix sat back with a smug grin half-hidden by clasped hands.

Lucretia contemplated him. He reminded her of a small child with a secret they can't wait to reveal, and she half-expected him to start jigging about. There was a time for games and a time for coming to the point. Favorix had never worked out which was which. Putting on a show could be crippling, but Max was rich. His daughter was betrothed to a rich man's son.

His lands and the lands Eira had inherited were fertile and he patronised a mosaic maker, claiming part of the profits. His house was well-appointed and his food lavish. But now she was less tired, Lucretia remembered Max as a youth, flush with cash one moment, the next with an empty purse, complaining that his otherwise indulgent father was keeping him short.

'Now you see it, now you don't,' said Favorix.

'Whatever are you talking about?'

'He's not doing as well as you think, desperate as he is to get votes. If he pays the circus, maybe he won't want to pay you.'

'Then Deryn can. Either way, it's better than nothing.'

'Deryn won't. He's hoarding his money to leave to Berenice. I think you deserve more than the paltry sum I daresay they're offering.'

Lucretia rolled her eyes. 'Well of course I do.'

'I thought we'd see eye to eye,' said Favorix, sliding along the couch to put his arm round her shoulders. 'You don't need some failure of a Roman stuck out in the sticks - you could move here, have me and -'

'Favorix!' A tremulous wail came from the other room. 'Where have you been, Favorix? Is there a girl in the house? What's she doing here? How could you leave your poor mother? You and your father - just the same!'

Lucretia wriggled out of Favorix's embrace and rose. 'I thought your father would be dead by now.'

'He is,' sighed Favorix. 'But Mother's forgotten. You needn't mind her. She's no bother. If you marry me, I'd put her in the country house with a slave or three. As I said - you deserve much more than you have!'

'But what do you suggest I do about it?'

'We,' said Favorix. 'Not you. We.' He tapped his nose. 'I can suggest to Max - just suggest - that the gods may look more favourably on his enterprises if he does what's right by you and atones for what he's done. Remember: I know what people pray for, why they offer sacrifices, what they worry about, who makes them miserable.'

'And you'd use that knowledge to manipulate someone?' cried Lucretia. 'That's terrible!' She grinned. 'I love it!'

Chapter 8: Diggers

'Nice knife,' said Dun. 'Sharpen up lovely, that will.'

Gris ran his mud-smeared thumb along the corroded blade and nodded. In the shade of oak, he wiped dirt from the hilt. Golden leaves floated around him to land in the pool of autumn where he crouched.

'Gems?' said Dun. 'Prise them out, shall we?'

'Maybe,' said Gris. He glanced around and shivered. Fallow fields stretched in stubbly slumber in all directions, dotted with copses, hedged with shrubs. The ramparts were a way off, smoke drifting into the still sky, occasional pricks of light sparking in the dusk. Villas, roundhouses and farmsteads were scattered out of sight, hunkering down for the evening. The squeaking, clattering, lowing, singing sounds of distant households filtered through the clear air.

'There's no-one for half a mile,' said Dun. 'Same as usual, if anyone sees us, we're looking for turnips and got lucky.'

''Snot that,' said Gris. 'It's him.'

He nodded into the centre of the grove, where it was just possible to discern the edges of relaid turf.

Gris spat on the knife and wiped the mud off with the edge of his tunic. It was a pretty thing; dainty, if you could say that about a knife. There were carvings in the bone hilt and yes, stones of some sort, gems or pearls or pebbles or glass balls. Probably not glass. He looked at the grove again. Maybe there had been more standing stones once. There were only five now, the height of a man, and two of those leaned against each other like two drunks at the end of a long night in the tavern. The trees circled them, dancers with clasped branches holding them in. Dun wondered if, before the Romans came, anyone could recall what it meant. If it meant anything. For all anyone knew, these places had been some sort of forum or tavern or something. No-one could truly be sure any more. He shivered again.

''Sall in your head,' said Dun. 'Superstition. We bin robbing graves and sacred groves for long enough. If we was gonna get haunted, it would've happened by now. And I reckon -' He pushed the leaves about with his foot where signs of charred twigs lay in a shallow dip. 'Someone camped out here recently. Course, they could have got took by the spirits.' He grinned at the expression on his friend's face. 'Only kidding. They cleared up, didn't they? Ghosts don't do that. Come on, let's take that knife home and have a proper look in the light. We could take it to bits if you think someone might reckernise it. Masner is canny. Let's ask him tomorrer.'

Gris grumbled, his face paler than usual.

Dun rolled his eyes. 'Look, I'll pour a bitty beer on the skellington, just to make you happy.' He stepped into the stone circle and upended his flask onto the turf. A breeze blew up and rustled in the trees. More leaves fell and a conker dropped on his head.

Gris swallowed and stood, shoving the knife deep into the stale loaf he'd brought and plugging the hole. If they were searched, there would be nothing to see. Dun was right. Probably. The skeleton didn't need his things any more.

'Reckon it was *his* knife?' He nodded to the grave.

'Dunno, but...' Dun sniggered. 'He'd have trouble holding it now.'

Gris frowned and shook his head. 'Yeah well, that was shocking that was, what you did. Not respectful.'

'Wasn't my fault his hand snapped off,' said Dun. 'You'da thought a bracelet would come off a skeleton easy. Anyway, by rights we shoulda buried his skull elsewhere, to let his spirit out - assuming it's still in after an 'undred years - but you wouldn't let me and

46

now you're wondering if he's gonna walk. At least we buried his hand elsewhere.'

'How does that help?'

'If his spirit *does* walk, he can't strangle us.'

Gris snorted. 'It still don't sit right. There's rules about burials. Don't tell no-one, but my granny was one of them Christians. She made us promise to bury her all in one piece, pointing some which way. Can't remember which.'

'Christian, eh? Wondered where you got your criminal tendencies from.'

'Cheek,' grunted Gris, starting back towards the road. 'I'm not that bad.'

Chapter 9: Lucretia

Lucretia had never paid much attention to pious people but with some effort, before returning to Max's house she composed her face into a demure downward stare and pinched her lips into rigid unkissability. That would surely indicate someone who'd been communing with the gods, rather than someone who'd been canoodling with their staff.

'I hope that spirituality keeps off hunger, since you've missed breakfast,' sniffed Eira as the slaves helped them into a wagon. Max was taking them on a short ride to his farmland. It lay alongside Deryn's, but Deryn himself was absent. Lucretia's curiosity was piqued, but only a fool would try to play some sort of game either with her emotions or money. She flexed her mental muscles.

The countryside was drying out. Ditches were still filled with rain but otherwise the land was bright with autumn under the deep blue sky. In fields stripped of crops, ploughmen trundled behind slow oxen turning the rich soil. Birds stalked behind, sifting, picking and rejecting like housewives in the forum. Copses and groves dotted the landscape. Hedgerows glistened with berries and trees with late fruit.

Proud Durnovaria looked down from the hill, a hub in a wheel of roads.

Max's farmhouse was small and functional, since he had long since moved his family inside the town, leaving the day-to-day farming to a steward. Lucretia glanced about the homestead, from the fertile pastures to the doubtless fecund orchard, to the still-burgeoning herb garden. Sturdy horses grazed, plump chickens pecked, fat cows lowed.

'How ridiculously bucolic,' she sniffed.

'Come now,' said Eira, retrieving Nux from the groom. 'It makes a lot of money. I'd have thought you'd appreciate that. That's why you're here, isn't it? Because of money.'

'Humph,' said Lucretia. 'It's easy living in this part of the world. Neither the animals nor the people have the character of those from Pecunia.' Despite the fact that she hadn't dirtied her hands since girlhood, Lucretia was fully aware that at home, the tussle between farmer and land was a game in which the dice was loaded in the land's favour.

She looked around and tried to work out if anything had changed. Not that she had known Max's family lands very well. The only thing that she had never forgotten was the incongruous copse in the middle of neat striped fields, between his land and the land that was now Deryn's. Hidden in a heart of oak and ash, ancient stones huddled inward in brooding conference.

Now, in mid autumn, surrounded by rich fields and berry-bejewelled hedges, it was gloriously majestic. A hundred oranges and golds adorned the branches and fluttered down to crown the standing stones.

'It was spring when you came all those years ago, wasn't it?' said Max. 'Bluebells and blossom. It's gaudier now but just as beautiful.'

'Early summer,' said Lucretia, who had been thinking how much the leaves' colours resembled her new auburn wig, and wondering if the addition of an intertwined string of garnets and some yellow braids would be too much.

Yes, all those years before the ridge had blossomed with meadow flowers. She had lain buxom and alluring in sun-warmed grass, competing for Deryn's attention with the larks as they danced against the blue overhead. The larks were stupidly noisy and whizzed about in an irritating tangle. He had been more interested in listening to the birdsong than her: reason one hundred and two why she hadn't married him.

'Can you imagine the grove in winter?' Max continued. To her alarm he bent into a peculiar shape and pulled a face. 'Imagine a group of hags hunched over secrets, dark against heavy skies in the midst of snow-laden pastures, while starving creatures dig and prod for something to eat in the frozen soil. Even this fertile place sleeps sometimes.' His voice dropped to a sinister monotone. 'And yet the *Other World* is watching. Don't forget: you must never dance within the circle - especially when it's full of bluebells - for fear of being enslaved and disappearing into *The Beyond.*'

Lucretia glared at him. 'What utter and absolute nonsense. If you're that worried, plant a couple of yew trees round the outside, chuck in some horse-shoes to lock the Other World out, and dance to your heart's content. Even without the yew and iron, anyone trying to drag me into the Beyond is likely to get their pointy little ears ripped off.'

For the second time that day Lucretia wondered what her teenage self had found attractive in a man who could talk so much about scenery. She shuddered at the thought of what it would have been like to stare at a romantic face every day for thirty-five years, waiting for it to finally say something interesting. Thank the gods she'd had enough sense to marry someone with no poetry in his soul whatsoever. At least Porcius had had his priorities straight: Lucretia, Lucretia's money, Lucretia's wine cellar. She almost felt a pang of affection for the drunken old goat. Almost.

She glanced at the grove again. Memory nagged, but it was hard to be sure what was real and what imagined.

She frowned. 'Is someone in there?'

Max followed her gaze and pondered. 'Cats. They're always up there looking for mice. Come along, ladies, I expect you're hungry.'

'Since, er, Justicia and Tranquillitas summoned me to the temple at the crack of dawn,' said Lucretia, 'I can safely say that's the most sensible thing anyone's said all morning.'

***

Back in town, lunch was superb.

'This venison is particularly fine!' said Lucretia.

Max nodded. 'All credit goes to Petros. He's a fine hunter.' He nodded to where a young man lay reclined with Olivarius, both speaking with Berenice. 'I'm glad your escort could join us,' he continued. 'He seems rather less tense today.'

'Rain is apt to annoy,' said Lucretia. 'And I gather Amicus suggested he spend some time getting to know the place today, rather than practice whatever it is secretaries do for duovirs. Why Olivarius has to get to know the place with *me* I have no idea.'

'Amicus was to have joined us too,' Max explained. 'But since the other duovir died he's quite busy dealing with criminals alone. Not that we have many. And obviously, when I'm elected -'

'When you're elected you can sort out the beggars,' said Lucretia. 'The one by the temple has quite destroyed my appetite.' She speared another piece of venison and dipped it in sauce before swallowing it whole.

'Stump?' said Max. 'I suppose we don't really notice him. But perhaps you're right.'

Lucretia turned her attention to something more interesting. She approved of Petros, his features more pleasing to her than Olivarius's, reminding her of someone from long ago. His thick long lashes curled over eyes as deep and dark as burnished jet, yet warm

51

and laughing. His mouth, ready to laugh, was red from wine, or perhaps always that way - as if he'd been kissing long and with passion. Beside him, Olivarius, with his reddish hair and secret green eyes, looked sneakier than ever. Between them reclined Berenice, waving her pale hands as she talked.

'Just think, Lucretia,' Max said as he followed her gaze. 'The Empire is represented here, from Britannia to Tarsus to Palmyra.'

'I suppose it's a little true of Petros,' said Eira. 'But Galyna says they left Palmyra and Egypt when he was little more than a toddler and made their way north. He's well and truly settled now. All the same, I'm glad Berenice is betrothed to Ieuan. I want her to stay here. It's quite bad enough that her brother shows no interest in coming home from Iberia.'

Petros was busy declaiming. 'I'd like to see Egypt again. I haven't seen the Nile for years. But after a while these indecisive British skies enchant us. As for young Olivarius here, he's got a girl back in Pecunia, but whether he ever gets her to Tarsus or not is anyone's guess.'

Lucretia snorted and turned to Max. 'I think Berenice is quite safe from whatever nonsense they're telling her. They're making most of it up. From what you say, Petros hasn't seen Egypt since he was about five, and I know for a fact that Olivarius was born in Londinium and has never actually been to Tarsus regardless of his ancestry.'

If Berenice was listening, she gave no sign. 'Petros,' she said. 'Is everything as dull in Egypt as it is in Durnovaria?'

'Nothing is dull in Egypt,' Petros said, illustrating his enthusiasm with a crumbling pastry. 'Everything is bleached by the sun, the land nothing but dry sand. Flat-roofed houses grow square from the baked earth.

And in the boiling evenings, canopies of silks and linens waft on their roofs and maidens bathe behind them. Ah, but after the river floods, after the rains, the land bursts into such colour, such grass and grain, such vegetables and legumes, such fruit and flowers in hues so deep it is like looking into pots of ink. And the girls in veils of red and gold dance with bells on their ankles.' He sighed.

'It sounds marvellous,' breathed Berenice. 'Nothing changes here in Britannia, not really.'

'I beg to differ,' said Olivarius. 'It changes constantly.'

'But what of Pecunia?' Berenice wondered.

Olivarius crumbled some bread.

'Are you missing your young lady?' persisted Berenice. 'Is your heart quite broken?'

Olivarius turned a grunt into a sigh. 'We won't be apart forever, as long as she keeps her feet on the ground and doesn't do anything rash.'

'Ah.' Petros nodded sagely and called a slave over to fill their goblets. 'You're not around to keep her focussed. Difficult.'

'Mmm.'

'Are there dragons in Egypt, Petros?' said Berenice. 'Like there are in Pecunia?'

The two men looked at her and then each other.

'There are dragons in Pecunia?' hazarded Olivarius.

'Of course there are,' said Berenice, shifting into a different position and popping an almond into her mouth. 'You must have seen them. Cousin Porcius was eaten by one, wasn't he, Cousin Lucretia?'

Lucretia dropped a garlic snail down her cleavage and glared. 'Up until now,' she snapped, 'I had thought it was only my male relations who were idiots. It's clearly time to reconsider.'

'Dragons are wonderful,' breathed Berenice.

'Tarsus is full of them,' confirmed Olivarius.

'Egypt has more dragons than anywhere,' said Petros, 'and they're bigger and more golden.'

'Do you suppose Egyptian dragons are golden so they can hide against the sand?' mused Berenice. 'Or is it the other way round? Is it all sandy because the dragons have burnt the grass up?'

Lucretia retrieved the snail and chewed it with vigour before turning back to Max.

'I understand you're paying for the circus to put on a show,' she said. 'I hope Contractes puts on something exciting. The show he put on for us in Pecunia last year was over-dramatic. Admittedly the terrain was very much against him, not to mention a murderer running amok. But even so, the plot was...'

As Lucretia searched for a word suitable for polite company, Berenice interrupted. 'I'd like to see a tragedy. Star-crossed lovers, suspicious parents, angry gods.'

'I prefer blood,' said Lucretia.

Petros chuckled. 'Doesn't everyone? But who knows - perhaps the play will contain all of those.'

'How do you know?' asked Berenice.

'Met Contractes in the baths,' Petros answered. 'He plans a spectacular in which people might actually die, but if they do, it'll be ... what did he say? "A real money spinner, provided I don't run out of actors in rehearsals."'

'Things are looking up,' said Lucretia.

There was a clash of cymbals from the musicians in the corner of the room. The conversations stopped and everyone turned.

'Ieuan!' exclaimed Berenice, starting to rise.

A young man stood on the threshold with a small slave at his side, carrying a dainty pillow on which was a tiny wooden box.

'Stay where you are, darling!' cried Ieuan. 'I've brought a surprise! Until we are one, here is a gift to remind you of my love in those quiet days when we are apart!' He turned to the slave. 'Take it to my beloved.'

Lucretia rolled her eyes.

Ieuan shoved the slave in the direction of Berenice. The girl sat up and pressed her hand to her heart as if she'd never clapped eyes on either Ieuan or a slave before. 'Me? For me?' She reached out and lifted the box from the pillow. A carved ouroboros circled its sides, tail in mouth below the aperture. The top was carved with an intricate knot.

The musicians played a gentle hopeful tune as Berenice opened the box and lifted out a ring. She gasped and Ieuan knelt to slip it on her finger.

'I know it's a little big,' he said. 'But we can have it altered.'

Berenice perused her finger then held it out for Lucretia to see. The ring was made of gold. A piece of carnelian was set in it, engraved with something which looked like a winged lion. 'Isn't it lovely?' she said. 'Isn't it? Look, Mother, look!' She walked across to where Eira reclined. Nux, dozing against her, blinked himself awake as his mistress sat up. 'Look, Father! A dragon!' Berenice strode over to Max and held out her hand. The ring swivelled on her middle finger until the carnelian faced the floor. Max twiddled it round again.

He frowned and went pale. Eira inhaled with a gasp and Lucretia realised her own mouth was open.

Perhaps Max glanced at her. Perhaps Eira glanced at him. Lucretia didn't care to check and somehow, she had a feeling no-one was looking at anything but the ring.

Chapter 10: Lucretia

By mid afternoon Lucretia was relieved to have something else to think about. Max and Eira had probed a little further until Berenice became truculent. Only the offer of a trip to the amphitheatre to see Contractes' troupe cheered her up, but Eira declared she had a headache and would stay at home.

'Don't worry, Lucretia,' she said. 'I've made sure there's someone to keep you company.'

'Deryn?' suggested Lucretia. 'I really do need to talk to you both about your mother - and pay my respects to her memorial, of course. I'm sure she -'

'You must surely still be too tired from your journey,' interrupted Eira. 'I've sent for your friend.'

'Friend?'

'You speak as if you have none. How very sad.' Eira smirked. 'I mean Tryssa, the lady who travelled with you, and of course her sister-in-law Galyna. After all, they're virtually next door.'

'In a smaller house, I presume.'

Eira shrugged.

'This promises to be a very dull afternoon,' said Lucretia.

'You've forgotten what the amphitheatre is like.' Eira's indifference was overlaid with something approaching pride. 'And Amicus will be there too. You didn't get the chance to meet him properly yesterday. He's a citizen, quite the most eligible man for miles, and actually within your age bracket.'

***

Eira, for once, was right.

Lucretia had forgotten how magnificent the amphitheatre was, and was pleased to note that the Durotriges weren't so Romanised that they insisted on separating the women from the men and seating them with slaves. Amicus, sitting beyond Max, turned out to be quite acceptable too. He was taller than average, his hair a light brown which suggested German blood in his ancestry, and had strong arms that she imagined could hold a woman very tight.

Lucretia thought of her fiancé Anguis, with his bony frame and distaste for embraces. How wonderful that he was all those miles away in Pecunia. She fluttered her eyelashes at Amicus and was gratified to see him flush before he was drawn into conversation with Max.

On her other side, Galyna tapped her arm.

'Thank you so much for bringing Tryssa with you to Durnovaria,' she said. 'It's delightful to become acquainted.' She dropped her voice. 'And it's turned out quite beneficial, since the only experienced wise-woman has recently died and left us in a bit of a fix.'

'She can't have been terribly wise then,' said Lucretia.

Tryssa rolled her eyes.

Lucretia turned to stare down into the empty arena. 'At least they don't seem to be planning a play as their first performance.'

'Classical scripts can be very dull,' said Galyna. 'They miss the essentials. People say that writing is for men, but I bet a woman could pen something better and capture the ebb and flow of months as they pass, the rhythm of ...'

'I hope no-one ever writes a play to include that sort of thing,' Lucretia said, appalled.

Max looked smug. 'Never fear. I've asked Contractes to give a taster of what they can do to drum up interest for the main event. Something to bring the voters in.'

Lucretia nodded. Contractes was no fool and knew the audience preferred action.

Before anything more could be said horns sounded, and riders, drivers and acrobats burst into the arena. Within minutes, chariots and dancing horses swirled among tumbling men in a dizzying pattern. At any moment they must surely collide, and yet they never did. Men leapt over not only each other but also the backs of racing horses, spinning and twisting in the air to land within inches of chariots that passed within a hair's breadth of each other.

Lucretia was enraptured. Her eyes flickered as they followed the dance and her cheeks were hot. Her hands clenched and flexed as if she too were reining in those horses, or preparing to launch into the air. The excitement and the rhythm of the thudding hooves made her remember a pounding of blood, a welling desire, a restlessness she had long put aside in case it impeded her common sense. Unfocussed passion rarely made much money unless you were making it out of someone else's. Now she recalled not whatever she'd seen in the amphitheatre forty years earlier, but how she'd felt when she'd arrived in Durnovaria, bored with the boys she'd grown up with, weighing up the new young men she met.

They called her a sparrow. She'd been tiny if buxom. Bright and cheeky, not sulky and shy like Eira, not precisely a full-grown woman, but certainly not a child. In those days her dark hair had glinted with gold when the sun shone. All those boys had lapped up everything she said whether true, exaggerated, or downright lies. She knew how to sparkle and hint, she didn't need to redden her full lips or smooth her cheeks. She knew without question that every one of them longed to span her tiny waist, pull her soft, curvaceous body towards him and run his hands over her full bust and hips. But she had been no fool. She had danced and spun between all the boys, always promising but just out of reach. It had been fun being a spell-caster. The whirling chariots reminded her of that dance. She felt as alive now as she had then and the certainty that not only Amicus but Max were now glancing at her made her heart beat even faster.

One by one the riders, the charioteers and finally the acrobats galloped or tumbled out of the arena and the audience sat back.

Lucretia exhaled, trembling with excitement. A slave appeared with a tray of snacks purchased from the vendors outside. Little parcels of honeyed pastry, tiny cheeses encrusted with nuts, and savoury breads dribbled in oil and garlic were proffered. Lucretia waved them away.

'They are the finest in the province,' Max assured her.

'Doubtless,' Lucretia murmured back. 'I'm watching my figure, although I'm not watching it as much as you are.'

'Seeing you just now was like seeing the years drop away. Do you remember what it was like when we were free?' said Max. He pondered for a moment. 'Well, I was already free. You had to sneak a bit, if I recall, but nothing stopped you, not even a high window or locked door. If you like, tomorrow I could take you to the sea like I did back then. Eira will join us of course, the air might help soothe her headache. We can start by standing on the ramparts of the old hill fort and summon up the echo of our ancestors, then we'll go to the coast and we look towards Armorica. On a good day the sea sparkles like turquoise, and in the morning the mists swallow the world.'

Minerva save me from poetry, thought Lucretia. 'Turquoise doesn't sparkle,' she pointed out. 'And I'm not walking about in mists on hill forts, I might break an ankle. But I suppose it would be nice to see the sea.'

Determined to retain the throb of excitement she had felt during the display, she leaned forward to address Amicus. 'You may not realise it, but Contractes' troupe was trained by the horsemen of Pecunia last year. We have the best in the Empire, you know.' It wasn't true in the slightest, but that was irrelevant.

Amicus was clearly fascinated. His mouth kept dropping open as she spoke and then closing. Clearly astonished. Speechless. It was wonderful.

She bathed in his gaze for a moment and then said, 'But I have to say that this was a very fine performance. How I love to see manhood displayed in its full glory.' She twiddled a curl that had escaped its braid.

Amicus blinked and then smiled. 'Yes indeed, though if your townsfolk trained them it must be familiar to you. Anyway, what about other entertainment in Pecunia?'

Lucretia sighed. 'It needs improving. Apart from executions - the interesting ones of which are few and far between - there hasn't been anything of interest since last summer, and even then the lion was disappointing. Chariot and horse racing happen across the hills on a sort of cross-country course. It's quite thrilling waiting for the winner, but sadly we can't witness how someone was trampled or managed to get their arm bent backwards. Of course there's "whack a rat".'

'The farmyard game with the tube and the ball and a race to stop it rolling across the ground? Sounds a little tame.'

'Ball?'

'Oh, do you use actual rats? And the contestants have to whack 'em before they run away?'

'Goodness no, how dull. That's just normal household management. No, whack the rat is a punishment for disobedient children. It's a bit resource-intensive, admittedly, as the children tend to resist. Someone usually has to prod with a long stick at the top of the tube to dislodge the brat while others wait at the bottom to whack. But it's character-forming.'

'For the children?'

'If the children had characters they wouldn't need whacking. I meant for the competitors.' Lucretia sighed. 'My intended would like more refined performances: Greek tragedies, comedies, dances with scarves.' She pulled a face.

'You don't like dancing?'

'I prefer those dances where someone dies at the end. Nowadays they do it in mime. Occasionally someone's sword slips, but that's less to do with assuaging the gods and more to do with vendettas. In my grandfather's time it was a great honour to be the victim. Nothing's ever been the same since they banned sacrifices.'

Amicus laughed and rose. 'Oh my lady, I do love your humour. I'll be back in a moment. I must just speak to someone before the next display.'

Lucretia watched his departure then turned to Olivarius, who was sitting behind her with Berenice and Ieuan. 'Have you had word from Pecunia?'

Olivarius shook his head. 'No.'

Lucretia gave a smile. 'Not even from Camilla?'

Olivarius inspected his thumbnail. 'Camilla was fine last time I saw her. Bit unrealistic, bit argumentative, bit excited. Pretty much as normal.'

Tryssa gave a softer smile. 'She seemed a little downcast when she knew you'd be away. I should have brought her too.'

'Nonsense, she needed to stay behind,' said Lucretia. 'And if she hasn't written to Olivarius, she must be quite content.'

'Why -' Tryssa's voice was drowned out by trumpets as men dressed as warriors from across the empire entered, bearing a variety of lethal weapons and ready to start a display of fighting. When the noise died down a little she shook her head and started again. 'As Olivarius says, it's a little early to expect a letter and Camilla still finds writing hard. But forgive me, Lucretia, I imagine you're eager for word from Anguis.'

Lucretia, scanning Amicus's shapely form as he returned, put up her chin and readjusted her veil over the black wig. 'One can hardly expect a decurion to write every two minutes. He'll be busy keeping law and order and hopefully keeping an eye on developments at the baths, since Marcellus can't keep his mind on anything but writing poems for that wretched baby. I can wait. Now, I think I need proper support for the next display in case I swoon - a man on either side.' She rose and settled on the other side of Max so that Amicus found himself sitting directly beside her.

'Ooh I forgot!' said Berenice, making everyone jump. 'Amicus Sonticus, look! I forgot to show you. See what Ieuan bought me!'

She pulled off her glove and thrust her hand into Amicus's face. He blinked in surprise and then focussed on the ring, taking her fingers in his and staring at the engraved stone.

'Ieuan,' he said gently, 'it's lovely. May one ask where it came from? I'd like to speak to the jeweller.'

There was a clash of cymbals.

'I didn't get it from a jeweller,' said Ieuan, over the noise of shouting from the arena. 'It's an antique, you see. The trader, Masner, said it possessed a history of great luck and much joy.'

'Did he now?' said Amicus. He rubbed his hand over his face. 'Did he now?' Unaccountably, he looked past Lucretia as if he locked eyes with someone else.

'Never mind that old ring,' said Lucretia, patting his knee. 'Let's watch the display. Help explain it to me. I'm sure I'll be terrified if there's blood. I may need comforting.'

She looked across at Tryssa and grinned.

Chapter 11: Tryssa

Outside the amphitheatre, Tryssa stood for a little with Galyna and Berenice, listening to them coo over the ring that seemed to disturb Amicus.

Max sneered a little at the story of the second-hand find on a junk stall in the forum. Ieuan's family, according to Corryx, was another prominent and therefore rich one who could afford anything they liked, but the young man himself seemed to know what would please his betrothed.

'Galyna, isn't it romantic?' breathed Berenice. 'Such a pretty thing from so far away and long ago. Ieuan's given me lots of new things of course, but as soon as he saw this, he knew I'd love it and could imagine its story. I think of a foreign princess who...'

Max's face softened a little as his daughter chattered, joining in the story-telling after a while.

Lucretia was fluttering at Amicus. 'I hear you lived abroad for a while, do tell me - what could I add to my baths to make them appeal to visitors from across the empire? A cosmopolitan man such as yourself...'

Amicus listened, his face polite but his hands slightly clenched. His eyes darted across to Tryssa just as she rolled her eyes, and the tiniest lift of his mouth mirrored hers.

'Max,' he said, 'didn't you want to show Lucretia the sunset from the top of the amphitheatre?'

'I certainly did.' Max grinned. He turned to his guest. 'You came in summer before. I don't think you were allowed out late enough to see the sun go down.'

'It didn't stop me,' said Lucretia. 'Provided Eira was asleep and didn't see me sneak out of our room.'

'Really?' Max raised his eyebrows.

Lucretia ignored him, eyeing the height of the amphitheatre with doubt as if hoping that in the absence of flight, someone would carry her to the top.

'Oh don't be like Mother, cousin Lucretia!' Berenice said. 'She's never brave enough to climb to the top, but I bet you are!'

Lucretia's scowl turned into a smug grin and she allowed Max to bear her away. All but Tryssa and Amicus followed.

Amicus came forward. 'Do you want to go too?'

'Maybe on another evening,' said Tryssa.

'When it's quieter and someone isn't expressing their views about the quality of the sunset or the steepness of the climb?'

Tryssa chuckled. 'Something like that.'

'Forgive me,' Amicus hesitated, and she noticed his hands clench again. 'This may seem like a strange thing to say, but I saw you noticing.'

'Noticing?'

'When Berenice showed me the ring, you only gave it the briefest of attention.'

'It was pretty enough, but I'm no great jewellery-wearer. I'm a wise-woman. It's a practical occupation and fussy rings tend to be annoying.'

'That's as may be.' Amicus glanced at her hands and Tryssa felt aware of them for the first time in years - hardened by work, unlike Lucretia's, despite the lotions she used to soften them. 'It's not really what I meant. You looked at the ring very briefly and then you started watching *me*.'

'Oh.' Tryssa felt her face warm. 'I'm sorry. I didn't mean to be rude. You just seemed rather taken aback.'

Amicus smiled and shook his head. 'I'm not in the least offended. I recognised a kindred spirit. You were trying to work out what was bothering me. And you were looking at everyone else to see how they were reacting too.'

'Force of habit,' Tryssa admitted. 'I have to diagnose things and often I can only go by working out what people are not telling me, rather than what they are. Again, I'm sorry.'

'Don't be. I just wonder - would you be offended if I asked you to use those skills to help me? I could do with a woman.'

Tryssa raised her eyebrows. Now it was Amicus's turn to blush.

'I mean an observant woman. I want to ask a few questions about that ring in the forum and I can't be looking everywhere. Petros will help, but we only have a small guard here and besides they might not see the same things, and people will be looking out for them. They won't be looking out for - forgive me - yet another woman doing her marketing.'

Tryssa bit her lip. 'You think the ring was stolen?'

'I just want to know where it came from. I'm sorry, I shouldn't have asked.'

Tryssa looked into his eyes. They seemed not only as honest as Corryx had said but also troubled. 'I'm not sure what use I'll be, but I might have a little time before Galyna takes me to see your new wise-woman.'

Amicus suddenly grinned. 'Of course, if *you're* not interested - do you think Lucretia would be any use?'

Chapter 12: Amicus

Amicus stood in the shade of a house and scanned the scene before him.

The forum had different moods depending on the time of day. First thing in the morning it was brisk and focussed, humming with haggling. Slaves and good housewives selected the best of the fresh produce. They peered into the eyes of fish, choosing those that seemed simply petrified by shock and about to come alive, leaving the soft-bodied, dull-gilled offerings for the lazy, incompetent and poor. They sniffed at vegetables to see if they were damp with dew or sluiced with well-water, and into the barrels of dried goods and spices to check for mould.

It was not the vague indecisive tangle of people it would be later. There was a swift efficiency in the way shoppers traversed and argued and elbowed each other out of the way. The poor hovered, waiting for their turn to buy offcuts and broken pieces. The desperate sent their children under the stalls to grab anything they could, knowing their time would not come until the market was packing up and there was nothing but the softest turnips, the slimiest fish and the mustiest dried fruit for the traders to more or less give away.

Amicus could see at least some of the guard ambling through the stands. Most of them were off duty, stocking up on hot street food after a night on the tiles. Two, however, were there under his orders, keeping an eye on things from a distance. Everyone knew who they were but their languorous amble kept things light. He waited until he saw Tryssa enter from the east side with a slave in tow.

She was barely taller than Lucretia but less rounded, more simply dressed and without arrogance. She merged with the other shoppers, drawing no attention to herself, but he recognised without hesitation that she was already another set of eyes and ears.

Tryssa walked with some purpose and then, as planned, she bumped into Petros who for all intents and purposes was nursing a headache on the way home. He stopped to lean on her shoulder as if steadying himself. She patted his arm and they separated, both changing direction. Petros slumped at a food stall. Tryssa stopped by a ribbon-seller who was just setting up next to Masner's jewellery stall and started a conversation. Amicus ambled in the same direction, but made no acknowledgment of her.

'Morning, Masner,' he said.

The trader straightened up. He too was just setting out his goods. At the front were pewter bowls and plates, too heavy to steal easily, cheap enough not to matter if they were. Closer to his person were bracelets, pendants, rings, brooches. For a moment Amicus could have sworn he saw an old bronze torc, small enough for a child who had been dead for centuries. Before he could be certain it disappeared from view into the sack under the table to be sat on by Masner's slave.

'Good morning, Amicus Sonticus. How may I help you?'

Amicus picked up a brooch designed to look like a marvellous creature and turned it over in his hand. Its intricacy was astounding, the silver twisted and twisted again into a knot and when the brooch was closed the creature would appear to bite its own tail. It was quite beautiful and, unless it was a replica or someone had resurrected an older style, it was ancient. 'Been digging again?'

'Not me,' said Masner. 'I trade. I don't get my hands dirty. Bought in good faith from an old fellow.'

'Really?'

'Yup. Been in his family for years, but now he's getting on a bit and his daughter-in-law prefers the modern style. He thought he might as well get a few *as* for it and buy the girl something she'd like.'

'You bought it for a few *as,* eh? And how many *denarii* are you selling it for?'

'Gotta make a living.'

'Mmm.'

'Do you fancy it yourself, sir? Some of the ladies like an old thing.'

Amicus raised his eyebrows, but Masner's face was straight, his eyes open wide, his hands busy as he arranged his display. 'They do indeed,' he said. 'In fact I know a young lady who received an old thing yesterday. A ring. She was delighted. I gather her fiancé bought it from you.'

Masner scratched his chin. 'I daresay. Sold a lotta stuff yesterday. Lots of rings. Lots of young men.'

'It was young Ieuan Paryn Silvestris. You must know him. Gwin Silvestris's son. Betrothed to Berenice Maximilia.'

Masner shrugged. 'I know the lad you mean, but it was busy yesterday, sir. Can't say I remember everything I sold or to whom. Maybe it wasn't me.'

'A gold ring with engraved carnelian. Very pretty. I admired it a great deal.'

The tradesman chewed his lip and frowned as if in deep thought. 'Sort of rings a bell. The lady was pleased with it, I hope? It might need resizing. She's dainty from what I recall and -'

'And it's a ring for a bigger finger than she's got, yes indeed. I was wondering...' Amicus threw the brooch in the air and caught it with one hand while with the other he reached over the table and picked up a long bronze hairpin with amber trims. He twirled it in a way

69

that kept the long sharp teeth outwards. 'I was wondering if you had any matching pieces.'

Masner shook his head. 'Nope. Or at least not that I know of.'

'And who sold it to you? Another dear old gent?'

'What's with the questions? I've been trading here for ten years and apart from a couple of misunderstandings you've let me get on with it. So I sold a ring. It was a nice ring, unusual. I sold it for a fair price. A man's got to live. I've got a household to feed. Tell you what, I'll put some feelers out. See if anyone else has seen anything like it. Or better still, there's Nyn the jeweller, he'll knock you up a replica soon as you like if you give him the wherewithal.'

Amicus didn't reply but beckoned to Petros and then scanned the scene around them. The forum was crisscrossed with people coming and going. Tryssa had moved away from the ribbon-seller and was inspecting some olive dishes. Two rough-clad men passed her as they made for Masner's stall, and at the sight of Amicus made a sudden right turn. Just as he'd expected: Dun and Gris - the grave-robbers.

Tryssa fell into step with them as they increased their pace towards the main thoroughfare. Amicus's men were closing in, but the housewives and slaves were getting in their way. With one small sideways step, Tryssa tripped up Dun and knocked him into Gris. The two men sprawled on the pavement at her feet and waved her apologies away as they struggled to get up, hindered by her foot on Dun's cloak. Amicus grinned as he watched his own men step smartly forward and haul the grave-robbers to their feet. He was not surprised when Tryssa wandered back if she had an urge to buy ribbon after all.

'Who says there's no place for women on the guard?' said Petros with admiration. A slight squeak came from below the table. 'Oh sorry, lad.' Petros lifted his foot off the slave's wrist, which had been reaching for Amicus's ankle.

Dun and Gris were marched up to Masner's stall and turned to face him. Masner crossed his arms, his face bored. The slave's eyes flickered from one to the other as he nursed his wrist. The grave-robbers looked at their feet and shuffled like cattle.

'Dun and Gris, isn't it?' said Amicus. 'Weren't you involved a couple of years ago in what Masner here called "a little misunderstanding"?'

'Can't you take it elsewhere?' said Masner. 'You're putting people off coming to my stall.'

'Nonsense,' said Amicus. 'We're making you look busy.'

'You're making me look dodgy. What have *they* got to do with me?'

'Suppliers of raw materials, perhaps?'

'Not any more. Not after that business you just referred to. Haven't seen each other for ages, have we lads?'

Dun and Gris shook their heads.

'Saw the three of you in the tavern a couple of evenings ago,' said Petros. 'Talking over old times, perhaps.'

'No crime in that,' said Masner. 'But it's dark in the evenings now, so I can't see how you could be sure who was meeting who. Even so, as I say, there's no crime in having a drink and getting things straight. "I'm an honest man," I said. Didn't I lads?'

'The point is,' said Amicus, 'I want to know where you got that pretty bit of jewellery from.'

'Another trader at the market by the ford in Vadumlutra, a few miles north-west of Vindoclavia.'

'That's half a day's walk each way and the guard reports you've been safe in a bed, or at least inside the town, every night for the last six months since the last "misunderstanding".'

'Oh, so you're keeping tabs on everyone are you? Is this a police state now?' grumbled Masner.

'Yep,' said Amicus. 'You know it is. Especially at the moment but I don't think that's relevant. Shall we try again?'

'You can let me, us go though. It's got nuffink to do with us,' said Dun. 'We was just off.'

'Off where, exactly?' Petros picked up a small folding knife from Masner's display and started to clean his nails. 'You didn't seem to know. One minute heading this way, the next heading the other. Too many turnips giving you brain-ache?'

'Nothing in the forum caught our fancy, did it?' grumbled Gris. 'There's no law against changing your mind is there? Thing is, that ring ain't nothing to do with us.'

'Who said anything about a ring?' said Amicus, leaning down to flick through Gris's beard with the comb before he put it down. He pinned the brooch to his cloak and threw a couple of denarii on the table.

'I'm a reasonable chap, so let's stop wasting time,' he said. 'Petros here needs his breakfast or he'll get tetchy, and you don't want to see him when he gets tetchy. We can do this the fun way or the boring way. Where did that ring come from?'

Dun gulped. 'What's the fun way?'

'Weeell, I've got a couple of new torturers who need training up, and Petros here has a dog which needs to learn when to let go of miscreants on command. Hasn't got the hang of it yet. Tends to leave a lot of chew marks. And didn't I hear Contractes' circus has a lion? It might need a bit of practice.'

Masner drew a breath and put the denarii in his pouch. 'Now I think of it, I'm getting confused. I got

72

the ring from these two here the day Contractes' crew were chalking up their graffiti. Someone was talking about Vadumlutra and perhaps I was casting my mind back to springtime when I was last there. Or maybe Dun and Gris told me that's where they bought it before selling it on to me.'

All eyes turned to the grave-robbers. They looked and smelled as if they had grown from the clod. There was dust in their hair and beards; grime clogged their fingernails. A money pouch hung loose on each of their belts.

'If a member of the gentry handed that ring to either of you two,' said Amicus, 'he'd have to have lost all his senses or been at knife-point. Perhaps we should take you separately to find out what you have to say. Who'd prefer the torturers first and the dog second?'

Dun and Gris swallowed, then both started gabbling at the same time.

'Slow down,' said Petros. 'One at a time. You - ' he prodded Dun with the folding knife, 'spit it out.'

'We was out in the fields,' said Dun. 'Minding our own business. Looking for food, gleanings, sticks. That sorta thing.'

'And lo and behold, there was a bejewelled ring among the stubble.'

'No, course not. Er. sir. There was this -'

'Geezer,' chipped in Gris. 'Slinking about, limping, eyeing up the west gate. Sly-looking cove, weren't he Dun?'

'Yeah,' said Dun. 'Yeah he was. Hard to make out on account of...'

'The dusk. It was dusk. Just about when the sun goes down. And foggy. You know how it was the other evening.'

'It's been raining for about a month,' pointed out Petros. 'Only stopped two days ago.'

'I mean drizzle. Same difference. Low cloud, gloomy and sunset. And people.'

'People?' said Amicus.

'You know, going into the town before nightfall. I mean, we were with them and all, heading home.'

'Do you *have* homes?'

Gris sniffed. 'A wall's as good as a roof when you're as poor as us. Better'n woods.'

'My heart bleeds,' said Petros. 'Get on with it, because my dog's not getting any better-trained while I'm wasting time with you.'

'Well, he was slinking in and out of the wagons and people but he wasn't going in,' said Dun, looking over Petros's shoulder as if staring into his memory. 'Probably cos he was lame - hunchbacked or something. I thought he looked suspicious, cos we were all heads down cos of the rain 'cept for him. He was looking up at the ramparts and muttering to himself. I nudged Gris, didn't I Gris? And we tried to tail him but it was that busy and anyway, before I could get a proper look he slipped and fell and picked 'isself up and turned tail and went off again back the way we'd come, and soon I couldn't see him no more. And then, when we got to where he'd fell, there was the ring. And well, seemed like the gods were smiling on us sorta. So we collared it.'

'You didn't think to report any of this to the guard?' said Amicus.

'Who'd listen to us?' Dun shrugged, his hands spread. 'We coulda handed in the ring I suppose. But you know, there was a chance of a night on a mattress in Bella's with stew and everything, so we sold it to Masner. Told him to keep it for a day or so, just in case someone came asking for it, then he could hand it in and get a reward. That's right isn't it, Masner? Never thought there'd be any trouble over it. It looks old enough.'

'It is,' said Amicus. 'But it's very curious. Are you sure about this stranger?'

'On my mother's life,' said Dun.

'I'm not sure I believe you ever had a mother,' said Petros. 'I think you were just dug up with the rotten beets one day.' He turned to Amicus. 'What do you reckon, sir?'

'Take them to the baths, get them stripped, searched and above all washed, find them something clean to wear and we'll see if they stick to their story afterwards.'

Dun shuddered. 'Would we lie to you?'

'Is the sea wet?' said Amicus.

'Wot?'

Amicus waved them away. 'Go on, Petros, see to it. I'll question them again at the tenth hour. Now then, Masner. Anything else that you remember, just let me know and don't make any plans to leave for a while. Understood?'

'Of course, Amicus Sonticus,' said Masner with a small nod. 'I am, as ever, at your command.'

Amicus turned and stepped away. He paused to survey the forum again. The slight lull in the noise disappeared as people hastily turned from staring to continue about their business. Amicus walked towards the ribbon-seller and fell into step with Tryssa as she started to walk away.

'Thank you, Tryssa Doethion,' he said. 'Can we share thoughts? There's more to this than I've had a chance to explain.'

'I had a feeling there might be,' said Tryssa. 'And I'm more than happy to help.'

Chapter 13: Lucretia

Lucretia looked into the mirror and twisted her head to and fro. It had to be admitted, Nia was wonderful with hair and cosmetics. Lucretia wondered if the girl would work as well if she were gagged, or better still had her tongue removed. There was a possibility the constant chatter helped her creativity. If Nia came home as a new body slave then Lucretia would have to find some way of transporting her separately. She felt certain that if Nia sat talking at Ondi the whole way back they would all end up in a ravine, even if Ondi had to drive somewhere specifically to find one. Perhaps Nia could ride pillion with Olivarius and take his mind off Camilla.

She was hungry, but picking at the sweetmeats on the table before her risked cracking the cosmetic before it had dried. Nia stood back. With a sigh Lucretia removed the wax plugs from her ears, and the flow of Nia's monologue she'd thus far blocked spewed forth like water from a cracked aqueduct.

'And Riona turned to me and said "well it was so romantic" and I turned to her and said, "Well you needn't be so smug, just cos my mistress can manage without someone fussing over every little thing and wants to give her maid a rest," and she turned to me and said, "Well some of us are indisposable," but really I am a bit disappointed, truth to tell. I just don't like letting that Riona think she's got one up on me but fancy missing that. It must have been so romantic. I wish someone would give me a ring. I mean someone give me one once but it was just an old green bit of metal really, it was all he could afford so I suppose I should be grateful but all the same, it would have been nicer if he'd made some effort and whittled me one out of wood. The one he give me looked like it had been in a drain for six months or maybe years. I wouldn't be surprised if he didn't buy if off that Masner too, only from what Masner calls his lucky dip. You pay an *as*, dig your hand in a sack and if you're lucky you pull out something you can use and not just a stone with the pattern of a shell or leaf in. Just you remember that, Mistress Lucretia. If you want to get hold of something nice don't go rummaging in Masner's sack. Oh but it was a shame I missed Master Ieuan giving Mistress Berenice that ring. It's ever so pretty, don't you think? Next time you go to dinner, don't worry about letting me rest, Mistress Lucretia. Just you remember, where there's a wig, it's best to have a maid. See, I could have kept it straight and made sure it didn't slip and all sorts. There now, what do you reckon?'

'It's not bad,' said Lucretia, marvelling at how twenty years (according to the mirror) had been wiped off with Nia's ministrations. 'With a little more practice you might be worth keeping.'

She rose, loaded Nia with everything she needed and went to find her cousin in the main room. Eira sat bolt upright in a cushioned chair, Nux nestled as ever against the bony plateau of her chest.

'Are we finally ready?' said Eira.

'Well, I can't speak for you and the rat,' said Lucretia. 'But I am.'

The slaves handed round the dishes of sweetmeats.

'I'd think twice about smiling with all that cement on your face,' suggested Eira as she took one without looking at Nia.

'Smiling is for fools and children,' pointed out Lucretia, waving Nia away. 'Whereas if I were you I'd think twice about offering an embrace to anyone you don't intend to impale on a rib.'

'One doesn't embrace.'

'One must have embraced at least twice,' said Lucretia, allowing Nia to arrange her clothes ready for the outside. 'One has three adult children. Although if you told me Berenice was found in a nest of dragon-obsessed squirrels I wouldn't be surprised.'

'At least one has borne children and retained one's figure.'

'At least one of us looks like someone who can bear children without snapping in half.'

'Or be used as a mattress. To each her own.'

'Better a mattress than a plank of wood.'

Eira opened her mouth, then closed it as Max entered the room.

'Have you seen the like of the ring what Master Ieuan gave Mistress Berenice, Mistress Eira?' interpolated Nia.

Eira swallowed and her eyes for one second sought something in Lucretia's. Lucretia, still calculating whether she wished she were slender or was proud of a figure which suggested fecundity, shrugged.

'I might have once,' said Eira.

'What about you, Mistress Lucretia?'

Lucretia, aware that whatever she did should not involve extremes of head movement, nodded in a vague manner. 'Maybe some time ago,' she admitted. 'But now we are going to the temple to...' She thought for a moment. 'To give thanks for a safe journey here and ask for a swift conclusion of business.'

'Christians gives thanks and asks for forgiveness.'

'Do they now?' said Lucretia. 'How very odd of them.'

'Isn't that the same as being sorry for angering the gods?' said Eira, turning to go.

'Not really, Mistress,' said Nia, joining Riona as they prepared to follow. 'It's more like being sorry for not being perfect or something.'

Lucretia and Eira exchanged glances. 'But I am perfect,' they said in unison.

'Course,' said Nia, and bowed. Lucretia narrowed her eyes.

Berenice slipped into the room and sat on the edge of her father's chair. 'Why doesn't anyone like my new ring?' she pouted. 'Everyone went very quiet yesterday. Is it because it's old?'

'It's beautiful, darling,' said Eira. 'Ieuan has wonderful taste. It reminded us of someone, that's all.'

'Someone from the olden days?'

'Really,' said Eira, 'you make us sound ancient. And besides, it's not the same as the one we thought of. Just very similar. Don't you think, Lucretia?'

Lucretia shrugged. 'I've no idea,' she said, leaning forward to peer at the ring. 'It's very pretty indeed, but I am fairly sure I've never seen its like.'

'Not recently,' insisted Eira. 'But you did when you were here last.'

'I can hardly recall every jewel the ladies wore back then,' said Lucretia, sitting back and twirling her hair. 'I was busy. As I intend to be now. I thought we were going to the temple.'

'Yes, you were busy,' snapped Eira. 'Busy flirting. And it was one of the young *men* who wore a ring like this.'

'Was it?'

'Yes, but I'm sure it's not the same.'

'If you say so. I don't recall it either way. I don't recall flirting either, simply making conversation. What was the boy's name?'

'G - girls like you were are nothing but trouble,' said Eira, pressing Nux so close to her chest he yelped. She rose. 'And how can anyone recall the names of all those men who tried to get your attention?' She glared at Max, who went a deep red. 'I have a headache and we were supposed to be setting out for the temple,' she continued. 'I need to fetch my votive. After lunch, you can take whichever slave you need when you go to the mosaic-maker. I hope he has finally designed something you'll approve. I'm sure you're finding this place far too full of memories you'd prefer to forget.' She swept from the room.

Max sighed. 'I'll escort you both to the temple. I've business to attend to.'

'Whatever's wrong with Mummy?' said Berenice. Her wide eyes perused Lucretia as if marvelling that a withered rose might once have been a bud. 'Cousin Lucretia, were you really fascinating to men when you were young?'

Lucretia raised an eyebrow and glanced at Max. 'The key thing it to ensure you always are.'

'Young?'

'Fascinating,' said Lucretia.

Chapter 14: Tryssa

On the north-east road, Tryssa and Amicus waited on horseback in the forlorn shelter of a memorial stone for Olivarius to join them. Amicus was deep in thought, which gave her the chance to consider him objectively. He was like her, getting on in years, but it hadn't diminished him either. Olivarius glowed with youth but to Tryssa, the grey flecking the light-brown of Amicus's short hair and the lines that spoke of laughter on an otherwise serious face were more attractive.

'I just want to know where they found the ring,' he explained when the younger man joined them. 'I don't really like to believe anything those two clods say, but something about their story rang true. I'm just not quite sure what.'

'I meant to ask, sir, was the ring stolen from someone important?' said Olivarius. 'Poor Ieuan was upset he might lose face with Berenice.'

Amicus blinked, then drew a breath and looked across the farmland surrounding them. 'Someone important?' he said. 'I suppose that depends. Unless two identical rings were made, the owner was a friend. A man called Galen.'

'You think Dun and Gris broke into a memorial?' Tryssa asked.

'Oh, they do that all the time. The fact that they can sleep without haunting from the shades of a hundred ancestors seems proof that ghosts either don't exist or don't care about their grave goods.' Amicus ran his hand over his face. 'But even though Galen left Durnovaria in disgrace I'd always hoped he was still alive. He was a good friend once.'

Olivarius nodded. 'You'd have liked to speak with him again.'

'Ah, as to that,' said Amicus, 'I suppose not, since then I'd need to arrest him and then see him put to death. He stole a great deal of money.' He straightened on his sidling horse and his face grew solemn. 'But all the same, if he is alive, I'm sorry he's fallen on times so hard he's had to sell that ring. Part of me wonders if it might be possible to get him a pardon and find him something to do. He's a citizen, after all. But the description Dun gave was not hopeful. "A man in rags, wasting away."'

'Perhaps he's a leper,' said Olivarius, 'in which case, best left alone and the ring burnt.'

'Maybe,' said Amicus and shrugged. 'All the same, see what you can find out on this road, will you? People come and go all day long; someone may have seen something.'

'Dun and Gris said it was near the western entrance,' pointed out Tryssa.

'Those two couldn't tell a straight story if you paid them for it. As I say, something in what they said is true but I'm not sure what. Masner, in this instance, is as innocent as it's possible for a man like him to be. The guard are asking which way Dun and Gris entered from. Not that I expect anyone to know. Tryssa, thanks for your help. I'll escort you back to Galyna's now.'

'Don't worry,' said Tryssa. 'Olivarius can do that. I'd quite like to stay with him and see what he finds out.'

Amicus bowed. 'Of course. But if you discover nothing, don't feel you have to bother further. I'm chasing hares, I daresay, but I'm going to threaten Dun and Gris with watching the torturer go through his paces, and see if that clears what they like to call their minds.' He nodded at Olivarius and turned his horse to return to the town.

There was virtually no one on the road. The sky was overcast and threatening something but not yet prepared to decide what. Presumably all who had business in town were already there or had done it as early as possible and gone home to prepare for winter.

After a few yards Tryssa and Olivarius came across a beggar huddled under the meagre shelter of a hawthorn. He was twisted and bent as if he and the tree had been formed by the same cruel wind. A scar ran down his face through a damaged eye.

'Alms,' he said, holding out a bony hand. 'I'm a seer. I'll give you return for your coin. Just an *as*.'

Olivarius threw a couple of small coins. The beggar, hunched as he was, caught them midair. 'Thankee,' he said. 'Sir is kind.'

'What do you see?'

The beggar scanned Olivarius and Tryssa and then closed his eyes before announcing 'Things are not as they appear.'

'Whenever are they?' said Olivarius.

The beggar, without opening his eyes, gave a wheezy laugh. 'True that. But these are troubled times. Two respectable folk on horseback seek something ... or someone ... when they should be inside, dry and warm. I see money. I see worry. I see...'

Olivarius held up a *denarius*. 'As I say, none of that is new. See this.' The beggar opened his undamaged eye and focussed on the coin. 'This could be your future if you can tell me anything about the past.'

'Whose past?' said the beggar. 'Mine? That's easy told. My name's Blue. I had a proper name once I think, but can't recall it. Can't recall a lot, truth be told. I've walked a long way for a long time, but this way seems familiar. I can recall enough when I need to.'

Olivarius grunted.

Tryssa said, 'So today's the first day you've been along this road for many years.'

'I didn't say that. I've been back and forth along here for a few weeks. Back and forth lots of places -bin in Gaul for years. I expect I've seen things you wouldn't believe, only my memory you know...' He tapped his head and shrugged. 'Sometimes it pays to wait by the stones, sometimes it don't. Besides, I likes it out in the country. I can forage better most of the year. And towns - they give me the chills. But not now. Now I'm getting old. I'd sell myself into slavery for the sake of a regular roof and a meal, but who'd buy me? It'll soon be bitter winter and there's nothing to forage. The trees are sleeping like the stones, and old bones grow colder by the day. You're the first to stop for days. I keep having to go in there.' He glared at the town ramparts as if they were a cell. 'I hates it, but maybe I'll do well by the temple over the winter. Someone'll pay if I keeps asking.'

'That's hard,' Olivarius said.

'No-one's sure of life, are they? Even the rich will die, but there's a fuss and they get to do it in the dry. Usually. Been like that for always.'

'Maybe. But it's the more recent past I wonder about,' said Tryssa. 'Three days ago - the last time it rained hard - did you see a lame man, thin and ragged, trip and lose a ring near town?'

The beggar shrugged. 'More fool him for not wrapping it with thread if it was loose. Me, I'd have sold it the moment it became so. But if it happened three days ago, it was on a different road. I was on this one morning till nightfall, much good as it did me. I was pushed out the way by fat farmers and kicking soldiers and wagons full of ladies with slaves to drive them, but everyone just wanted to be inside the town and no-one gave more than an insult. Anyhow, I'm off into town now. I'm hopeful.'

'Hopeful?'

'I'll get what I deserve.'

Olivarius handed him the *denarius* and Tryssa dug in her money bag and added a *sestertius* to the open hand. 'Take care going back.'

Blue shrugged.

They watched him trudge back to Durnovaria, hunched and slow on bandaged feet. It was impossible to tell how old he was. A wagon coming towards them paused. The driver slowed to exchange words, dropped a coin into Blue's hand and then came on. When he reached Tryssa and Olivarius he stopped again, the road too narrow to pass easily.

'Good morning,' said Olivarius.

'Morning.'

'Do you know that beggar?' asked Olivarius.

The man shrugged. He was very thin; the wrists just visible between ragged sleeve and meagre gloves were bony. A crutch lay alongside him.

'In a way. I met him a couple of times on this road over the last week.'

'Is he trustworthy?'

'That's an odd question.' The man's lips narrowed.

Tryssa smiled. 'Someone lost something and we're asking people who might have found it.'

'Well...' The man shifted on the wagon seat, wincing as he straightened his leg. 'I can't say in truth if Blue's trustworthy. But to me, he's luck.'

'It sounds like life's been hard,' said Tryssa. 'I'm glad things are improving.'

The man relaxed a little. 'I'm a carpenter. Things have been - anyway, I met him while tramping for work a long way from here. He put me on to some villas thereabouts where I might find work. Nothing permanent, but it saw me through and let me come this way.'

'Where are you headed?' said Olivarius.

The man shrugged. 'I'm getting wood from the forester to do a job.'

'So you've found work here.'

'That's what I mean by luck. Now it's autumn there's no work to be had. I'm not one to beg, but it was getting bad. Then the other day on this road I met Blue again, and he mentioned a circus was at Durnovaria and needed carpenters.' His hard face broke into a sudden smile. 'So trustworthy or not, he's been good luck to me. Maybe my life's changing at last.'

'That's good news,' said Tryssa. 'I wonder if you were along this road the day we were. Or rather evening. I'm Tryssa, a wise-woman, and this is Olivarius. We're visiting Durnovaria from a long way away.'

The man's face brightened. 'From the west? Isca?' Then it dropped. 'Of course, if you were coming this way it would have been from the north.' He sighed. 'I'm Morgan. Where I'm from is a long story. All I can say is Blue has done me a good turn. If you came from the north along this road, you'll have seen that grove, I guess.'

'Sort of,' said Olivarius. 'It was pouring with rain.'

Morgan shivered. 'Maybe you passed one of us. Blue said he liked to keep company with the stones, and since passing travellers often chuck money to assuage any spirits, he does all right. Not that he'd say that.'

'He thinks he deserves it for keeping them company, you mean,' said Olivarius.

'I imagine so,' Morgan chuckled. 'This is the circus's wagon of course. I've been walking up to now.' He stretched his bad leg again. 'It takes me a while.

86

When Blue saw I was struggling, he told me he'd made a shelter under the trees and I could use it as long as I took it down the next morning. He'd been going to stay, but it was too wet and he changed his mind. I was happy to take up the offer. It beat lying in a ditch like I had the two nights before.'

Tryssa looked around at the low hedges, the sleeping ground, the copses. There were plenty of places for people to hide unseen. *Something about their story rang true*, Amicus had said, *I'm just not quite sure what.*

'During the time you were in the ditch, before you found the shelter, did you see anything odd?' she asked.

Morgan contemplated her before replying. 'Maybe.'

'Did you see maybe a thin, ragged man who lost a ring?' said Olivarius.

Morgan waggled his head, his eyes turned to the country around them. 'Nothing to do with a ring,' he said.

'What then?'

'Not one but two thin men, a little ragged. The sort who could get an honest trade if they wanted, but don't.'

'Those men,' said Tryssa carefully, 'what did they look like?'

'Small, weaselly, grubby. I'd seen them once before near one of the villas, digging about. This was different.'

'What was different?'

'This time they were burying something. Something small. I'd been asleep under a hedge, a bit feverish.'

Olivarius straightened in the saddle. 'Did you go and see what they'd buried?'

'None of my business.'

'Can you show us where they did it?' said Tryssa.

'If you like. It's not far.'

Morgan drove the wagon ten yards along the road, then alighted to hitch it to a hazel near a narrow lane. Olivarius and Tryssa dropped to the ground and, leading their horses, followed after.

A few feet along the lane, Morgan stopped where a small tree marked the corner of a field. They squeezed through a gap and stepped onto the turned earth. It was rich, soft, like the soil near Glevum and quite unlike the boggy, hostile earth of Pecunia. Mud sucked at their boots. Morgan stopped and turned.

'I was over there,' he said, pointing to the far hedge. 'Tucked down low with some branches pulled over. The men were messing about over here. Couldn't tell you where exactly.'

If she hadn't been looking, Tryssa wouldn't have noticed anything unusual. Among the roots was a pile of stones. Barely discernible among other small rocks thrown from the field during harvest was a small cairn, neat under the hedge. She crouched and lifted the stones carefully one by one, feeling a fool, but then she found a the edges of a square of turf. She dug with Olivarius's knife, and a few inches down the tip of the blade caught on something and then slipped. She could see a bundle made of rotten cloth wrapped around something. Tryssa dug around it until she could lift it out.

Inside the bundle was a skeletal hand, bones barely connected, the little finger looser than the others as it dangled on one remaining sinew.

Chapter 15: Lucretia

Odours of fat and burnt feathers filled Lucretia's nostrils as she stood with Eira at the small altar on the portico steps. The stench was overlaid by the sickly tang of rotten apples piled at gods' feet. The temple was shadowy, cool and slightly damp, a forest of looming statues, with flecks of light from small high windows catching on votives and offerings.

Lucretia surveyed the gods with disdain. They, being in the Roman style, surveyed nothing, their eyes blind and their anger frozen in stone. Back in Pecunia, the elusive Diffis was British and open-eyed. There was no image of her. If Diffis actually existed, she would feel the small joys and fears of the people around in her very bones. She peeked from under branches and breathed in a stream of water, sharing the human world, knowing whether it was hot or cold, raining or dry, looking down over a valley and knowing if this year was unusually fertile or distressingly barren.

Any gods who might lurk in the ancient hollows of Britannia belonged to Lucretia, and she to them. Their images glowered or laughed with open eyes. She was indifferent to them, but she understood them. Slender Roman idols with their inadequate clothes were utterly ridiculous.

All the same, doing what was expected by society made better contacts.

Favorix appeared from between Minerva and Jupiter and smiled in welcome. Lucretia considered simpering, but it was far too early. She settled for an aloof nod.

'Lucretia Silurenis,' said the augur as if they hadn't met the previous morning. 'You once came from the wilds to settle, and then returned to the wilds to marry that Londoner. Back then, we never expected to see you again, although some of us hoped. Do you recall me?'

'Good morning, Favorix Mellitus,' said Eira.

Lucretia smiled. 'Ah Favorix. It's as if we met yesterday.'

He gave her a frown, then turned to Eira. 'And here is dear little Nux.' He leaned forward and tickled the dog under his chin and put on a childish voice. 'Are you here to tell me how you're feeling and save me the bother of reading a chicken's entrails?' Nux nipped his fingers and Favorix withdrew them with a grimace.

'Can't we just read Nux's entrails?' said Lucretia.

Eira fixed her with a stare but Favorix bit his curving lip.

'It's joyous to have you back, Lucretia,' he said after straightening his face. 'Our temple is burgeoning. In a way it's a shame I can't bring you within to see. We only had Jupiter, Hera and Minerva when you last visited, but now we have many more. A grateful sailor paid for the one of Neptune. Do you think he feels all at sea this far out from the coast, ha ha? And we have an ancient depiction of Ooser, our local god. You can take the druid out of the countryside but you can't... I think I have that mixed up, but you and he know what I mean. Who is your local god again?'

'Diffis,' Lucretia declared. 'Water goddess. But anyway, may we?'

Favorix waved his arm airily towards another statue. 'And that of course is the divine emperor. Imperator Caesar Lucius Aelius Aurelius Commodus Augustus. God of ... well, being a divine emperor.'

'Are you sure it's not just the one of Hercules that used to be in the forum?' said Lucretia, squinting at the effigy of a man in a skin who was apparently trying to tie a somewhat bored lion in knots. A laurel wreath was askew on the statue's head, giving him the look of a man staggering home drunk who'd tripped over a large cat and wasn't too happy about it.

'Tsk,' said Favorix, nudging her in the ribs and giving her a small wink.

'Are there any *signs*?' whispered Eira.

'Very hard to say, dear lady,' said Favorix, becoming serious. 'There are many reports from Rome. These are troubled times: famine, fire, faithlessness.'

'Pshaw.' Lucretia flapped her hand. 'Rome is a long way away. Your temple is marvellous, Favorix, and I have a votive I wish you to put at Diana's feet.' She handed him a small flat piece of lead scratched with marks, and watched him squint at it before tucking it among some withered berries staining the goddess's toes. With a minuscule smile which would crack nothing on her face Lucretia said, very low, 'My own code, you know. Only she and I know it. But it has to do with hunting the future, not the past. Should she grant my desire, I will arrange for an image of Diffis to be sent here.'

Favorix made a small bow. 'Very kind. Perhaps she and Ooser can become acquainted.'

'Yes, perhaps they could.'

'While *we* could become re-acquainted. Mother's bound to be asleep again.'

Lucretia restrained the urge to grimace. 'That would be delightful.'

'Perhaps…' murmured Favorix, 'I could take you home to discuss a suitable spot for Diffis after Eira Junia makes her prayer.'

'Wonderful idea,' said Lucretia. 'I'm sure my cousin won't be long.'

Eira clicked her fingers and Riona stepped forward with a small purse. From it Eira withdrew her own votive. It bore three words. Lucretia restrained herself from spelling it out. She had just about learnt to read Latin, but she struggled with handwriting. The third word seemed to be *promissum* - it might have been

91

promise, plight, vow - who could say? The first appeared to read *Nem* - the end? *An* end?

Eira indicated the piece of lead should be placed with Minerva, nodded to Favorix and walked out of the sheltered portico into the thin autumn drizzle. A light breeze flapped her cloak, making it cling to her thin body as she stood at the top of the temple steps, raising one slender hand to a pale brow.

What a performance, thought Lucretia. Favorix was clutching at her arm and she turned, ready to share a smirk. But he looked earnest. 'Lucretia Silurensis - I can't tell you how much I -'

Before he could finish Riona let out a screech and Nux a kind of strangled yelping. Spinning around Lucretia saw Eira crumpled on the steps, half-crushing the dog. Her face was a strange suffused purple, and drool stained the corner of her mouth.

'Get a doctor! She's been poisoned!' wailed Riona. 'She's dead!'

Chapter 16: Amicus

Amicus pointed at the skeletal hand on his desk. 'Well, Tryssa Doethion, what do you make of this?'

'I don't know. Do you think it's Galen's?'

'Somehow, yes.'

'But all the same, how can you be certain after all this time that the ring Dun and Gris found was your friend's?'

Amicus drew something from his pouch and handed it over. It was a small portrait on wood. The tanned young man it portrayed had a mop of curls and a neat beard and moustache. His mouth was full - about to smile or blow a kiss - and his hazel eyes were teasing. It was so lifelike that it was almost as if someone had pressed his face to the wood and the essence of his person had been transferred. He wore a simple tunic with a red stripe from shoulder to hip and his arms were folded with his right uppermost. 'Galen's mother was Egyptian. This was something he commissioned for her. She thought it a bad omen since this sort of thing, as perhaps you know, traditionally often goes on a shroud to cover the face. But he wanted to leave her something to remember him by. Perhaps it was a premonition, I don't know. But look.' On Galen's little finger was a ring, identical to the one Ieuan had given Berenice.

'He must have been ambushed on the road,' said Tryssa.

'And the ring not taken then?'

'You said it wasn't especially valuable and that he'd stolen money. The cash would have been of more interest to any robber, surely? This hand looks as if it's been cut off. Perhaps it fell when he was attacked, and he ran away. Then the attackers got the money but hadn't even thought about the ring on the hand, and both were lost until those grave-robbers found it.'

Amicus leaned forward. 'Do you know, I think you could be right. It's not easy to escape with that kind of injury, but not impossible. Yet…'

'If you knew where they found the hand, you could be more certain?'

'Yes. That's why I want to talk to our guests again. But without them knowing we've got it.'

***

'The lady says I should give you one last chance without pincers,' said Amicus. 'Where did you get that ring?'

The room was cold, with rushes on the floor. A thin, grey light seeped in through high narrow windows. It was barely more than a cupboard really. The prisoners' cell was warmer, but from Amicus's point of view, also malodorous. To the men it might even have felt cosy, nestled in the dark like the two rats they were, and he didn't want them cosy. Better within this stark, indifferent room where he could see them properly. He cursed inwardly, wondering if he should have kept them apart.

'It was just a ring,' protested Gris, as animated as his shackles would allow. 'We found it. We didn't kill no one for it. We're not that sort. And we didn't thieve it or rob it. We just found it. It's what we do, we find things.'

'Magpies are usually prettier,' said Amicus, sitting back for a moment to consider each man. Curious that even without the dirt, they still somehow looked like small, burrowing creatures. Gris was quite young, barely mid-twenties perhaps. His facial hair almost concealed an overbite and indefinite chin. Above a very definite nose, small eyes glittered, but they were reddish and ringed with grey. 'Let's assume for one

94

moment that what you assert so passionately is true. You found it, you didn't kill, thieve or rob for it. What I want to know is where and in what circumstances. I've reason to believe the original owner of that ring is dead. I knew him.'

Amicus fell silent, a sudden image of himself and Galen younger than Gris, stumbling from a tavern, arms round each other's shoulders, laughing, singing in the moonlit street, someone cursing them, so young, so full of life. It wasn't hard to make his face sad. 'I knew him,' he repeated, his voice low, his eyes downcast. Then he leant forward, looked straight into Gris's eyes and in a colder, deeper voice he said, 'His spirit will be watching. Where ... did ... you ... get ... that ... ring?'

Gris swallowed, his Adam's apple bulging through his beard then disappearing. 'There was an 'and,' he whispered.

'Anand?' said Amicus. 'Who's that?'

'No. An 'and!'

'Han hand,' clarified Dun, flapping his own in their chains. 'We found a hand and not far away, buried in the mud down an 'ole, there was a ring.'

Was there a tiny glance between the two men? Amicus couldn't be sure.

'We didn't know if the two was together,' persisted Dun. 'Looked like maybe someone had dropped the ring and couldn't get it out. Gris's got long fingers, ain't you Gris? But we did the right thing by it. I mean we kept the ring cos, well, why wouldn't you? But we buried the 'and proper after. We showed its spirit proper respect.' The last words seemed addressed less to Amicus than to the air about them.

'Then let's go hand-hunting. I assume you can remember where you buried it?'

This time there was a definite glance between the two men. Dun and Gris nodded.

'A mile or so north of town,' mumbled Dun. 'It'll be easy enough if you make us.'

'Maybe that can wait,' said Amicus. 'More to the point, where did you find it in the first place?'

'Under a tree.'

'By a brook.'

'Which?'

'Both,' said Dun. He stared at Amicus's eyes but Amicus took in the whole of Dun's broad face. The flattened nose twitched like a rabbit's just once and his left ear, which looked as if someone had once taken a bite, moved slightly.

'Which tree? Which brook? It's a long way from the North Gate to a river.'

'Well all right then, it was more of a trickle in a ditch really,' Dun said. 'By an 'awthorn, at the edge of the road. We was just taking shelter from the rain and there it was.'

'A dog musta dug it up,' said Gris. His face was green. Amicus hoped there were enough reeds on the floor.

'It was 'orrible, all mangled. It wasn't right,' said Dun. He'd moved closer to his friend, stepping on his foot in his efforts to comfort him.

Gris suddenly shouted 'We're sorry!' There was no mistaking it this time; the young man's head was turned up to the window. He was not addressing anyone who could be seen. Despite twenty-five years in the army, Amicus shivered.

Tryssa touched his arm and he bent his head to her whisper. 'They seem scared enough for some of that to be true. If you let them go, will they go back to the same place to make amends or in the opposite direction to get away?'

'Either is possible. I could keep them in tonight and see what they do tomorrow, I suppose. It goes against my principles to let rats run for cover.'

'I think these rats will squeal eventually,' said Tryssa. 'But not yet, and somehow I think it's not you they're most scared of.'

He raised his eyebrows.

'Sorry,' she said, and grinned. 'It's only because you're not a ghost.'

He tutted and shook his head. 'Very well, I'll -'

The door burst open. 'Sorry, sir.' Petros saluted. 'Sorry Madam. There's something going on at Maximilian Hygarix Agricola's. They refused our medic, said only Tryssa Doethion would do. Or at least that's the message I got and I've been looking all over. Eira Junia's been poisoned.'

***

Amicus waited in Max's study while Tryssa tended to Eira. The steward was still out looking for his master, but Deryn had just arrived. His fastest horse was lame and he'd been slower than he'd intended. Apart from a brief greeting he ignored Lucretia and was pacing the floor when Tryssa came out, wiping her hands on a cloth. Deryn stopped, his face white.

'Don't worry,' said Tryssa. 'Your sister's all right. Whatever it was did her little harm. She must only have ingested a tiny amount. The emetic expelled it before there was any real harm.'

'Do you know what it was? The slaves said they served mushrooms this morning. Or was it the beans they had last night?'

Tryssa's face was non-committal. 'Nothing in the, er, remnants of the episode indicated what it might be. Of course I'd advise the cook to be careful about any mushrooms he's not certain about, or even mildewed nuts which might be masked with some coating or

97

other. It's been so damp recently and these are easy mistakes to make. Then again, it's possible Eira Junia was simply reacting to something that wouldn't affect someone else. I've told Riona how to make a posset and to care for her mistress. I suggest as much sleep as possible for the next twenty-four hours will be the best thing.'

'That needn't stop us talking, need it?' asked Lucretia.

Deryn stared. 'I'm not lolling about at a dinner party with my sister ill.'

'It wouldn't be a dinner party,' Lucretia replied. 'It would be a business meeting.'

'Have you no shame? Eira nearly died and all you care about is money!'

'Well it's my money and she's not dead. Perhaps we could discuss it over lunch.' Lucretia settled more comfortably into a chair. Some of her cosmetic had fallen away, but the skin underneath was almost as white.

Deryn made an exasperated noise and stormed from the room.

Tryssa broke the silence. 'I'm going back to Galyna's, Lucretia. Maybe I'll return early to Pecunia. I'm sure no-one needs me here.'

Amicus felt his heart sink. It was a sensation he hadn't had for longer than he could recall. He felt his face flame and coughed to cover his confusion, although neither woman was looking at him, but rather sizing each other up as cats might. Lucretia, he noticed, was pale, and her hands twitched slightly. With evident effort, she relaxed.

'Of course, that's up to you,' she said. 'But what if it had been *me* who was poisoned?'

Tryssa opened her mouth and then shut it. 'Well, Lucretia, let me know if you are and I'll be sure to help.' Turning to leave the room, she winked at Amicus, her eyes twinkling. 'But for now I have something else to see to. Good-day.'

Outside Galyna's house, Amicus paused. Most people were now settled in for the midday meal but a pair of slaves rushed between them bearing packages. 'When do you intend to go home, then?'

Tryssa smiled. 'Not till spring. I just wanted to see how Lucretia would react. Besides, I'll be busy later. Sila the wise-woman has asked me to train her, and Galyna and I would like to get to know each other better.'

'I'm glad,' Amicus said. 'I mean the wise-woman situation needs improving. I mean… Anyway, I'll be busy myself this afternoon, and by the time I finish it'll be too dark to see properly. But would you come back tomorrow and look at the hand again, if you don't find it too gruesome?'

'I thought you'd never ask,' said Tryssa.

Chapter 17: Lucretia

Lucretia had no time to lose. She needed to talk with Deryn before he went to ground again.

A small bronze hand mirror lay on Max's desk and Lucretia held it up as Nia straightened her wig and smoothed the cosmetic into something less cracked. The bronze surface made her appear dream-like, young. Her face was not as slim as the one Deryn would perhaps recall, now filled out and soft. Lucretia regretted the loss of her tiny waist rather more than those bony cheek-bones. Her bosom was even finer. Deryn hadn't altered a great deal, but his frowning face had matured well. And he'd been a widower for years, apparently. Talking him round couldn't be hard. It never had been when they'd been betrothed and she'd persuaded him to steal from the pantry at dawn and ride towards the sea, coming back laughing to irate Aunt Ursula. Well, Lucretia had laughed. Deryn had skulked. Or sulked, or something. Presumably he was now doing the same somewhere in the house. He just needed cheering up.

She peered into the hall and saw him leaving Eira's room. Riona followed, bearing Nux. A look of horror crossed her face, shortly followed by a stench that could have removed the fresco from the walls. The girl held the dog out at arm's length, muttered something about finding a cork - the larger the better - and marched towards the back of the house.

Without any comment Deryn turned the other way, grabbed a cloak and stormed out of the front door.

Lucretia snapped her fingers at Nia, bundled herself up in her own cloak and rushed out after him. He was striding towards the forum, shouldering pedestrians out of the way in his hurry. The midday sun was making its last attempts to warm the street but in the shadows of the houses, she shivered.

Deryn was nearly at the temple by the time she caught up. At the foot of its steps he came to a sudden stop as the beggar stumbled close, shoving a cracked wooden bowl into his chest. Deryn rummaged in his coin purse, recoiling as the beggar muttered into his face. Above them in the portico Favorix peered out, and seeing them, hurried down the steps.

'Away with you!' he cried to the beggar, and drew Deryn away just as Lucretia arrived beside them. Favorix was pale. 'How is Eira Junia?'

'Recovering,' said Deryn.

Lucretia put her hand on his arm. 'How worried you must be,' she murmured. 'But Tryssa is right, we should leave her in utter peace to recover.'

'What did you do to her?' snapped Deryn.

Lucretia blinked. 'What?'

'She says it's your fault she's ill.'

'Oh, come now,' said Favorix. 'How could Lucretia have done anything? It's hardly as if she's required to cook.'

'Quite,' said Lucretia. 'Eira is probably ill because she barely eats. Max should take better care of her.'

The beggar sidled up and grabbed Lucretia's cloak. 'Mistress, what will you give me? I remember a pretty thing with a pretty thing, flashing in the sun.'

'Whatever are you talking about?'

'An old man am I and my memory is blurred, but the spirit talks to me.'

'What spirit?'

'The stones.'

Lucretia narrowed her eyes. 'Do they speak in a gravelly voice, by any chance? Give him a coin, Favorix, I'll pay you back when I next visit the temple.' She wrenched the cloak free and tucking her arm

101

properly into Deryn's, steered him away from the temple steps at speed. Favorix reached out his hand and gave her a hopeful leer. She mouthed 'What can I do? Later,' and marched towards the market stalls.

'Where's Max?' she asked.

Deryn's eyes slid away from hers. 'Oh, drumming up support for his campaign, I daresay. Though why he has to pick now…'

Lucretia shrugged. 'He's putting a lot of effort into staging entertainments to encourage votes.'

'Effort. Mmm.' Deryn's face flickered.

'Gaining power is hard work, you know,' said Lucretia. 'Back in Pecunia I spend all my time keeping people focussed on making the place richer, and does anyone thank me?'

'It must be terrible for you,' said Deryn.

Lucretia took courage from the sympathetic smile which she sensed lay under his scowl as sun lies below cloud. 'Deryn,' she said. 'Let's leave Eira Junia to rest and talk like old friends. That can't be so hard. Why not take me for a walk around town and show me how it's changed? We could pretend I'm still leading you astray by letting you buy me street-food like you used to.' She considered putting her head on one side, remembered the wig and settled for a wink instead. 'Do you remember how annoyed Aunt Ursula used to be?'

'She blamed me because I couldn't tell her it was always your idea.'

'It was fun though, wasn't it?' Lucretia surprised herself with the words. In Pecunia she had been the daughter of a man the locals still referred to as the chieftain, even though he'd long taken up with the Romans. It had been her job to show the townsfolk how sophisticated people behaved. Then she'd come to Durnovaria and there was more than one important family and they were all so stuffy. It had been her job to

102

show them how to run wild. Not that Eira ever would. For one tiny moment the memory of the summer breeze caressing her bare face and tangling her hair made Lucretia's cosmetic and wig feel heavy and dirty.

'Sometimes,' said Deryn.

'Perhaps ... perhaps the time was just wrong for us.'

Deryn closed his eyes and swallowed. Lucretia imagined him looking back over the years and wondered if at any moment he'd risk pulling her to him now with the passion he'd signally failed to display back then.

His eyes snapped open. 'Did you love him?'

Lucretia blinked. 'Porcius? Of course not.'

Deryn stopped walking.

Lucretia wished people would concentrate on the important things in life. The scent of fresh buttery bread and roasted chicken wings basted with honey and spices filled the air. It had been a long time since breakfast.

'Let's eat and talk as if we were humble people,' she urged, wafting her hand at Nia to dust down one of the seats near the food vendor for her.

'My sister's been poisoned,' said Deryn. 'I'm not hungry.'

'Well *I* am. I know your mother left me land and I want to know where. If you're unkind her spirit might...' She struggled to imagine what her aunt's ghost would do. The one time they'd met, Aunt Ursula had been barely in her thirties, mostly worried about what the neighbours were thinking. 'She might cry.'

'No,' said Deryn with a grim smile. '*You* might. I wrote to say we'd send money as your inheritance. Wasn't that enough?'

'Why would you hide what she really intended?'

'Why would you want land instead of money?'

'Because it's land.'

'You should have written and asked about it before rushing down here.'

'You should have told me what I'd inherited.'

With a cold laugh, Deryn gave Nia some coins to buy Lucretia a filled pastry. 'It's the tiniest bit of useless land. Everything else she divided between me and Eira.'

Lucretia opened her mouth to speak but was interrupted as Max's voice called across the forum. She looked up to see him striding across, his face full of smiles.

'Deryn!' he said. 'I didn't know you were in town. I'd have taken you with me!' He patted his money pouch. 'I've had a good morning playing *tabula*. Fortuna has smiled on me. I presume you two have finally spoken, so perhaps we can come to some arrangement. We'll give you more than that piece of land is worth, Lucretia.'

'Land's land.'

'You can hardly farm it from Pecunia.'

'I could rent it out. I could have a winter house built down here, since your winters are a little warmer and less wet. I could...' Inspiration struck. 'If there's a spring, I could have a second bathhouse built - and start a bathhouse empire!'

Deryn gave another cold laugh. 'It's no good for any of those things.'

Lucretia stamped her foot. 'Why not? There's never been a piece of land you can't make *something* of.'

'Unless it's a grove with a stone circle, Lucretia,' said Deryn. 'That's what Mother left you. Untouchable. Like I said, you should have stayed in your nice little backwater with your attentive fiancé - a man you no doubt love with all your being - and counted up the cash we sent in exchange.'

'Don't be ridiculous.'

'About which bit?' said Deryn. 'Us buying the land, you loving your fiancé or you inheriting the grove?' He turned to Max and pulled him aside to explain about Eira.

Lucretia looked at the filled pastry proffered by Nia, its savoury scents filling her nose. For once, she had no appetite at all.

7th October
Chapter 18: Diggers

Where's he to? thought Dun. He hugged himself in the cold outside the stables. His breath warmed his lips as he exhaled, the air cooled them when he breathed in. This was no weather to be abroad. A small part of him missed the town lock-up and the knowledge that some sort of slop would be handed to them. He had stuffed his shoes with straw, but all the same, the chill of the stones came up to the soles of his feet. He stamped softly. He was still a little dubious about the way Amicus had released them so readily. Gris needed to hurry up. The sooner they got away the better.

A padding in the darkness came near. For a second Dun stood still and held his breath. In the pre-dawn gloom it was impossible to tell who was approaching until they were close enough to kiss. But it was all right. Even though it was very low, he recognised the tuneless humming of a love-song. Talking of kissing...

'What kept you?' he grunted.

''Ad to say goodbye, din I?' said Gris.

Dun could imagine the soppy smile on his friend's weaselly face. 'It's not *goodbye* you nirrup, we're coming back when everyone's lost interest in us.'

'Yeah, but Amicus is still unhappy. We mightn't be able to come back afore spring. And she says...'

'Nah mate,' said Dun. 'We'll be back by Saturnalia, you watch. It'll be heaving then: good pickings. I'm sure you can both wait a couple of months.'

'Yeah but...'

'Shhh.'

'Wot?'

'Thought I heard summat. Come on, let's get outta this place afore Amicus changes his mind.'

'If we can find the way out to the west road.'

'Don't be a fool. You can see the torches at the edge of town from here.'

'Look uncanny, they do.'

It was true. The flickering flames splodged, as if they'd soaked into the dark of the sky.

'You worry too much,' said Dun. 'Did she give us anything to eat?'

'Bread, cheese and a coupla small cakes. They're a bit dry, but it's all she had. They haven't started baking yet. She said she'll give us eggs if we wait. She din want me to go.' Gris sighed.

Dun pulled his hood over his head, shouldered his bag and clapped Gris on the shoulder as they walked forward. 'No time for all that. We need to be off, lad,' he said. 'It's a long two days' walk to Isca. We'll have to stop at Moridunum tonight.'

'Why west?' muttered Gris. 'Why not north? Why not east? Up to Sorviodunum or Venta Belgae? I heard there's nothing at Moridunum but soldiers.'

'We won't go to the fort, you fool,' snapped Dun. 'We'll find a tavern before then. But at Isca...' He rubbed his hands. 'We can make a fortune and no-one will know us. Then we'll come back.'

'Will I have enough to get my girl?' whispered Gris. Their feet clumped on the cobbles. A cat slinked and darted in front of them, making him stumble. He swore.

'Course you will. Come on.'

They paused at the edge of town. There was barely any change in the darkness. The torches on the nearest building sputtered. It was like stepping into a cave. A misshapen lump emerged from the gloom, making them cringe back until there was enough light to make out a farmer, lugging produce towards the forum.

'Sure about this, lads?' he said. 'Don't want to wait till sun-up? That's if it ever does come up. It's gonna be one of them days, I can feel it. Never can decide if I prefer it warm and wet or cold and sneaky.'

'Got someone waiting,' said Dun. 'We'll be fine.'

'Make sure you keep to the road then,' said the farmer. 'You'll end up over an edge else. Or worse. It's not a day I'd pick to travel west.' He shuddered.

'Wot's 'e on about?' whispered Gris as they made their way down the slope.

'Dunno.'

They walked in silence for a mile until the town was well behind them. From time to time they turned, expecting to see the sky lighten, but the sun seemed reluctant to rise. Ahead, the night seemed even more reluctant to retreat.

'It'll be a fine day in no time,' said Dun, more to himself than his companion. 'It'll be clear. We'll be able to see for miles.'

'You sure we're still going right?' said Gris.

'We're climbing, ain't we? That's the way the road goes when it goes west. Up hill, down dale, between…'

'Between wot?'

Dun tried to recall what he'd been told. 'Slopes.'

'Old places? You mean old places, don't you?'

The route continued to climb. The road was slippery under their feet. When they turned now, they could just make out a thin layer of pale sky gilding the edges of the town behind them, the torches still flickering on its ramparts. But from every other direction a low fog was creeping towards them. It climbed up from the sea to the south and crawled across the fields, it rolled from abandoned hill-forts and sucked from hidden dells in the north, and it swirled ahead of them westward like a whirlpool.

'I just remembered,' whispered Gris. 'You know that knife? The pretty one wot I found? I forgot to get it outta the hidey-hole. We need that to sell, don't we?'

Dun swallowed. 'Did you say your girl said there'd have been eggs and fresh bread if we'd waited?'

'Yeah.'

'Maybe we should go back and collect the knife, have a think and go north instead. Vadumlutra. Go and see my dear old mum. She warned me about the west, she did. Shoulda listened. What you reckon?'

'Thought your mum said if we showed our faces again she'd have us birched.'

'She was just joshing mate, just joshing. Don't be fooled by that red glint in her eyes. She loves me really.'

'But then we won't make a fortune, will we? Not in Vadumlutra. This fog'll clear once the sun's up, won't it? We could be brave and go on to Isca like you said, and make a fortune.'

In the road, the men spun. Behind them the world was slowly waking. Ahead of them it was being sucked into an abyss.

The fog moved and coiled and then, in the light of another strike of Dun's flint, they saw a thin strip of vapour detach to form into something tall and thin, unbalanced, asymmetrical, drifting closer and closer in utter silence towards them, and something like a foreshortened arm reached out…

'Peg it!' shouted Dun. He whirled Gris round and they ran back down the slope until the ramparts came into view.

'Was it 'im? It was, wasn't it? It was 'im,' gasped Gris, as they staggered towards the town.

'We keep quiet about this, you hear,' grunted Dun, his chest heaving. 'We never say a word about him. He wants his hand back, that's what.'

'Well I ain't...'

'Nor me.'

Dun and Gris slowed as the buildings closed around them. They made an attempt to swagger into the forum, their legs shaking.

'Thought you'd be back, lads,' said the farmer. 'Was there *things*? There's usually things in the fog.'

'Forgot to have breakfast,' said Gris, his voice rasping.

'Course you did,' said the farmer, peering closer now that there was enough daylight to see by. 'You're the two what Amicus questioned, ain't you? Better keep your noses clean else you'll be in the lock-up again.'

Dun turned to look west. The hills and the road were invisible, engulfed in white.

'Suits me,' he said. 'Right now, I can't think of anything I fancy more than nice thick walls till the sun's up good and proper.'

Chapter 19: Tryssa

Tryssa leaned close to the hand, her eyes narrowed as she gently touched the bones. The middle finger was almost straight, while the thumb, forefinger and ring-finger were curled. All the joints in the little finger, from the tip to the metacarpal that would once have been under the palm, were loose, attached by the slenderest of sinews. 'Didn't you say Galen wore the ring on his little finger?'

'Yes,' said Amicus. 'It was small for a man's hand. I believe it had once been his grandmother's. He wore an old bracelet too, but that was just bronze. I suppose Dun and Gris took that too.' He ran his hands through his hair and then peered closer. 'Was I wrong to let them go?' He spoke more to himself than to Tryssa. 'Is it all lies and they *did* kill him? But if that's the case then it can't be Galen.' He turned to her. 'If he'd returned he would have sought me out. We were close friends.'

'Can you tell me about him?'

Amicus paced away and looked up to the high window as if seeking permission. Then he turned. 'He disappeared around forty years ago, in the summertime. I'd joined the auxiliaries and gone abroad. Galen wrote to me once or twice after I went away, then stopped. I thought nothing much of it. A letter is a rarity, isn't it?'

'Very true,' said Tryssa. 'Corryx wrote once a year.'

Amicus nodded. 'Galen wasn't really the type anyway. He ought to have joined the auxiliaries like your brother and me, but his father was a retired legionary and wasn't happy just to be an average citizen. He wanted Galen to help make the family wealthy, get in with the local leaders, that sort of thing. Galen wasn't really interested. But he was happy to run with a gang of lads from the richer families.'

111

'Including you?'

Amicus shrugged. 'Including me. It didn't matter to us, of course, except when Galen flirted with the girls we fancied.' He chuckled. 'He was much better at it than most of us and had the looks to help.'

Tryssa watched his face, warm with memory, firm mouth on the verge of smiling, eyes twinkling, and found herself imagining running her finger along the fine line of his cheekbone as she wondered how anyone could be better-looking than Amicus was.

Her face flamed and she shook herself. Fortunately Amicus was still recalling the past and paying no attention to her. 'I suppose I assumed he wasn't writing either because there was nothing to say or too much going on. He'd mentioned girls - not just the ones I knew, like Eira, but Lucretia too. Though he generally called her something else…'

'Rhee?' Tryssa frowned.

'That's it. A shortening, I assume.'

'No,' said Tryssa. 'It's her real name, or rather her original one. She took a Latin one when she was twelve or so. How curious! She refused to answer to Rhee in Pecunia. She said it made her feel like a peasant.'

'Galen liked her spirit. He implied she was a bit wild - riding around the country with her hair down.'

'Lucretia?' Tryssa stared back into her own memory. 'Even curiouser. She went away sophisticated and came back even more so.'

Amicus chuckled. 'If anyone could dig out the inner peasant it was Galen. None of us stood on ceremony when he was around, even Eira. I'm sorry, that was unkind.'

'Maybe, but we won't find anything out if we're polite about everyone rather than honest. So when did he disappear?'

The smile dropped from Amicus's face. 'Sometime that summer. It was hot and dry. When the lads could get away from whatever their fathers needed them to do, they flirted with girls, they drank, they gambled, they fought sometimes - Deryn and Galen for certain, I gather.'

'Because he was flirting with Lucretia?'

'Or she was flirting with him - and everyone else. It seemed to be one of her, erm, pastimes.' He coughed. 'Still does.'

Tryssa rolled her eyes. 'True enough. But go on - what happened next?'

'They told me a stranger came to stay in the town and joined in all the gambling and drinking etcetera and Galen lost a great deal of money he didn't have. A few days after that, when the stranger was still waiting for him to pay up, Galen left before dawn and never came back. The stranger asked around to see who Galen's father was, but everyone closed ranks and said Galen was an orphan so the stranger left - whether to hunt him down or because he'd given up I don't know. Shortly afterwards money was found missing - money held by one of the quaestors.'

'He stole from funds for public works?'

'Apparently so - though I can't think of Galen as a *real* thief. I like to think he took it to gamble with, planning to win big enough to pay his debt, then put the money back before anyone found out. The quaestor was a hen-pecked old duffer with his head in the clouds - I'm surprised he even noticed the money had gone.' Amicus fell silent, peering once more at the anonymous skeletal hand. 'It broke Galen's father's heart. The family was disgraced after the disappearance and faded into obscurity. And I confess it broke my heart too. Galen was like a brother to me. He was always a chancer, but I had no idea he might be a thief.'

113

'And if Galen came back now?'

'I'd find a way to help him. But the truth is -' Amicus ran his hand over his face. 'He'd be safer staying away. If he came back and someone else remembered him they might not be so well-disposed towards him.'

'Do you mean the old quaestor?' asked Tryssa.

Amicus cleared his throat. 'He's long dead. His son is an augur and he - no that's nonsense. The theft didn't disgrace *his* family and he's just as henpecked as his father.' He pointed at the hand. 'Maybe this isn't even Galen's, even though I'm sure the ring Ieuan bought was his. And besides, this isn't a recent severing; the hand's too skeletal.'

'I agree,' said Tryssa. 'These are old bones. There are no marks from chewing, the flesh has gone cleanly and it's stained from earth as if it has been buried for many years.'

'But who would kill, cut off a hand, bury it and not take a ring?' mused Amicus. 'It's not extremely valuable, but it's valuable enough.' His brow cleared for a second. 'If someone's hand is severed they can survive, if they take care of the wound. Could this be a sacrifice? I mean, do you think Galen could have done it himself to placate some god?'

'Does that seem likely? You knew him.'

Amicus slumped. 'No. Not at all. And besides, if he was on the run, he wouldn't want the risk of infection.'

'Mmm.'

'Perhaps he sold the ring to raise money for gambling, tried to get it back in exchange for the money he'd stolen, then there was a fight, and the *other* person's hand was severed and fell into a ditch like those two idle wasters say. Maybe, against all the odds, Dun and Gris are telling the truth.'

Tryssa shook her head. 'I doubt it - or not entirely, anyway. I'm pretty sure they didn't find a neatly severed hand.'

'What do you mean?'

Tryssa used a stylus from his desk to touch the point where the carpals would once have connected with the radius. 'See here,' she said as they bent to look closer, 'it's a completely clean cut. If the wrist had been covered in flesh, then unless the person severing it was highly skilled, it's likely there would have been scratches on the bone where the knife missed the joint.'

'But you say it's been buried a long time.'

'Even so, I think any marks would be visible. I think this hand was severed from the skeleton, not the body.'

'Why would anyone do that?'

'I don't know,' said Tryssa. 'Although looking at this, I'd guess Dun or Gris broke the little finger to remove the gold ring.' She glanced up. 'I'm sorry, Amicus. I appreciate this might have been your friend.'

No emotion crossed Amicus's face as he shook his head. 'Continue.'

'I think someone cut the hand off at the wrist a long time after death. It's quite neat, as if they knew how to do it - or more likely, it was easy to do.'

'You're suggesting someone severed it on purpose rather than that it ... um ... fell off.'

Tryssa nodded.

Amicus clenched his jaw. 'You mean someone killed him, dismembered his body and scattered it to stop the spirit wandering? But then - isn't it usually only the head that's removed for that purpose?'

'Yes about the latter. No about former. I think there might be a simple explanation.'

'What?'

Tryssa straightened. 'I think Dun or Gris severed it.'

Amicus slammed his fist on the desk, making the hand jump and turn over. It looked like a wounded beast trying to crawl away. 'I should never have let them go.'

'They won't have gone far, and they'll come back.'

'How do you know?'

'Rats like their own nest.'

Tryssa watched Amicus wrap the bones in the cloth as carefully as if they were made of glass, and then looked into his face. His ire appeared to be replaced by consternation, his eyes flickering as if following the thoughts trickling round his mind.

'You said the last thing you expected was that Galen would steal money,' said Tryssa. 'Who told you he did?'

Amicus pondered and then scowled. 'That's a good question. It was forty years ago, give or take, and I was young. My father was a fair-minded man. He wrote to tell me Galen had run away, but nothing else. When I came back on leave it was old news. I accepted what everyone said, grieved, and then went back to my legion. In the next twenty-four years I always hoped I might meet him somewhere else in the empire, but I didn't. So I hoped he'd made a new life, and maybe the shock had stopped him from letting gambling destroy his life like it does for so many. But now I think about it… He hadn't got to that stage then - so what was different about that time? Someone must remember. I haven't talked about it with the old gang since that first leave. But…'

'Shall we see what we can find out?'

'We?'

Amicus stood in a shaft of light, his skin warmed by the russet of his cloak. Tryssa could imagine how he'd looked as a young man and wondered if he could see beyond her own greying hair. *I'm being ridiculous*, she thought. *It's not as if he's the only good-looking man I've seen. But - he's one of the most loyal.*

He frowned again as if trying to read her mind. A loyal man.

'Who was in the gang?' said Tryssa. 'You said that apart from Galen, they were all from the prominent local families.'

Amicus took a breath. 'Max, Favorix, Deryn, me. Perhaps I shouldn't be dragging it all back up again. Perhaps it doesn't really matter. There's no chance of finding the stranger he owed money to. And that stranger won't want to be found since he must have killed him for the money. If this is Galen, there's nothing to be done for him - and if it isn't, I can only hope he's still alive out there somewhere and we'll do our best by this poor fellow.'

'If it will settle your mind to find out what really happened, then it won't hurt to ask,' said Tryssa. 'But it's not for me to interfere.'

'I'm more than happy for you to interfere,' Amicus said. 'We'll start with Deryn. He always tells things as they are without embellishment. He'll be fair, even though he and Galen fell out.'

'Over Lucretia?' Tryssa rolled her eyes again. 'She was only here for a month.'

'That's all it took, apparently. If you're happy to help, let's do it now, although I'm not sure what excuse I'll give.'

'I've got one. Deryn mentioned a lame horse yesterday. I helped Sila prepare an embrocation for it and I planned to send it over, but we could take it instead.'

'Good. I'll have Olivarius see if he can find anything in the records about the quaestor's accounts and send Petros to find Dun and Gris.'

'Oh, I don't suppose they're too far away. As I say, they'll want to be in their nest by nightfall.'

Chapter 20: Diggers

'Shoulda stuck it out for Isca.' Dun stamped the ground to see if any of it was dry. Mud oozed up the sides of his boots. He glared around at the marketplace. The locals knew the best spots from which to sell. They had tables for their wares and benches to sit on. With arms folded, they stared at the two newcomers, watching to see what they'd do next.

Gris shivered, hunched inside his cloak. 'Nah.'

'It was just fog,' said Dun.

'No it wasn't,' said Gris. 'It was *him*.'

'It couldn't have been him. It was the wrong road. We buried him good and proper on the north side. If anything, he should have followed us here.'

Gris shuddered again. On a cold, foggy autumn morning it wasn't hard to imagine the townsfolk of Vadumlutra as wraiths: grey, hollow-eyed, threatening.

'We shoulda moved a leg too,' Dun added. But then an image came into his mind of a ghost hobbling towards them with a crutch, or worse, hopping or crawling across the mud. 'It's not fair. We never done him in. The blood's on someone else's hands. We just relieved him of a ring and a bracelet, and Masner took them off us no trouble. And we treated him respectful.'

'Yeah,' said Gris, his voice wobbling. 'What's he got against us?'

'Why be scared of a skellington?' murmured Dun. 'I'm more frightened of *her*.'

A woman had risen from the log she was using as a stool and clumped towards them. Her feet were so mud-encrusted it looked as if she was using platters for shoes. Bundled from head to toe in brown and barely tall enough to reach Dun's chest, she looked as if she'd been moulded from clay by a small child.

'Wot you want?' she said, her arms still crossed.

119

'Hello, Mum,' said Dun, bending to kiss his mother's dry cheek.

'Don't you "Hello Mum" me.' She turned her glare to Gris.

Gris swallowed. 'Hello Wena.'

'Why are you still hobnobbing with this waster?' she snapped. 'I told you to keep away from my son and get a trade.'

'Don't be hard on the lad, Mum,' pleaded Dun. 'He just wants to sell enough stuff to be able to get his girl.'

'At least he can find one willing to take him on.'

'Don't be like that, Mum.'

'And why did you follow your father into grave-robbing after what happened to him?' said Wena. 'You'll be the death of me, you and your stolen goods.'

'They're not stolen,' said Dun, affronted. 'They're reclaimed.'

'Yeah well, let's hope the original owners don't reclaim them back, hey?'

The two men shivered. Gris glanced westwards. 'Don't say that, Goodwife Wena,' he begged.

She humphed. 'Well you better watch out or it'll serve you right. Remember what happened to his father. Anyway, why are you back?'

'Got something to sell,' said Dun. 'Thought we'd try a different market.'

The three of them took in the scene. The town was small, huddled in a rough circle of houses around a marketplace. Nearby was the fording place where people from the other side could walk across the broad river. Sometimes in deep winter it froze enough to cross. Otherwise, if the water ran too deep, a ferry on a pulley would bring you across, but right now even that was no good since the river was in flood, lapping the gardens of the houses, furious as it tumbled and over-spilled its channel. The market traders were already competing for a sparse selection of customers and at the sight of additional potential competition, were pushing up their sleeves ready to send Dun and Gris down the swollen river without a boat.

'Why here?' said Wena. 'Why not Vindoclavia? There's Romans there.'

'Can't a man miss his mother and want to come home?'

'Huh. What you got?'

Dun nudged Gris who unwrapped the knife and held it out on his palm. It was bronze, polished till it gleamed like gold. Twists and intricate swirls covered its handle and an image of a woman holding ears of wheat in her hands, her hair flowing around her shoulders. The blade was carved with dragons and knots on one side and a bull on the other.

'What a lot of old junk,' said Wena. 'Who's gonna buy that? Even your granfer would think it was nothing but rubbish, and people could persuade him a cowpat was treasure if they gave him enough mead. I suppose someone might buy it to melt down.'

'It's beautiful,' said Gris.

'It's fancy nonsense,' said Wena. 'Did you get it out of an old grave?'

'N-no,' said Gris. 'Not *in* one. Near one maybe, but not *in* one. It was just buried. Someone musta dropped it.'

'Yeah? No risk of it haunting me?'

'No Mum, would I do that to you?' said Dun, shocked.

'You'd sell *me* if you thought you'd make any money,' said Wena. 'But Gris seems sure it ain't haunted.' She turned the knife over and then rummaged in her purse. 'Tell you what,' she said, 'I'll pay you a *denarius* for it, and I'll sell it when I find someone fool enough to buy it. But you'd better go back to where

121

you came from. No one's going to put up with you pitching a stall here today. Trade's slow. Take or leave it, lads: a *denarius* and go, or just go.'

The two men exchanged glances and sighed.

'We'll take it,' said Dun. 'But any chance of lunch first, Mum?'

'Just like your father,' she grumbled.

Chapter 21: Amicus

Deryn walked his horse up and down the yard to see if Tryssa's embrocation had taken effect. Meanwhile, not for the first time, Amicus admired his villa which faced south, with a painted portico and no attempt at a Roman atrium within. The windows were glazed and the sun glinted off the ripples in the glass, turning them into molten gold.

'Thank you Tryssa Doethion,' said Deryn as he returned. The horse reached out her nose to nuzzle Amicus and he ran his hand down her neck, feeling her warmth transfer to his hand, the smoothness of her chestnut hair under his hard palm. The mare tossed her head and then turned to lock eyes with him before turning again and nudging Tryssa's shoulder.

'There's enough liniment to last a while,' said Tryssa. 'I've taught Sila the recipe and she'll be able to make more when you need it.'

'Wasn't she resentful that you'd be taking the credit for this?'

'It's not how we work. Any wise-woman who cares more for her pride than her patients' needs can't be trusted.'

Deryn patted the horse and clicked his tongue. She nuzzled into him and gave a gentle whicker before the groom led her into the stable. There was barely a trace of a limp.

'Thank you, Tryssa Doethion,' he repeated. 'I could not have borne to lose her.'

'The injury is still there,' said Tryssa. 'She must be allowed time to heal and build up her strength.'

'Of course. But that liniment is almost...' Deryn swallowed.

'Magical?' Tryssa laughed. 'Not at all.'

There was a pause. Amicus had known the other man all his life. Deryn had always kept his own counsel, preferring farm to town, animals to people. He was a quiet man and an honest one. If anyone tried to cheat him, Deryn would never do business with them again. If someone *actually* cheated him, that person could expect to lose a tooth or two. But he was fair. If Lucretia had truly broken his heart all those years ago, he didn't seem to tar Tryssa with the same brush for being connected with her.

'Will you both come inside?' he offered. 'It's not very homely I'm afraid, but it's freezing out here. I expect you could do with warming up before you go back to town.'

Without thinking Amicus went to lift Tryssa's heavy bag, but before he could, she'd shouldered it. She hugged herself, slightly blue with cold. The sky was heavy with the fog which had not quite lifted, the air damp, droplets sparkling in the braids she had wound round her head.

She and Amicus followed Deryn to the villa and were ushered inside, handing their cloaks over to be hung up before entering a small room warmed by a crackling fire.

'I'm sorry, Tryssa Doethion,' said Deryn. 'I didn't mean to imply anything untoward about your liniment.'

'I'm not easy to offend,' she answered, her eyes twinkling. 'And trust me, plenty try.'

Deryn laughed and scratched his nose. 'Take a seat,' he said, indicating the chairs in front of the fireplace. 'I'm afraid this is the only room I bother to heat, as there's only me here usually. I don't really entertain, you see.'

His hounds spread out on the hearth, one of them putting her head on Deryn's feet. 'Who would want to offend a wise-woman? It seems a little unwise.'

'To someone I'm only the wise-woman when she needs one. Otherwise I'm just the person she's known since childhood.'

'Ah, Lucretia. It doesn't seem like the sort of thing a friend would do,' said Deryn. It was more of a question than a statement.

'Lucretia isn't a friend,' said Tryssa. 'Just someone I've known all my life. If I really did have magic powers I might have been tempted to turn her into something by now. Sadly, however...' She gave a small wicked grin.

'I'm not sure I entirely believe you,' said Deryn. 'That liniment did work wonders very quickly.'

'Ah,' said Tryssa, 'that wasn't just the liniment. It was when the mare stopped noticing her pain. Once she started to relax, the liniment and massage could start the healing.'

'So what made her relax? It was as if you could talk to her too.'

'Too?'

Deryn blushed despite his weather-worn cheeks but didn't answer. Amicus knew he had a special way with horses. He wondered if Deryn and Tryssa had even more in common, and felt a small, unexpected pang. He should leave and let Tryssa do the questioning, since the two of them were getting on so well. But then she turned as if to make sure he wasn't excluded.

'Deryn's cousin Camilla can talk to horses much better than I,' said Tryssa. 'She learnt when she came to Pecunia. It's very handy. Perhaps it's in the blood.'

'Camilla?' said Deryn and Amicus together.

'Lucretia's niece,' said Tryssa. 'Tullia's daughter.'

Deryn screwed up his eyes. 'I never met Tullia. She was only five or so, wasn't she? Too young to travel down.'

125

'She's quite different from her sister,' said Tryssa. 'Rather lost in Glevum I think. Very much prefers the wilds.'

'Is this Camilla the same?'

'No. Camilla is simply herself. A tendency to act before she thinks. A bit unpredictable and as I say, very good with horses.'

Deryn grunted. 'Sounds too much like Lucretia. All she and I had in common was horses. She'd borrow some leggings and we'd ride south across the fields and we didn't have to talk. She had very lovely hair I remember, streaming out behind her. But then we'd have to slow down and she'd treat me with utter disdain. I could never think of one solitary interesting thing to say to her.'

Tryssa was watching him, warming her hands on an earthenware beaker of spiced cider. The flickering fire and the reddish-brown of her dress made her face glow.

'Camilla is nothing like Lucretia,' she said. 'I'm sorry for what you suffered back then.'

'Humph.' Deryn shifted in his chair and the dog resting on his foot gave a soft woof. 'Our mothers were sisters. Mine thought it would be a good match without really finding out what Lucretia was like. It was a bad summer, but in the end I got over it. Everything feels like the end of the world when you're young, doesn't it?'

'It does.'

Deryn's gaze moved from the fire to Tryssa, and he frowned a little. 'I suppose I shouldn't blame her. No-one pretended it was a love match - they just hoped it would turn into one. Lucretia was sent down as a prize. The idea from my parents' side was that if she sold her land, she'd bring me a great deal of wealth. I've no idea what her father was thinking. She seemed excited to see somewhere new. I suppose she just wanted to feel free to explore it her own way, rather than have her life all set out for her. In the end she refused to sell her land, and when she suggested I sold the rights to mine and went back with her, I refused. Not that that was the only problem. I found her energy exciting, but she thought me very dull and rather strange. I was better at drawing than talking.'

Amicus glanced up at the fresco around the study walls. Deryn had painted it himself, breaking every classical rule. A woman peeked from behind an oak tree, holding a basket, her head to one side. It was a simple sketch but Amicus knew it was Deryn's late wife Elli. He wondered what she would look like now, apple-cheeked perhaps, plump maybe, grey like all of them. The right woman for Deryn - one who wouldn't waste time with wigs and cosmetics. Perhaps the basket was supposed to hold the baby who'd died with Elli, tucked up safe, just out of sight. It wasn't the sort of thing you could ask. And he wasn't any closer to discovering the things he needed to.

'That summer -' he began, but Tryssa tapped his foot with her own.

'This is a lovely room,' she said. 'I like the mosaic. It's a very unusual design. It's the four seasons, isn't it? Nothing but white and grey in that dark corner representing winter. In that one fresh greens and pastel pinks indicate spring; by me, rich reds and dark greens display the fullness of summer, and by you, tumbled autumn browns and oranges. Our two corners catch the light of the fire. And where Amicus sits, in the middle, is a never-ending circle.'

Deryn blinked. 'No one has ever realised before. People think it's nonsense.'

'It's your design, isn't it?'

He gave a small laugh. 'Yes. The mosaic maker thought I was mad. Grumbled. Offered me a goddess for half-price instead. I drew it many years ago. I never had the chance to show Lucretia before she upped sticks and went home. Although she'd already told me what she wanted for her house. Her ideas were quite different. Gods, dolphins, who knows what. The usual. Never did find out if it was made. There was some difficulty...' He ground to a halt. 'For a long time I thought of how strange mine was, and was embarrassed to think I'd nearly shown her.'

'Mmm,' said Tryssa. 'Yours is original. Lucretia's looks just like every other mosaic I've ever seen.' She paused. 'Maybe it's not for me to say, but...'

A slave entered with a platter of savoury items which he placed on a low table between them, then replaced the jug of mulled cider with another and withdrew.

'That summer -' Amicus said eventually. 'Forgive me Tryssa Doethion, I want to speak of things from long ago and I fear you'll be bored.'

'Everything is interesting if you look at it the right way,' said Tryssa. 'And I love stories.'

Amicus chuckled then grew grave again. 'It's a hard thing to explain, but recently Galen came to mind.'

Deryn's face paled and then flushed again.

Amicus turned to Tryssa. 'I know you come from the same village as Lucretia Silurensis. Did she mention Galen after that summer she came here?'

'No. She said very little about her visit here when she returned.'

Deryn snorted. 'I'm surprised she didn't make something up. I imagine there must have been gossip. Are you sure she didn't make me out to be a monster?'

'There was a great deal of talk,' said Tryssa. 'But all credit to Lucretia, she simply raised her head and ignored it.'

128

Deryn's face burned. 'I'd like to sympathise, but I can't. I'm not sure which is worse: being a forsworn boy or a forswearing girl. What did she tell you, Tryssa Doethion?'

'Nothing,' said Tryssa. 'As I say, we aren't remotely close. After returning she never once explained to anyone, other than to say she didn't want to leave her land to live in Durnovaria, and you didn't want to leave yours to live in Pecunia.'

'But now she's back. Why do you think she couldn't just accept money instead of coming down to argue?'

'You'll have to ask her. We're no closer now than we were then.' Tryssa frowned. One of the dogs lifted his head into her lap and she stroked its ears absently. Amicus wondered what was on her mind. Whatever it was, she shook it off and turned her smile back to him in encouragement.

'I'm sorry, Deryn,' Amicus said. 'I'm digging very old bones.'

Deryn scowled but then shook his head. 'Lucretia had a sort of fascination - probably because she was from somewhere else. But she and I weren't a good match. I didn't realise it at the time, just thought I was a failure for not being more interesting. And dented pride...' He bit a honey-cake and choked on a crumb.

'Dented pride makes men of us.' Amicus played with the beaker, tipping it to watch the dregs roll round the bottom. 'But going back to Galen. He was my friend,' he explained to Tryssa, again as if she didn't know. 'I was away when he disappeared.'

'Disappeared?' she said, leaning forward to withdraw a spindle from her bag and start that slow measured teasing and spinning which women did rather than sit idle. The dog sniffed at the wool and licked the end of the spindle.

'I'm making it sound too mysterious,' said Amicus. 'I confess that Galen was in disgrace. He absconded.'

'He was a criminal,' said Deryn, his face closed.

Amicus made a rueful gesture. 'Yes, indeed. I promised his mother I'd try to find him, but of course I never did. Did you have any idea where he went?'

'Surely he'd have gone to Armorica,' said Deryn. 'Galen had the whole empire to lose himself in once he got across the sea. Maybe he even went outside the empire and took his chances there. He was the kind who would.'

'Perhaps,' said Amicus. 'What do you recollect of him just before he ran away?'

Deryn scratched his head. 'It was forty years ago. I can barely remember last week.'

'I meant his demeanour. What do you recall of his behaviour in general?'

Deryn glanced up at his mural even though Galen wasn't depicted in it. He seemed to seek inspiration in the painted skylarks flying above willows and the stylised cat sunning itself on a lightly sketched window-ledge.

Amicus closed his eyes and tried to remember for himself those evenings when the young men had gone out on the town together.

He recalled Galen clapping Deryn on the shoulders, offering more wine, telling him not to worry so much. If he mocked it was to Deryn's face, since he wasn't the sort to laugh behind someone's back. But he'd tease without understanding how a different mind might work. Galen would never have painted a mural or designed a mosaic. His sole creative skill was the ability to bring an evening to life. He never understood how hearts might break, but he cared. Galen and Deryn weren't kindred spirits, yet they'd been friends. Once.

Only Galen was a gambler. If he won money or a girl's attention it was open, fair and square. He'd expect the other man to accept things as they were without offence. What if the other man hadn't?

Amicus opened his eyes.

Deryn shrugged. 'Galen was one of the lads, wasn't he? Drinking, flirting ... good at gaming just like Max. Better than me. I wasn't foolish enough to bet against either of them in *calculi* or *tabula*. Galen wasn't a cheat, though. Straight as they come. He wanted what he wanted and he bet big. When he won, he won big and when he lost, he lost big.'

'And you weren't surprised when he stole that money?'

'He owed money, he left, the money was gone. There was no other explanation.' Deryn's eyes, despite his assertion, were turned away.

'Do you remember the person he owed it to?'

Deryn snorted. 'A stranger? In Durnovaria? Picking out one sparrow from another would be easier, although they said afterwards something about him was quite distinctive.' He frowned.

'They?' said Tryssa.

Deryn grunted. 'You know. People. Gossip. Makes a better story, doesn't it? I wasn't paying attention. I might not even have been there when they were gambling, or more likely drowning my sorrows and oblivious.'

Amicus bit his lip, looking briefly into the fire and then directly at Deryn. 'I know Galen angered you. I was away, but I heard how he pursued Lucretia.'

Deryn gave a short laugh. '*Everyone* pursued Lucretia. She was new, she was from somewhere else, she was a whirlwind. And she treated everyone like dirt. That was the thing. She was a challenge that every young man thought he could win. None did.'

'Yes, but you were the one who was betrothed to her.'

Deryn took a swig of cider, his hand trembling. 'It was a family arrangement, a mistake. Even Mother could see it and she didn't insist the marriage went ahead. So Lucretia went home. As for Galen, he was straight, like I said. He made no pretence that he was attracted to her, and she responded to him the same as she did to all of us - as if he was less than a speck of manure on the sole of her shoe.' The dog at his feet let out a small surprised yelp as if his master's foot had jerked and Deryn leaned down to comfort him, his expression hidden but his face red nonetheless. 'None of that would make me answer you differently. You know perfectly well that Galen was one of the lads. Always short of cash, often brawling. One minute he was here and the next minute he was gone. Everyone said he lost a game with the wrong sort of person and panicked. If you're wondering if I know what the game was or who it was with, then no, I have no idea. I wasn't fool enough to compete with him for anything. Not for anything.'

Chapter 22: Tryssa

They were silent as they left Deryn's house. The two ponies walked side by side back to Durnovaria in a gentle rolling walk. After a while Amicus said, 'Tell me about you and Lucretia.'

'She's not my friend.'

'I know. That wasn't what I meant.'

Tryssa contemplated the man beside her, then looked away and recalled Pecunia in the spring when Lucretia had left.

A small town - little more than a village - between a marsh and a forest. Tryssa is fifteen. Brown curls bounce on her shoulders as with smooth strong hands she pounds roots in a pestle to her mother's satisfaction. A thousand other chores besides wait to fill her day.

Some extra sense makes her heart quicken, and she looks outside.

Smoke coils from the roofs of roundhouses into a sky of the perfect blue which remembered skies often are. It's somehow no surprise when her view is blocked by a young man beckoning from the doorway, but her heart lurches anyway. He is middle-height, muscled and dark-haired.

Just remembering his laughing eyes makes her smile all these years later. She can still recall the scent of him - wood smoke and earth - a huntsman's smell.

'Go on with you,' says her mother. 'You can take this ointment to the chieftain.'

Tryssa puts her work away neatly, not just because of her mother's scrutiny but so Rhys doesn't think she's as eager as she really is. He catches her hand when she emerges into the sunshine.

It's a long walk to his homestead up the hill, but not long enough. The house is daunting: part Celtic, part Romanised, the worst of both. Slaves are everywhere. It is the wealthiest house for miles. In a year's time she will be its mistress, but she's already determined she won't sit idle letting others do what she could do herself.

Rhys's father Lyn is an old man to a fifteen year old girl - over sixty, white-bearded, narrow-eyed, gruff.

'Regulus?' he barks at Rhys. 'Have you no work to do?' He scans Tryssa as if willing her to quail but she stands straight and stares back, handing him the ointment. Lyn couldn't manage without Mother's lotions and tinctures. There's more than one way to be important.

'I've told you before, Father,' says Rhys, 'I won't take a Roman name.'

'If I had more sons and didn't need you to run this place I'd make you join the auxiliaries,' says the old man. He glares at Tryssa again, then back at Rhys. 'You won't get rich without knowing how to use the Romans.'

Rhys shrugs and puts his arm round Tryssa. 'We're rich enough already. And think of the grandsons we'll give you.'

His sisters come out of the house. Little Tullia, pirouetting barefoot in the dust, is just five. Rhee is a few months older than Tryssa and her hair is braided in what she tells everyone is the latest Roman style. Once her hands were strong and scratched from learning to berry and bake with the other girls. Nowadays her hands are soft, smooth and unstained.

'Hello, Rhee,' says Tryssa.

'You know I go by Lucretia now,' says Rhee, scowling. She looks Tryssa up and down, then turns her glare to Rhys. 'Shouldn't you be hunting?'

'Later,' says Rhys. 'Shouldn't you be packing? Your bridegroom is waiting.'

Rhee's face reddens and her eyes flash. 'If there was a boy worth having round here, I'd stay to make this place what Father wants,' she snaps. 'And you could leave and marry our girl cousin. She's the right sort.'

A chill goes through Tryssa, but Rhys's arm is warm around her. 'I've got the right sort already,' he says.

Rhee tosses her head. At the same time and with the same intensity, she and her father stare at their land. Lyn's mottled, knotty hand rests for a minute on his elder daughter's shoulder. Do her eyes glisten? And if so, with distress or anger?

'Deryn will give you the luxury you think you deserve,' mocks Rhys. 'And you'd better learn our "girl cousin's" name since she'll be your sister-in-law.'

Rhee repeats 'Shouldn't you be hunting?' but Rhys laughs and pulls Tryssa away to sit in the orchard.

She will always remember the taste of his kisses that day, the sparkle in his eyes, the reluctant walk home and saying goodbye at her own door before rushing inside to her duties.

Her mother tuts but does it with a proud smile. 'That's a good lad you have,' she says. 'He's like his mother. He'll give you a happy life.'

'We'd run together in the pack as children,' said Tryssa, shaking herself. 'But after Lucretia's mother died she grew apart from the rest of us, and became more romanised. Not that we'd ever been close. Then I became betrothed to her elder brother and it looked as if we would be sisters. She wasn't very keen on the idea.'

'Were you?'

'Lucretia and I have this similarity: we don't let what other people think stop us.' Tryssa heaved a sigh as the image of the two girls squaring up to each other faded away. 'It wasn't just because I wasn't grand enough for her, but because she knew she'd have to leave her land and I would be mistress there. Even if we'd liked each other, that would have been hard for both of us.'

Amicus rubbed his chin. 'I can see that. And her match was made so far away.'

'Yes. She didn't want to go, but could see it might be worthwhile. To this day I think Deryn's right: she had some hare-brained plan of bringing him back to Pecunia and running the Durnovaria land with stewards.'

Amicus frowned. 'I don't understand. I thought you said you married her brother. Isn't the land yours?'

Again the scent of woodsmoke drifted through Tryssa's memory. And the rich smell of undergrowth … and the tang of blood.

'No. I never had the chance to marry him,' she said. 'Rhys died a few days before Lucretia had been due to leave for Durnovaria, killed by a boar when he went hunting alone. She was the one who found his body. The visit to meet Deryn was delayed but Lucretia came here anyway, then rejected him after all. It was a complete waste of time. I shouldn't have been surprised by the way you described the Rhee Galen knew. I think now that she never intended to stay in Durnovaria. She just wanted to get away from the forest where Rhys had died and be someone else. Not the chieftain's daughter, not dead Rhys's sister, just a young girl with no responsibilities. I would have too if I could have. With Rhys gone, Lyn left the land to her.'

Amicus said nothing. The only sound was the steady clopping of hooves and occasional squawking crows. Tryssa could sense his sympathy, but was glad he wasn't saying the usual trite things people said. It was no good his being sorry. It had been a long time ago. The pain and grief had long been replaced by warm memory.

'Anyway,' she said, 'Lucretia came back, was introduced to a man with alleged good connections who wanted to live in Pecunia despite its many drawbacks, and married him. To be fair, she *has* made the land pay - despite Porcius rather because of him. She thinks her son is a dreamer but left to his own devices I think he'll do well, if she could stop interfering.'

'It's hard to imagine her being of interest to Galen the way she is now.'

'She wasn't *quite* so self-absorbed then. But she was self-contained. A challenge, perhaps?'

Amicus chuckled. 'That sounds possible. And maybe he just meant to tease Deryn or maybe even break it up, because it would have been a disaster and he was actually trying to help a friend.' He gave her a soft smile. 'It must have been terrible when Rhys died. I suppose after that…'

'I should have gone away, perhaps, but I didn't. I stayed to train under my mother. But all in all, life has been good.'

'And you and Lucretia have had little to do with each other.'

'Not much,' said Tryssa. 'Childbirth, sickness, bad winters or harvests when the village had to pull together - that was about it until last year. Then her husband died and, well, a few other people, and we sort of fell back into each others' spheres.' She took a deep breath. 'But one thing is certain; she couldn't have severed that hand. We'll have to let what Deryn said sink in before we work out if it has any significance. Who shall we speak to next? Max or Favorix?'

'Max,' said Amicus. 'I've invited his family to dinner tonight. If you would do me the honour of coming too, perhaps we can dig a little deeper.'

'I'd be delighted,' said Tryssa. 'And beforehand, as soon as they're back from their travels, a little chat with Dun and Gris.'

'Ah yes,' Amicus gave a small grin. 'Let's look on it as an appetiser.'

Chapter 23: Lucretia

Ondi was lounging at the bottom of the temple steps watching the world go by, and jumped to attention as Lucretia reached his side.

'We was worried about you, mistress!'

'Were you now?'

Max was crossing the forum from the other side but also looking, thankfully, in entirely the wrong direction, and therefore was unaware she'd climbed a few steps and then come down them.

She gave one backward flutter of her eyelashes in the general direction of where Favorix was watching her, and her arm hooked through Ondi's elbow. If her thin shoes slipped on the stone, it would be his fault.

'Alms!' cried Stump from the shadow of the temple. Spittle sprayed. It glued his beard and dampened the front of a filthy over-tunic. He shook a slimy wooden bowl held between two bandaged wrists.

Lucretia, feeling nauseous, lurched sideways and knocked Ondi off the last step. 'Good morning,' she said.

Max turned a warm smile on her. 'Ah, here you are, Lucretia,' he said. 'It's nearly lunchtime! I see you were able to brave the weather.'

'A little frost never killed anyone important,' said Lucretia. 'And who would want to be holed up in the dark on a day like today? It's so wonderful to be alive and feel the blood pumping through one's veins! Does Eira still feel unwell? How many years, I mean, days has that continued?'

Max winced. 'I imagine you're used to more bracing weather in Pecunia. You must be missing your home. I was speaking with your slave earlier.' He nodded at Ondi. 'He says that you can see right down across a hazy valley as moss-like as a redhead's eyes, and the sound of the river in winter is like the tumbling of celestial lovers in a bed made of waves, and the forest behind you whispers secrets in a lost language.'

Lucretia blinked at Ondi in surprise. She didn't realise he could utter any long speech, let alone such a ridiculous one. Ondi flushed, but didn't meet her eyes. It proved everything she'd ever heard about the Ordovices. They were too fond of songs and too secretive.

She was about to say so when she realised that Max was dreamy with approval. Swallowing the disparaging words on the tip of her tongue, she cleared her throat. 'Well, the valley is definitely green and the others can be very noisy. I confess that I am too busy with to be poetic about them.'

Max chuckled. 'You sound like Amicus. He would say he was a practical person.'

'Practical people get things done,' said Lucretia. 'I do so worry about my son. He is apt to start overseeing something and then rush off and write a poem about it. And of course my daughter-in-law spoils the slaves. I fear the place will have gone to rack and ruin by the time I get back.'

'Can't your fiancé look into things for you?'

Lucretia batted her eyelashes. 'Oh, Anguis doesn't really understand, you know. He's not a man of action. He has staff to look after his other staff, if you see what I mean. And although he sent Olivarius as my escort, he has woefully neglected me since I arrived. Here I am, a poor widow - well not poor, I mean wretched, I mean, under-appreciated - still in my prime, needing a helpmeet. I wonder sometimes…' She lowered her gaze.

'Poor Lucretia,' said Max, taking her hand and patting it. 'I'm sure no-one under-appreciates you.'

She raised her eyes again and looked into his. His stare was very intense, his chiselled face enough to make a heart beat faster.

'Of course, Max,' she breathed, 'I'm sure you wouldn't.'

Max smiled and opened his mouth to speak. Before he could do so, Deryn appeared at his shoulder.

'Good day,' he said, flicking a cold glance at Lucretia. 'Max, shouldn't you be at home tending to Eira? I've just been round looking for you and Berenice is hammering on her door intent on bothering her. You've allowed your daughter to be far too wayward.'

'Oh, come now,' said Max. 'Berenice isn't wayward, she's just high-spirited. I wish more girls were. It makes them a lot more interesting.' He stuck his chin out.

'All this nonsense about the grove,' snapped Deryn. 'Who put it into her head that it was suitable land for building on? Or, for that matter, suitable land to wander over as if...'

'Oh, but Deryn...' murmured Lucretia. '*You* took me to wander over it when we were very young, don't you remember? And you promised you'd protect me from anything hiding in the stones.' She held his gaze for a moment, startling even herself as the years dropped from his face and he blushed as he once had. For a second Lucretia recalled lying in the long grass and Deryn looking down, unsure what to do next, while the warm breeze danced in and out of the stones only feet away, and the leaves of the oak tree rustled like gossips.

'Alms!' Stump's voice made them jump. 'Time was thozh shtanding shtones - guarded the spiritsh - shtones of our fathers - one, two, three, four...' Spittle flew.

'Oh for pity sake, let's move,' said Lucretia.

'Fivsh...Sixsh!'

'Here.' Deryn threw a couple of coins into Stump's bowl as they walked away.

Max's face had darkened. 'Well it wasn't *me*. Everyone knows you don't mess with that sort of grove. I can't imagine what modern ideas Berenice has been listening to which make her think it's safe.'

Deryn glared. 'People have sheltered there overnight. They've no respect.'

'People? What people?'

'Tramps, beggars, I don't know. Someone's been there. Which they did without our permission.'

'*My* permission,' said Lucretia. 'Technically it's mine.'

'Regardless of permission,' said Deryn, his expression unchanged. 'I caught a beggar named Blue breaching it a while ago and now it appears he's dead.'

'He died in the grove?' asked Lucretia.

'No,' admitted Deryn. 'He did it in an alley in town.'

'Oh him,' said Max. 'The slaves were muttering about it this morning. Eira's quite revolted.'

'Why fuss? It's the way of things,' said Lucretia with a shrug.

'Shacrifice! Shlaughter!' spat Stump, limping towards them and shaking his bowl, the coins sliding around inside.

'As I say, he sheltered in the grove and is now dead. It's been a sacred spot for generations.' Max ignored Stump, his expression still closed. 'No-one had any business messing about there, whoever they are. So maybe the proper rituals *should* be observed.'

'No-one can remember the proper rituals,' pointed out Deryn. 'But if you're still concerned, perhaps we can find a druid to assuage the spirits.'

'The Romans slaughtered all the druids years ago,' snapped Max.

'Dead! Dead! Deshicrated!' declaimed Stump.

'It's hard to imagine there's not a druid or two lurking somewhere hereabouts,' snapped Deryn.

'If not, we've got some in Pecunia,' said Lucretia. 'Perhaps I could have one sent down. Goodness knows we could do with thinning them out.' Max and Deryn turned to her in surprise. 'And I'm sure you're right about the grove, which is, may I remind you, mine. Therefore *I* shall decide what shall be done with it. But now I gather it's lunchtime, and then I need to prepare for the mosaic maker. Ondi, come on. Don't dawdle.'

***

'Haven't you finished yet?' demanded Lucretia out of the corner of her mouth. She sat bolt upright, draped in linen, her chin tipped. The latest wig, towering in auburn curls, was in stark contrast to carmine lips. Her hands tipped an earthenware jug in a pose which was starting to make her arms tremble. The itch on her powdered nose, which had become so unbearable that she would have kissed anyone who cut it off, had sent out little envoys to her elbows and cheek.

'Just a few more lines,' said the mosaic maker, his head on one side as he perused the charcoal sketch. 'Haven't quite got your feet right.'

'Bother my feet,' Lucretia snapped. 'Copy someone else's. They'll appear underwater anyway. As long as the goddess bears my facial likeness that's all that matters.'

'As you will, Madam.' The mosaic maker rolled his shoulders and, putting the sketch down, flexed his fingers.

'Well?'

'You can drop the pose now.'

Lucretia slumped and waved the jug in the general direction of the nearest slave. 'Fill that with something hot and bring it back.' She too flexed her fingers, willing the blood to circulate properly again, and then

143

with the tip of her fingernail scratched her nose as best she could without dislodging the cosmetic. She clicked her fingers at the mosaic maker. 'Let me see.'

'Oh my dear,' said Eira, entering the hall and staring over the mosaic maker's shoulder. 'He's captured you so well.' She was still pale yet energised from resting.

Lucretia narrowed her eyes and clicked her fingers again. The mosaic maker rose, blew stray flecks of charcoal from the strip of wood and carried it across to her. Nux squirmed in Eira's arms as she followed.

The image was perfect in its simplicity. With very few lines the mosaic maker had captured an imperious mature woman, looking down her nose with haughty black-rimmed eyes. What appeared to be Grecian robes clung to a full bosom and revealed plump arms which poured water from a jug to swirl over small incomplete feet. Lucretia saw a woman of influence who brooked no nonsense. She might have to start describing Diffis as a little more stern than she had hitherto suggested.

'It isn't bad,' she conceded. 'Although you have smudged a little, as if I'm - I mean *she's* old rather than eternal. And if you had brought a taller piece of bark, you wouldn't have had to make her look unnaturally short and wide. Still, it's a good start. Finally I'll have a new mosaic in my house.' She waved her hands in dismissal and with the tiniest roll of his eyes, the mosaic maker packed away his things, bowed to both women and withdrew.

'I thought it was for the baths,' said Eira. She sat next to Lucretia and accepted a proffered goblet, letting Nux snuffle at it before taking the smallest sip.

Lucretia pulled a blanket around her and drank from her own cup of hot wine. 'Did you?'

'I assumed your villa was tiled throughout.'

'It is,' said Lucretia, 'but one floor was never well done. There were tesserae missing, and a local dimwit

144

cobbled together some tiles out of what look like broken pots. I thought I'd replace it in honour of my dear grandson's birth.'

'Don't you have grandsons already?'

Lucretia frowned at her cousin for a moment, shivered and then turned to stare into the fire. 'Oh, Prisca's rabble. They are too much like their father. Their other grandmother is welcome to them. And as for you?'

She turned her gaze back on Eira. Nux was nuzzling against his mistress, touching the dribbles of wine with his tongue. Eira patted him. Lucretia could not for the life of her remember if she had ever had news of anything which had happened in Durnovaria after she'd rejected Deryn.

'As you know,' said Eira, with a grim smirk that suggested she was reading Lucretia's mind, 'I married Max two years after you left, once he and everyone else had finally cast off the incomprehensible spell you cast on them. Our eldest daughter married and went to Venta Bulgarum, our surviving son is abroad. When he returns, we will be introducing him to a suitable girl. Berenice as you know is our autumn child, but strong and healthy. I fully anticipate being a grandmother by this time next year.'

'Is that what you petitioned Juno for at the temple?'

Eira's face settled into its usual neutrality. She said nothing for a moment, then, 'Juno is also the best to give one the wisdom to be a good wife.'

'Hmph.' Lucretia motioned for more wine and demanded that Nia fetch more clothes.

'You should have just worn a proper dress for the pose,' Eira pointed out. 'I thought you abhorred Roman gods and their attire. The mosaic maker could have guessed arms and drawn them in afterwards. In fact, I bet you wish you'd worn a woollen under-tunic. He

145

could have made allowances for it adding a few ounces.' She smiled. 'I'm sure I hope you don't catch your death, wandering out to the temple so early this morning again and then sitting round half-naked this afternoon. There are a lot of nasty coughs about at this time of year.'

'It's for the summer bedroom,' argued Lucretia. 'Why would Diffis wear an undertunic? But right now I'm freezing to death. Nia, where have you been?'

The slave had entered with a woollen overdress in russet. Even when Lucretia rose, the young woman towered over her as she lifted the dress over her head, easing it past the auburn curls. She was disconcertingly silent.

Lucretia let out a yelp.

'Oh, I'm sorry mistress, did I catch your wig?'

Lucretia emerged, the curls slightly askew and the dress hunched on her shoulders. Nia reached to help adjust it, but Lucretia batted her away. The slave's eyes were red and her fingers trembling.

'What *is* the matter with you, girl?'

'The new beggar from the temple's dead.'

'I know. Why does that mean you have to maul me?' Lucretia shrugged herself into the dress more comfortably and the wig lurched forward over her eyes.

Nux growled at it and Eira kissed him, something approaching a smile on her thin lips. Lucretia glared at them both. Nia restrained a sob and reached to readjust things.

'Just take the wretched wig away!' snapped Lucretia. 'And what are you creating for? What's a beggar to you?'

'Blue's made her think of someone, Madam,' said one of the other slaves, helping Nia with the wig. 'No trouble, and a kind word if you gave what you could.

146

It's just a shock, I expect. You had a nice chat with him, didn't you, Nia?'

'He made me think of someone I miss,' said Nia. 'I thought if I was nice to Blue, someone would be nice to…' She cleared her throat. 'Anyone could be down on their luck.'

'Could they?' snapped Lucretia, batting at the girl's hands. 'Is that all you're fussing about?'

Nia took a shuddering breath and composed herself. 'Of course it is, Mistress.'

It was almost certainly Lucretia's imagination that she added, 'As long as it wasn't *my* fault.'

Chapter 24: Diggers

'Welcome back lads, couldn't stay away?' The farmer smirked as he passed Dun and Gris trudging up the slope.

What was left of the light was grey. Strange clouds, curved like grapes or soft breasts, gathered in pink over the western hills.

He gave a wheezy chuckle. 'Shoulda come back sooner. You've missed half the fun.'

'Wot fun?' Gris scratched his beard. He was still annoyed with his mother, but a jewelled knife is only as pretty as its value. A *denarius* was a *denarius*. They'd have a good night and have a rethink tomorrow.

'Know Blue? The new tramp? The one begging by the temple?'

'Yeah?' Gris frowned.

'Dead.'

'Yeah?' said Dun. 'Not surprised, this weather. It's too wet to be living rough, the damp gets in your lungs, in your bones... Anyway, poor old Blue. What did they do with him?'

'Chucked him on the midden, I expect.' The farmer shrugged. 'Dunno. Not like anyone's going to pay for rites. But I'm not sure it was the damp what did it. I heard there was blood. A scuffle, I expect, fighting over the best begging spot.'

'Yeah?'

'Hope he doesn't wander.'

Dun shivered. 'Come on, Gris.' He clapped his companion on the shoulder and walked through the gate.

'Yeah,' said the farmer, 'get along inside won't you. People are waiting.'

In the dusk it was hard to read his face, but there was something mocking in his voice as he continued down the slope.

'What people?'

A man stepped out of the shadows of the ramparts.

'Evening lads,' said Petros. 'Don't dawdle. Supper's getting cold.'

Chapter 25: Amicus

Amicus listened to Tryssa's probing. Dun and Gris were exhausted. They said they had walked seventy miles. Unpicking likely fact from unlikely exaggeration, it was a little over thirty. There was some garbled tale about *things* on the western road. Or maybe it was just one *thing*. Amicus shuddered, remembering marches in the fog when even the men at arm's length disappeared, and the only thing linking him to them was the steady thump of feet and the occasional muttered curse or prayer. Of everything the grave-robbers said, this was the part which rang true. He resisted the urge to slam his fist on the table and demand they came clean on the rest. He could see their shoulders relax despite themselves. It was unlikely they had had much experience of women being polite to them, and they had concluded Tryssa was a soft-hearted fool. Amicus restrained a smile.

'And no doubt your mother was so disappointed you didn't stay,' Tryssa said.

A flicker of a grin crossed Gris's face.

Dun grunted. 'Man's gotta work. I hadn't time to tittle-tattle all day. And I still don't.' Despite the half-eaten bread and cheese, his stomach rumbled.

Tryssa smiled. 'Just a little longer, gentlemen, and then you can go home and have a proper meal. I'm sure you must be very tired and yearning for an early night.'

'Yeah. Course.' said Dun.

'Now then,' said Tryssa. 'Let's see if I'm clear. You rose early, left for Isca -'

'Yeah, we fancied somewhere we're not persecuted every five minutes for wanting to earn a living,' Dun muttered.

'You left for Isca...' said Tryssa as if memorising, 'then felt warned to return by supernatural forces.'

150

'I ... er ... well … something like that.' Dun kicked Gris, who trembled beside him speechless.

'Then you headed seventeen miles north instead to visit your mother,' said Tryssa.

'Yes. Rattled I was.'

'And you thought there might be trading there.'

'That's right,' said Gris. 'But it was dead. I mean, there was nothing doing.'

'So you came back.'

'Yeah.'

'Although you've forgotten you came back before you went,' put in Amicus.

'What?' Dun blinked.

'For breakfast apparently, according to someone Petros met in the forum.'

'Oh yeah, that.'

'Which you got from...'

'Coupla eggs and some bread outta a kitchen door,' said Dun. 'That's all. We -'

'Not gonna say whose,' interrupted Gris. 'I'd get her into trouble. It wasn't more than five minutes and then we was gone again.'

'That almost matches what the man told Petros,' said Amicus. 'Only he said it was more like ten minutes.'

'Who's counting?' snapped Gris. 'She had to cook the eggs, didn't she?'

'Look, what's all this about?' growled Dun. 'You let us go. Now you've dragged us back. Is it any wonder we're trying to leave Durnovaria for good?'

'*This* is what it's all about.' Tryssa unwrapped the skeletal hand and pointed it at each man in turn.

The two men recoiled. 'We told you,' hissed Dun. 'We found it in a ditch.'

'B-by a river,' added Gris.

'And you broke the tendons in the little finger to remove the ring,' said Tryssa, putting it on the table.

Gris swallowed. 'We shouldna done it,' he whispered to Dun. 'I knew we shouldna. No wonder he came limping after us on the road.'

'Stow it, Gris. Cos of a finger? Give us a break.'

'You weren't so brave this morning.'

'Yeah well, maybe I was a bit spooked. Now I think of it in the hard light of day ... evening...' Dun leaned forward and made to stab his finger on the desk, contemplated the hand and waved his arms about instead. 'Listen, missus. We told Amicus Sonticus where that ring came from yesterday. We owned up. We found a hand and took a ring. And yes there was some damage to the pinky cos it was all curled up, for which I'm sorry. I even went to the temple and made amends. But it's not like we killed the geezer, is it? He was well and truly dead by the time we took the ring off of him, weren't he?' Dun sat back and crossed his arms.

'How do you know?' said Tryssa.

Gris looked at her as if she were several gods short of a temple. 'Well it's bones, ain't it?'

'Oh yes,' said Tryssa. 'The hand is dead. But how do you know its owner is?'

'Well it's obvious,' said Dun, shifting in his chair. 'It's not like you get people walking about who've had their hands chopped off.'

'What about Stump?' said Gris. 'And the butcher's lad, after that accident. And...'

'Oh yeah. Well, that's right,' Dun conceded. 'It's probably one of *their* hands. Now if that's all, there's a tavern with a table waiting for us.'

'May I see your knife?'

Both men jumped. 'Knife?' said Gris. 'What you mean, knife? I haven't got no knife. People aren't allowed to go about with weapons on them.'

'Of course you have a knife,' interposed Amicus. 'Everyone has them for eating with. Quite different from the kind my trainee torturer needs to test out.'

'Oh, *eating* knives.' Dun pulled his out of its scabbard and indicated to Gris to do the same. 'Here you go.'

Tryssa picked them up in turn and looked at them under the lamp. 'They're both a bit blunt,' she said. 'Which one did you use to remove this hand from the body?'

Gris started to tremble. 'Did his ghost tell you?'

'Shut up,' hissed Dun.

Amicus slammed his fist on the desk. The skeletal fingers spun around to insult the two grave robbers. 'So where's the body?'

'Buried good and respectful,' gabbled Gris. 'On my honour.'

'You haven't any honour,' snarled Amicus. 'Now where is it?'

'In the -' Gris glanced sideways at Dun who gave a begrudging nod. 'In the grove. You know. Where them standing stones are. Buried again proper.'

'Again?' Tryssa frowned. 'What do you mean, again?'

Chapter 26: Lucretia

'Thank you for coming to dine in my rather humble home,' said Amicus.

'It's perfectly pleasant,' said Lucretia as she reclined with Tryssa. 'It simply needs a woman's touch. I'm sure I could make suggestions.' She beamed at him with a tiny wink. His returning smile was startled but polite, and his gaze drifted to pause on her companion before taking in the other guests.

He was, presumably, comparing the effort the women in the room had put into their appearance. Lucretia compared her hands with Tryssa's as they reclined together and selected stuffed dates. Her own were soft and smooth, Tryssa's strong and hard looking. Tryssa, whose grey curls had escaped to coil on her cheek, seemed very still within herself. She was, Lucretia suspected, being sneaky.

'Where's the maid Eira lent you?' said Tryssa. 'I thought she'd be here tending to you.'

'I left her behind to be dreary,' said Lucretia. 'A miserable face is very annoying.'

'She does seem sad, though.' Berenice popped the pastry in her mouth and reached for another. Eira tutted. 'Poor old Blue was just chucked on the midden.'

'Blue?' said Tryssa.

'Didn't you hear? Died in the alley. Like a cat. A beggar.'

Tryssa frowned. 'One of those in the forum?'

'One of them,' said Max.

'The one-handed one?'

'No, that's Stump,' said Berenice. 'I don't like Stump.'

'He's quite a fixture, said Favorix. 'Tramps most of the year, comes back for winter and settles outside the temple. Blue only turned up recently. I imagine he long

154

since lost his living and somewhere along the way his mind. Maybe he thought someone would take him in for Saturnalia, send him to be scrubbed clean, and make him king for the day.'

'Do any of you do that?' asked Tryssa.

Max flicked his gaze to Eira. His wife's lip was curled.

'We don't,' she said. 'I couldn't bear that sort of nonsense.'

'One fewer beggar is a good thing,' pointed out Lucretia. 'There's nothing more disagreeable for a decent person than being pestered as they go about their business. It's quite bad enough having to give money to the temple. Apologies, Favorix.' She turned a warm smile on the augur and licked her lips a little. 'But you have to admit beggars make the place look untidy. And really, Berenice, who's going to pay the priest to do the necessary for someone like that?'

Berenice nibbled the edge of an almond like a mouse. 'Tryssa, you're a wise-woman. Do you think Blue will haunt the alleyway where he died, or do you think he'll haunt the temple?'

'Get a dragon,' said Lucretia. 'They deter all known ghosts.'

'Do they?' Berenice's face lit up. 'Could you send one from your forest when you go home?'

'Only the very small, weightless, invisible ones travel well,' said Lucretia.

'Ooh...' breathed Berenice. 'Is that what you'd recommend, Tryssa?'

'In answer to your first question, and in some way to your second,' said Tryssa, 'I don't think Blue will haunt anywhere. I've seen enough death in my time: some peaceful, some violent and some, like Blue's, symptomatic of a cruel world. But so far I've never encountered a ghost outside anyone's head.'

155

'I'm not sure I feel precisely the same,' said Amicus.

'I'm still sad about Blue,' said Berenice with a soft smile.

'He should have made more effort earlier in life,' said Eira.

Max stared into his goblet.

Lucretia looked into her own and waggled it at the steward. When not being ridiculous Max was as good-looking as he'd ever been, and Amicus was even more pleasing on the eye. Deryn looked as if he'd been left out in the sun too long. He met her gaze and to her surprise, she felt as if she were a girl looking at her betrothed for the first time and feeling like a wolf in a snare. His expression somehow mirrored her thoughts. It was most offensive. Favorix leered a little from his couch. He'd never really learnt the difference between lecherous and seductive.

She tossed her head and turned to Max, who reclined on the next couch alongside Eira and Nux. It was amazing how husband and wife managed to seem so close together and yet so far apart. Max's eyes kept turning to Lucretia as if he was searching for something in her face. She was glad she was wearing little cosmetic and in the lamplight she was confident her features must look young, fresh and enigmatic. She fluttered her eyelashes and bit her lips to redden them.

Eira was pale to the point of greyness. The skin round her downcast eyes was dark. She nuzzled the dog and throughout the meal had offered him tidbits but taken nothing herself, refusing even wine.

'Even if you're not hungry, I wish you'd drink something, Eira,' urged Deryn. 'This is aged water from Rome. Amicus had the amphora opened especially. It might help your head.'

'It's really quite astonishing how much aged water tastes like spring water,' said Lucretia.

'Even the stuff from Diffis's spring?' Tryssa murmured.

Lucretia narrowed her eyes and then gave a wry shrug. 'Thankfully it's better than that. Diffis's spring water is medicinal. That's why it tastes so unique.'

'I'd prefer not to risk it on my patients,' said Tryssa.

'Darling,' Max turned to Eira, 'maybe Tryssa would be able to find a remedy for your headaches.'

'I'd be pleased to,' said Tryssa.

Eira looked up and gave the tiniest of smiles. Her eyes were cold.

'I think I should escort Eira home,' said Deryn, starting to rise. 'She's clearly unwell.'

'Oh don't go quite yet,' said Amicus. 'I hoped to discuss the ring Ieuan gave Berenice.'

Eira's head snapped up. 'Why need we discuss it?'

'What ring?' said Deryn. 'Is it another thing Lucretia thinks she has a right to?'

'It's mine!' wailed Berenice. 'You don't want it, do you, Cousin Lucretia?'

'Certainly not. It's not my style at all.'

Amicus's commanding voice silenced them. 'The ring was Galen's.'

'Whose?' It was not just Eira who spoke but Lucretia. Nux yelped and snapped at Max. Deryn frowned.

'It's mine!' repeated Berenice.

'I'm sorry, Amicus,' said Deryn. 'I don't know what ring you're talking about or why it's suddenly important. Is this why you were asking about him earlier? It was a very long time ago. I can't recall his face, let alone his personal effects.'

'That seems a shame. Apart from Tryssa Doethion and Berenice Maximillia, all of you once knew him almost as well as I did. I am particularly surprised, ladies, that you have forgotten so easily. He wrote about both of you as if you were well acquainted.'

'Hardly with me,' said Eira. 'He was too busy with the more compliant girls.' She sat up and gathered Nux into her arms.

Lucretia rolled her eyes and took another sip of wine. 'Amicus Sonticus, if you want to discuss it, perhaps we could do so in private another time. Tryssa needn't be here. She was in Pecunia allegedly weeping over my brother. She can have no knowledge of either a ring or a long-disgraced miscreant.'

'I'm sure it makes no difference to Tryssa,' said Amicus. 'I'm just curious. All I know is that Galen disappeared around the time he was pursuing you, Lucretia Siluriensis.'

The room fell quiet. Deryn met Lucretia's eyes properly. His face had darkened to a deep red, but his knuckles whitened as they gripped his glass goblet. She stared back, her head high. She could still make him jealous after all this time.

'Who *wasn't* pursuing Lucretia?' Eira's voice broke the silence. 'Though goodness knows why. She was plain, teasing and cruel.'

'How dare you!' snapped Lucretia. 'I wasn't plain.'

Eira ignored her. 'Men are fools.' She sat on the edge of the couch and addressed Tryssa. 'Tell me, was Lucretia as much of a flirt at home? Or had she gone through all the men in Pecunia before she arrived here?'

'You needn't answer,' said Lucretia. 'Eira has already made up what she likes to call her mind.'

'Not that I noticed,' said Tryssa. 'To be quite fair, as I recall, Lucretia was busy learning about how to run her land after Rhys's death. Then she went away to meet Deryn. A few weeks later, she came back and eventually married Porcius instead.'

'Yes,' said Eira. 'Not content to have half the town drooling over her, she cottoned on to some visiting Londoner who had *just happened* to have known her brother, and whose own very rich brother was settling for no logical reason in some gods-forsaken place in the Silurian wilds, which *just happened* to be the same gods-forsaken place where Lucretia owned a lot of land and most of a village. It's just as well you were away, Amicus,' she added, 'or no doubt she'd have tried to ensnare you too.'

'There's still time for him to be ensnared,' said Lucretia.

Amicus raised his eyebrows. 'There is indeed,' he said and raised a goblet. 'But I'm not here to disparage my guest. I just want to know what you all recall about Galen's disappearance.'

'I remember him very well,' said Max. 'He was clever, really crafty. He got away with horses, money, you name it, and yet they never caught him. I imagine he got on the next ship to Armorica before anyone realised what had happened. I've often wondered where he is now.'

'He wasn't really our sort though, was he?' said Favorix, shovelling a handful of sausage-filled pastries onto his platter. It was neverendingly irritating how men could eat what they liked and remain scrawny. 'I mean he tried, but he couldn't keep his end up with us. That's why, presumably, he did what he did.'

'I think he's dead,' said Amicus.

'Nonsense,' said Eira. 'That sort of man is like an oiled pig. Nothing sticks to them. They get away with everything and people just laugh.'

'Eira!' said Max. 'Forgive her, Amicus, Galen was our friend. My wife isn't feeling very well.'

'He's not dead,' snapped Eira. 'He's out there somewhere stealing: brides, money, you name it. And

159

everyone assumed he went to Armorica. After all, that's what those sorts of people do. But no-one could find him, could they? Yes, he was clever. What if he went north instead, where no-one expected him to go? For all we know he's sniffing around a place like Pecunia where no-one could be bothered to look for him.'

'I believe he's dead,' said Amicus. 'I'm certain the ring Berenice has was once his. Unless he sold it - and I don't believe he would - someone killed him. I want to find out who and when.'

Eira snorted. Deryn summoned a slave for wine and proffered it to Eira, but she shook her head. Emotions were boiling under a face that was usually like a still pond. There was a storm brewing in her eyes.

'You can't,' she said. 'Galen's not dead, or if he is, he didn't die here. He was no fool. He'd stolen all that money and needed to lie low. That ring probably isn't his. The style is common enough, ask Petros's mother. And besides, Galen didn't wait around here to be arrested.'

'Why are you so sure, my lady?' said Amicus gently.

'Galen is far away, I tell you,' she insisted. 'I…' She stopped talking, swaying with Nux clasped to her chest.

'You what?' said Lucretia. 'For pity's sake spit it out, Eira.'

'Don't bully her,' said Deryn. 'Max, don't just lie there while your wife is bullied.'

'I'm not bullying her,' said Lucretia. 'I just want to eat with a more relaxing conversation.'

'I want to put this whole thing to rest,' said Amicus. 'Eira Junia, can you tell me why you are so sure Galen is far away?'

'Don't let him bully you!' snapped Deryn. The glass in his hand broke under his grip.

Eira rose from the bench. 'Because I saw him leave,' she said. 'He never noticed mousy people like me. But

I noticed him. I was glad he was going. I'd seen the games he was up to with Lucretia, the pair of them teasing my brother until she broke his heart entirely.'

'Eira...' Deryn's fingers were cut from the broken glass; blood was dripping onto the floor into the spilt wine.

His sister held up her hand. 'No, Deryn. Before you take me home, I have to tell them this. Amicus, I overheard Galen tell a slave he'd dropped the ring down a rabbit hole. I expect the truth was that he'd lost it in a game of bones while he was carousing.' She paused, rubbing Nux's head against her cheek. 'Or maybe he needed to make sure he was harder to identify, and sold it.' Her gaze left Amicus and settled on her cousin. 'As to when he disappeared, it was exactly the same time as Lucretia,' she said. 'Despite what she'd done, our parents insisted we wave to her from the ramparts. As usual, no-one but me was looking at anything but *her*. That's when I saw Galen. Sneaking out after her, following her north. Two days later everyone found out what he'd stolen. And he never came back.' She stormed out of the room, followed by Riona and Deryn.

There was a brief silence before Lucretia clicked her fingers for a slave. 'Thank heavens,' she murmured to Tryssa. 'She quite ruins one's appetite. I don't know why you bothered looking for what poisoned her. She's doing it to herself with misery.'

'Max, I'm sorry I've upset Eira,' said Amicus.

Max beckoned for more wine. His hand trembled a little but he was otherwise sanguine. 'Don't trouble yourself. She's not been well recently. I should have left her at home.'

'Don't mind Mummy,' said Berenice. 'She doesn't like excitement. Everything that's remotely interesting gives her a headache. I'm quite thrilled to hear the ring may have an interesting history! Daddy, what do you know about it?'

Max contemplated the wine in his glass. 'There's not much more to tell is there, Amicus?'

'I wasn't here, remember.'

'Well then, Favorix, you recall it.'

Lucretia fluttered her eyelashes at Favorix. His bald head grew a little red as he turned a smirk on her.

'Oh,' he breathed, 'I was too busy falling in love.'

'Go on, Daddy,' said Berenice, oblivious. 'What happened?'

'It's simple but sad, Berry. Galen lost a gamble with the wrong person, stole money and disappeared.'

'My father's money,' said Favorix. 'Or rather, money he was responsible for. It caused a great deal of trouble. A common boy like that should never have been given the chance to better himself.'

Max made a non-committal waggle of his head. 'He was our friend, Favorix. But maybe you're right. He didn't have the polish to be clerking for a quaestor. Anyway, he lost money to another gambler and then stole public funds. Whether he tried to pay the man off or not I don't know - whether he lost or sold that ring I don't know either. But the other gambler, I'm afraid to say, doubtless got his revenge. And as to Galen leaving when Lucretia did ... it probably made sense to go when people were distracted. The loss of the money was about to be uncovered, and the other gambler was still in town looking for him.'

'He was distinctive, wasn't he?' said Amicus.

'Oooh,' breathed Berenice, 'was he very terrifying?'

Max downed his wine and called for more. Then he sat up, said, 'Like this', and pulled a hideous face, pretending to loom over his daughter as she pretended to quail in fear before falling into giggles. Reclining once more, he gave Lucretia a wink. 'I'm sure you don't mind my describing your departure as a distraction.'

Lucretia licked a few crumbs off her mouth and winked back.

Beside her, for no discernible reason, Tryssa whispered under her breath, 'A distraction?'

And everyone thought her so wise. What fools people were.

8th October
Chapter 27: Diggers

There had been a frost overnight.

Digging in the grove at dawn was hard, the earth under heaped fragile leaves reluctant to release its embrace on the skeleton.

Amicus and Tryssa stood with the stones, watching as Dun and Gris, with Amicus's men, dug with trowels.

Gris was whimpering a little, periodically staring round to get his bearings. The grove was small, but even so the skeleton was not quite where he remembered. Had it inched its way, bone by bone, out of this ancient circle to find him?

Dun, however, was whistling very low through his teeth. The sun was cold but bright. No ghosts would dare to step out.

'Dig careful,' he whispered. 'Maybe there's still jewels. We'll do sharesies, yeah?'

'Hey,' called Amicus. 'Dun! Come up here, stand with me and point.'

Dun grumbled and rose to his feet. 'Here, who's that?' He pointed over Amicus's shoulder. Gris dropped his trowel, let out a whimper and covered his eyes.

Deryn strode past the oak and stood behind the two least upright stones. 'Amicus, this is - was - my mother's land. What's going on?'

'I'm sorry, Deryn,' said Amicus. 'I would have explained last night but you left before I could. We're looking for a skeleton.'

'This is a sacred grove,' said Deryn. 'It was once used for sacrifices. Everyone knows that. It's probably waist-deep in skeletons if you dig long enough.'

Amicus suppressed a shiver. Tales of Romans ritually slaughtered had been passed down from generation to generation for three hundred years. Where was that forest where the legion had been lost? Germania, wasn't it? Or maybe it was closer to home. And before that - sacrificed youths, slaughtered to bring prosperity to the tribe.

'It's more recent than that and not remotely sacred,' he said. He pointed at Dun and Gris. 'These two jokers dug it up and buried it again. This is where they found the ring.'

'Ah.' Deryn crossed his arms and noticing Tryssa, gave a small bow. 'Madam.'

'Good morning.'

'This seems rather grim for - but I suppose … anyway, the liniment is working. My horse is healing well; thank you.' He turned to address Dun. 'This is my family's land. What were you doing on it?'

'Not gonna lie,' said Dun with a shrug. 'We was looking for a body.'

'What?'

'Well, you know us.' He clapped Amicus on the shoulder without thinking.

'Yes, I do. But the torturer doesn't,' said Amicus. 'He's warming his pliers up especially, just in case he gets the chance to make your acquaintance.'

Dun removed his hand hastily. 'No offence, mate, no offence. But let's be honest, lads … and lady.' He nodded at Tryssa. 'You know and I know that me and Gris are grave robbers. It's what we do. And where there's a grave, there's usually a body. Gotta admit, we're happier when the body's turned to dust, cos jewels and stuff is what we're after, not bones.'

'Yes,' said Deryn, 'but this is a sacred grove, not a barrow.'

'Gotta diversify.' Dun shrugged.

'You mean you've robbed all the graves hereabouts,' said Amicus.

165

'Weeeell,' Dun shrugged. 'It's all flaming cremations nowadays, innit? And then there's the Christians. If anyone knew where they buried their people I bet you wouldn't find any grave goods, they're too busy giving things away to the poor. Unreasonable, I call it. Not a thought for us what are trying to make an honest living. So sacred grove we thought, who knows what's there, we thought. They used to sacrifice the best, didn't they? Princes, not slaves. Thought we'd have a look-see. Bit of a bronze torc we thought, touch of lapis, maybe a silver 'orse. That's what we thought.'

'*You* thought,' Gris moaned. 'It was your idea. And look what happened.'

'We found a body,' said Dun. 'Just a bit newer than we expected. A body and a load of trouble. I almost wish we'd never bothered.'

'Here!' called one of Amicus's men. The slender bones of a forearm had been revealed, shreds of dark cloth caught around it.

'There you are,' said Dun. 'There's the fella. Now you've got him you can give him back his hand and let us go. And he can stop haunting us. Not that he was. I mean, not that I thought he was.'

Gris glared up. 'You was just as scared as I was on the road to Isca.'

'No I weren't.'

'Yes you -'

'All right, all right,' said Amicus. 'Now get down there and help. And do it with respect.'

'We give him respect the first time,' grumbled Dun, 'didn't we, Gris? We just took the ring and a bracelet, and it turned out the bracelet wasn't worth an *as* and the ring's brought nothing but hassle. We didn't look to see if there was anything else to take -'

'You woulda,' muttered Gris. 'If I'd let you.'

'And we buried him again, nice and tidy.'

'Yes, and your reward for not telling anyone about it is to dig him back up again,' said Amicus. 'And if you keep anything but mud, I'm keeping you for target practice.'

'Where's the justice?' muttered Dun. 'It's enough to force a man to go and find a proper job.'

Chapter 28: Amicus

Tryssa stepped up to the table in the cellar and watched as Amicus carefully pulled back the sacking to reveal the skeleton. Earth still clung to the bones, apart from the handless right arm which was clean from the mid-forearm down. What clothing remained was no more than mere shreds of fibre, but the leather had partly survived. Shoes were loose on thin metatarsals, and a belt with its corroded buckle had collapsed against the skeleton's spine. A broken loop stuck to the rotting leather with what was hopefully mud.

Without touching them, Tryssa traced the bones one by one until she reached the skull. If there had been hair it had long since rotted into the earth. The head was rolled sideways, its jaw slightly open as if whispering an appeal.

'There's no way of telling if it's a man or a woman, is there?' said Amicus.

'I imagine there is,' said Tryssa. 'But I'm not sure. The hips look narrow for a woman, and the body seems too tall. What do you think?'

'Hard to say. The shoes must have been solid to have survived as much as they have, and even the nails in the soles have not completely corroded. They're long for a woman's feet but then...'

'You're being careful not to assume it's Galen.' Tryssa put her hand on Amicus's arm and gave him a small smile. He laid his own hand on hers. For a moment they both dropped their eyes to the touching fingers as if they belonged to other people, then stepped away from each other.

Amicus coughed, face hot and heart thudding, and bent to look more closely at the belt. 'If only the buckle was in better condition I might recognise it.' At the merest prod of a stylus, another flake of rust fell away. 'How many years, do you think?'

He braved a look at Tryssa. She was a little flushed. 'I have no idea. It depends a little on the soil, or so I understand. Ours is different from yours. It's not often I've seen a skeleton unearthed like this, but more than twelve I imagine, less than a hundred probably. There are still a few sinews and a little cartilage. So not very, very old. Like those two ruffians said, in the barrows the bones are usually little more than dust.'

'Forty years?'

Tryssa shrugged. 'I can't say for certain. But what I can surmise is this.' She pointed at the skeleton's ribcage. 'There's a chip off these bones. I think this person was stabbed. If he was, then the knife would most likely have gone into the heart.'

'So you think he was heading north, and along the road he was murdered.'

'I can't say that. All I can say is that he was stabbed, and he was buried near the road heading north.'

'It's the same... Mmm.' Amicus paced the room. 'I see what you mean. But whoever stabbed him didn't take the ring.'

'You said it wasn't especially valuable. Would Masner be selling it at a market rather than in a private sale if it were?'

Amicus went to lean against the wall, remembered how cold it would be and paced again instead. 'Well, that's a question. All this time I've been thinking of what that ring meant to him and his mother. But you're right and so's Eira. It wasn't that special. It had enough of a value to sell, certainly. Dun and Gris thought so and made a bit of cash from it, and Masner, obviously, even more. But value is relative, isn't it? Poor old Blue at the temple, he was glad of enough to pay for a bit of

169

bread and thrilled if he had enough to pay for shelter probably. Your Lucretia -'

Tryssa cleared her throat and Amicus chuckled.

'Sorry, but it seems to me that ten wagon-loads of gold carried by a legion of gilded godlings wouldn't be enough for Lady Lucretia.'

'Quite true.'

'So...' Amicus stopped to peer at the belt again. 'His money pouch has gone. It's been ripped away, look.'

'So it has.'

'And there was no sign of any other money bags.'

Amicus straightened his back and, without hesitation this time, put his hand on Tryssa's shoulder. 'I can't be sure if this was Galen but it looks that way ... so humour me. Let's assume he ran away with the money he'd stolen and on the way, he was attacked by the person to whom he owed a fortune. That man was only interested in the money. A ring meant nothing or - as Dun and Gris found - it might mean trouble. So he killed Galen, took the cash, and buried him in the last place anyone would dig. Does that make sense?'

'It does.'

'Alternatively, if these bones are not Galen, then perhaps they belong to someone who stole or won the ring, and fundamentally the same fate befell them. But in my heart I know this is my friend. I can't explain it, but...'

'Yes. I understand. Sometimes you just know.'

Amicus withdrew his hand and crossed his arms, turning his gaze from her to the skeleton. 'Do you remember what Dun said about Christians and their burial grounds?'

Tryssa tipped her head on one side. 'Yes.'

'I have a feeling if anyone could find the Christians in this town it would be you.'

'I'll take that as a compliment and not a threat. Yes, I probably could.'

'If you do, can you ask them to make whatever after-death prayers they make, for Galen?'

Tryssa raised her eyebrows. 'Was Galen a Christian?'

Amicus gave a short cynical laugh. 'I think that depends on the definition, but his mother certainly was and he made no secret of his connection. Knowing he had the right prayers would have made her happy. In the meantime, I'll pay the priest to have the bones cremated in the Roman way. That'll hedge everyone's bets and the matter will be at an end. As Max said, it's simple but sad. He owed money, he stole money, he was murdered for money. He was buried so the murderer could get away.' Amicus took a breath. 'Thank you, Tryssa. It can't be easy for you to look at wounds so similar to Rhys's.'

She looked down at the skeleton. 'Remembering Rhys and me as youngsters is like thinking of old friends,' she said. 'It's too long ago to hurt any more.'

'And there's been no-one else?'

'Never found the right man. May I ask...' He saw her swallow before she glanced up. 'Your wife...'

'Never found the right woman,' said Amicus, holding her gaze. 'Never thought I would.'

They stared at each other for a moment. He put out his hand again, and thought better of it. He felt too polluted to touch her again.

Better get to the baths then, you old fool, whispered the ghost of Galen, chuckling.

***

Despite all the years that Amicus had seen, and on occasion caused, death, it still seemed impossible that any corpse could have once been a living, breathing creature. It was worse still that he should see his one-

171

time best friend reduced to nothing but bones, earth sticking to his skull in cruel mockery of the curls that once sprung in a messy tangle.

It was unusual for him to attend the baths before late afternoon, but Amicus couldn't face the rest of the day without being cleansed. He went through the cycle of *tepidarium* to *caladium* to *frigidarium* - warm, hot, cold - twice before returning to the *tepidarium* to have his skin oiled and the dirt scraped from his skin with a *strigil*.

Perhaps Tryssa had already found whatever it was Christians used for priests and made the necessary request. Although it seemed more likely she would want to bathe first. *I wonder if, when she unbraids her hair, it's as curly as the little wisps over her ears suggest...*

Shaking himself, he forced his mind to the relevant facts. After all these years he had found Galen, and now he would do the right thing by him. *Poor Galen,* he thought. *You should have lived to sit in a tavern with me, remembering the old days and despairing over modern youths; claimed your mother's faith perhaps; settled down and married...* Amicus chuckled to himself. Galen married? He'd always had a string of girls on the go. It was hard to imagine any particular one could have really captured his heart. *But then,* Galen's ghost whispered, *it can happen when you least expect it, can't it?*

What had Galen said in his last letter? He'd mentioned several names from high-born to slave. Of the ones now identifiable, Eira was described as pretty but moody. Lucretia was spirited, challenging. Galen just lapped up the attention and laughed it off when girls fought over him.

You old fool! whispered Galen's ghost. *You're looking at this the wrong way! I'm back in the thick of*

172

things again! Amicus imagined Galen's face not full of horror but laughter. *You were lifting my bones like they were petals,* the ghost persisted. *When you and I wrestled, we threw each other onto the ground with no concern whatsoever for the consequences. And why should I care that Berenice is wearing my ring? A pretty girl of sixteen? I'm delighted.* Amicus grinned. Galen's imagined face sulked a little and then winked. *I'm just sorry I'm not sixteen myself and the one to gift it to her.*

Scraped so clean he felt flayed, his spirits lifted, Amicus rose from the bench and went to retrieve his clothes from the *apodyterium.*

There was someone - no, two men - close together in a dark alcove where a statue of Apollo stood in perfect naked mockery of those around him. The men were turned away, heads close. Amicus kept his eyes averted and made to hurry past, and then heard familiar voices whispering.

'It doesn't explain why she's here,' murmured Deryn.

'Someone must have told Lucretia we're cheating her.' Max's voice was muffled as if he were talking while chewing a nail.

'We're not. We're actually doing her a favour - offering her twice what Mother's insult of a legacy is worth.'

'Well then, pay her quickly and get her away from here.'

'*We* should be paying her, not me. Half of it should come from Eira.'

'I can't release funds just now. They're tied up.'

'Who with?'

'The election, the dowry ... you know how things are.'

173

'Really? I know Ieuan's father is casting doubt round town on whether Berenice will even have a dowry, and there are rumours about you raising money against Eira's land. How could you do this to my sister, my niece …'

'Calm down, Deryn. You're letting Lucretia get to you. She's quite fun, really. If you'd just tried to entertain her rather than argue with her all those years ago, you'd have had her eating out of your hand. I bet you could now, if you made an effort. She finds you enigmatic.'

'Fun? She's brought nothing but trouble. Favorix is digging, Eira's got sicker, and now Amicus has found Galen. I thought it was all safely buried. I still -'

'He was Amicus's friend. He was *our* friend.'

'Was.'

'So his body's been found. No-one cares any more except Amicus, and he'll be satisfied now he's found the body and we've reminded him about what happened. We can forget that. The key thing is getting Lucretia paid and going home.'

'And you want me to do that from my own funds. What about Eira's part? Which, it seems, is now yours.'

'It's all the same thing, Deryn old boy. You've no children. You've already said your land and money will go to Berenice. You might as well do it now. I was quite enjoying Lucretia being here but it's - she's getting pressing. Just pay her off, won't you? Then no-one will - I mean, we'll all be happier.'

'What -'

Another man bumped into Amicus and dropped a sandal.

'Sorry.'

'Sorry.'

'Shh,' whispered Max. 'Just play along. And we need to get to the amphitheatre before the performance starts.'

Amicus stepped away.

***

It was past noon when he emerged, wishing he could talk things over with Tryssa. The business of the forum had changed. Men were milling around, talking politics or news, purchasing hot snacks and spiced drinks and standing at makeshift bars to eat them. Masner's stall was quiet, his slave munching on a bun. Masner's and Amicus's eyes met for a second, and then each looked away.

Catching the scent of some fried pastries stuffed with spiced pork, Amicus realised he was hungry and walked over to the stall.

'Greetings sir, have you seen Tryssa?' Olivarius appeared beside him, holding some kind of hot flatbread, folded up with cheese inside.

Amicus felt his face glow up as the younger man's words broke into his thoughts, and hoped it would look as if the heat from the vendor's brazier and the exertions of the slave with the strigil accounted for any redness. He paid for the pastry and said, 'I think she's on an errand.'

Olivarius bit his lip and fidgeted a little, and Amicus nodded towards a stall selling hot spiced cider. 'Care to join me?' he said. 'I want to raise a cup in memory of a friend.'

'Yes, of course.'

They sat in silence for a while in the sun.

'To good friends!' said Amicus, and took a sip from his steaming beaker.

'To good friends!' responded Olivarius, and stared into his cup. 'I'm sorry that report has taken so long, sir.'

Amicus pulled himself back into reality. He liked Olivarius. He seemed loyal, knowing when to keep a secret and when to share it. His work was good too, thorough and intelligent. 'I didn't expect it to be a quick job. Have you found anything yet?'

'I'm not sure,' said Olivarius. 'The records are very hard to make sense of. Not a great deal of order in them.'

'That doesn't surprise me, but I'm sure you're doing your best. Why did you need Tryssa, particularly? Can I help?'

Olivarius slumped a little.

'Are you coming to the performance at the amphitheatre?'

'I thought I'd stay behind and finish the report,' said Olivarius. 'It's not the same going without -'

Amicus considered him more closely. 'What's your girl's name?' he said, after a pause. 'Camilla, isn't it?'

'How -'

'Experience. You're missing her.'

Olivarius swallowed. 'I thought she might have written. Or, well, got someone to write. She's not long learned. I thought Tryssa might have heard.'

'Do you have a rival?'

'I did last year. Camilla and I are betrothed - unofficially - but now I'm away... He's still there, no doubt still offering a life of excitement in the wilds, and here I am offering - I hope - the life of a secretary's wife. I wanted to talk with Tryssa. She's the only other person who -'

Amicus studied the misery on the other man's face, wanting to fill in the unfinished sentence: *understands, cares, knows, will help.*

'I'm sure if she's in love with you, it'll be all right.'

Who are you talking to? whispered Galen's ghost. *Him, or yourself? Can't you think of something less*

176

boring to say? Tell him to stop moping and do something.

'Do something,' said Amicus, surprising himself. 'Write to her yourself. Tell her you're helping investigate a murder.'

'Am I?'

Amicus drained his cup and stood. The shade of Galen was no longer laughing, and not yet at rest either. 'Sadly,' he said, 'I fear you are.'

Chapter 29: Lucretia

Looking around as she sat between Eira and Berenice, waiting for the play to start, Lucretia wondered whether instead of investing in a bigger temple, she and Anguis should build a proper amphitheatre for Pecunia. After all, entertainment could involve as much blood, devotion and downright insanity as religion, but with the addition of snacks, which meant you could charge more. The downside, of course, was that someone had to pay for it.

The amphitheatre at Durnovaria was set up for a full performance. Musicians were corralled near one end and at the centre of the display area, a framework like a box without sides had been erected. Ropes were hooked on corners, and a long table had been placed in the middle.

'I've never seen anything like it,' breathed Berenice. 'Usually it's horses or declaiming or executions. Where's the chorus?'

'Contractes has his own ideas,' said Lucretia. 'He doesn't precisely follow the classic tradition.'

'I heard there'd be wild animals! And romance!' Berenice squeezed Ieuan's hand under cover of the blanket covering their knees.

The day was clear, the skies above a deep blue, although on the hills to the west there lay a smothering fog. The air was freezing.

'You seem very tense,' Lucretia said to Eira. 'And where's Max? Gaming again?'

'How - No, of course not. He's with Deryn and the rest of the Ordo of course, gaining support for his campaign.' Eira pulled her cloak more closely round her. Her irritation turned to smugness. 'Speaking of escorts, whatever happened to Olivarius? I haven't seen him for days. Why didn't Anguis escort you? Was it because you want to keep Olivarius from your niece? Personally I wouldn't be surprised if you wanted him for yourself.'

Lucretia stopped checking that her make-up was still smooth and half-turned. 'What?'

'He's very good-looking.'

Lucretia considered Eira, who had composed her face into a mix of pity and triumph. Stupid woman.

Olivarius *was* very handsome, it had to be admitted. With that reddish hair and moss-green eyes, Lucretia could see why Camilla had been tempted. Even when angry amber glints sparked, they glinted with promise. She recalled the tales she'd heard of the folk beyond the veil, the ones who were supposed to inhabit places like the grove. Perhaps Olivarius's ancestors weren't from Tarsus after all. Perhaps he was able to lure people back to the other world when the time of year was right. Which it pretty much nearly was. *Perhaps it's just as well Camilla isn't around to be whisked off,* thought Lucretia. Then she shook herself. *Although it's all nonsense and if he was going to whisk her off, he's had several opportunities in the last sixteen months.*

'*You* might want to run away with a freedman's son,' she said. 'But some of us are more particular.' She watched the colour drain from her cousin's face, then return with vigour.

'If he were rich, you wouldn't care,' snapped Eira. 'His money would matter more than status, more than love.'

Lucretia shrugged. 'Dear me,' she said. 'Love doesn't feed you. Or keep you in nice things.'

Eira cuddled her fur-trimmed cloak closer round her head. 'I expected *dear* Favorix to be here dribbling over you.'

Lucretia scanned the packed seating and shrugged. 'Perhaps he's busy reading some entrails. And - erm - Amicus?'

'He's over there with Galyna and your friend Tryssa.' Eira pointed. 'But he's on his feet. He ought to be with the Ordo too, but it doesn't look as if he's staying.'

'Bored, I expect.'

Eira leaned until she was nearly nose to nose and dropped her voice to a low growl. 'Why couldn't you have just taken the money for the grove and stayed at home?'

Lucretia gave a short laugh. 'I might have if you'd been honest at the start. And perhaps if when I arrived you'd been more welcoming, I'd have settled things and gone home sooner. Never mind. It's much more fun watching you and Deryn squirm.' She turned back to the stage area. The musicians had stopped playing and were still, expectant, shifting themselves into more comfortable positions.

From her other side, Berenice nudged her. 'Look, Cousin Lucretia, the play's about to begin! What's wrong with Mummy?'

'I'm fine,' growled Eira.

'Ooh look!' Berenice grabbed Lucretia's arm and pointed.

As the music started, two rows of dancers dressed in green and brown flowed into the arena from opposite directions. They ran round the lower circle until they met, weaving in and out until they came to rest in groups, with their arms at strange angles.

'Dryads,' grunted Lucretia. 'Contractes is fixated with dryads. It's presumably supposed to be a woodland.'

'Why's there a table?' whispered Berenice.

Lucretia shrugged. 'Even dryads have to eat.'

180

'Ooh, what do they eat?'
'Badgers.'
The dryads started to sing:

In the forest where the hidden spirits dwell
Behold the hero's dwelling, he who
Dragons trained -

'Ooh,' breathed Berenice.
Lucretia rolled her eyes.

And elephants tamed
Once this jewelled fortress built
But woe woe woe
He is no more. His grey head lies beneath the turf

'Aw,' Berenice sighed.

His most precious jewel left to twinkle unperceived.

Lucretia blinked. 'What?'

Behold! She comes! The Princess!

A woman swaggered into the middle of the arena,
kicking out her full skirts with vigour. Long flaxen
braids stuck out on either side of a face obscured by a
fine veil. She pirouetted as well as she could in
hobnailed boots, while the chorus declaimed her beauty
and grace.
    'Oh what a *shame* they have to use a boy,' said
Berenice. 'Isn't it, Ieuan? That's the smallest charioteer
from the other day. There's hardly *anything* feminine
about him. In fact I'm surprised they didn't stuff his
bodice more. I could do that *much* better.'
    'Stuff his bodice?' said Lucretia.

'No, silly,' Berenice retorted. 'Act.'

Behold! A handsome prince from a neighbouring realm!
The Princess swoons for - Lo!
The first man she has ever seen
(Apart from domestic staff and tradesmen)
Dazzles her!

A horse galloped into the arena with a man in leather armour on its back. It made circuits and the man did acrobatics until on the third lap he leapt onto the wooden frame, caught hold of one of the ropes, and swung forward to land at the Princess's feet.

Oh beauteous one!

The chorus declaimed on his behalf.

You must be mine.

'Please gods, say no,' said Lucretia. 'Ask to see what's in his coffers first.'

Eira muttered something under her breath.

'Not to mention his antecedents,' Lucretia added, looking sideways. 'You don't want to be breeding with just *anything*.'

The couple canoodled at arm's-length as the dryads danced around them singing of love, and the horse tossed its head, as if recalling with longing battlefields where it could tread on severed limbs and perhaps its own slaughtered stablemates.

There was a clash of cymbals and another 'female' clumped forward to a long, low, flatulent sound emitted by a *buccina*. The new woman was short and dumpy, dressed in mud-brown, large breasts heaving, grey locks stiff about a face which had been painted to accentuate bad temper.

'Oh look,' said Eira. 'An evil old witch. Who does she remind me of?'

'Your mirror,' said Lucretia, and sat back to see what happened next. She was fairly sure that Contractes had intended a play delicate with inference. A battle of wills between an old queen and her beautiful daughter; a determination to retain the freedom to rule her realm as she chose. It was a major relief that his playwright was too inept for dainty metaphors.

Woe woe the miserable old queen arrives!
Unhand her maiden girl!
Do not besmirch her for she is promised elsewhere!

The hero whistled and his horse appeared to heave a sigh before trotting over to nip at a group of acrobats who had tumbled out, armed with kitchen implements in support of the queen. As the chorus sung a discordant argument, the old woman and the prince tussled for the princess, pulling an arm each and half dislodging the wig to reveal short dark curls.

'I mean,' said Berenice. 'If you're going to have a boy play a girl, you should make him grow his hair long. That just looks terrible.'

Eventually the old woman lost her grip on the princess, who collapsed against her beloved. He staggered a little before flinging her bodily over the horse and swinging up behind her. He galloped three times around the ring, pursued by tumbling slaves, while the queen wailed and tore at her clothes. The lovers dismounted and prepared to fall into each other's arms 'hidden' by a group of dryads.

Another 'girl' sneaked up. She had an undersized dress which revealed hairy ankles, an anatomically

183

impossible pair of breasts, and a wig of scarlet curls which grew more lopsided as she pushed the dryads aside to peer in.

Beware! Oh lovers, you are betrayed!
Cometh Nemesis in the form of a spurned Maiden!

The redhead ran around the arena twice staggering to a halt before the wailing queen.

With a clash of cymbals and a thunderous roll on a *tympanum*, the redhead towered over the old queen waving her arms.

One of the breasts fell out of her sleeve and rolled away, while the other escaped the cross-bindings and slipped to the actor's waist. As the queen ululated, a bugle made a rallying call, and through the entrance galloped a second man. He too galloped three times round the arena, ignoring the canoodling lovers, before swinging to the ground before the queen and bowing to her. His face had been painted into an evil, bad-tempered leer.

'Why does everyone keep going in circles?' said Berenice. 'It's making me giddy. And why didn't that nasty man spot the prince and princess?'

'They're supposed to be a long way away in a different part of the forest.'

'But they're right there. Shouldn't they be further away so it's obvious?'

'Then we wouldn't be able to see them.'

'Oh.'

Woe, woe!
The man to whom
The Princess was promised
Is full of ire!
Flee sweet lovers

184

For he will not rest till you are discovered!

Goaded and directed by the two angry women, the evil prince remounted his horse and after another three circuits, arrived at the 'glade' where the lovers hid, dismounted and unsheathed a sword. The good prince seemed to be embracing the princess a little tighter, and she had either started some complicated dance move or was trying to kick him in the shin.

'Finally!' said Lucretia. 'Less wailing and more action. Besides, the princess isn't going to remain unbesmirched for much longer at this rate.'

Berenice giggled into her veil.

The evil prince threatened the dryads, who fell to the ground to the accompaniment of an eerie cacophony of harp, *buccina* and wailing commentary by the chorus.

'Has he actually chopped them up?' said Lucretia, leaning forward. 'No. What a shame.'

The lovers were separated with enough force for the good prince to stumble sideways. The princess squirmed in the villain's arms.

Do not think you can capture this maiden of the forest!

The chorus were now somewhat behind. The actors froze for a moment until the chorus caught up and wailed:

Oh woe! woe! He has overcome thee!

The villain grabbed the princess awkwardly and tried to lift her onto his horse.

Oh maidenly girl so cruelly treated, thou swoonest!

The princess punched the villain in the face.

'I'm not sure that's swooning,' said Ieuan.

'It's the kind of swooning I approve of,' said Lucretia.

The good prince leapt onto his own horse and the two men raced round the arena with the princess flung like a sack of turnips over the villain's shoulder.

'I'm not terribly sure at this distance,' said Berenice, 'but there's something about the way she's bouncing that makes me think she's not enjoying this.'

After the second circuit the evil prince reined in his horse, unslung the princess from his shoulder, and pushed her into the arms of the gangly spurned maiden, who tied her to the wooden structure.

'It's getting better,' said Lucretia, 'but it's still a little tame.'

'Wouldn't you like to be fought over, my ickle precious?' murmured Ieuan.

'Who, me?' said Lucretia, looking across Berenice to give him a wink before turning back to the arena, where the good prince made a running leap onto the back of his horse as it cantered past.

Ieuan spluttered. 'Er - well - no.'

Lucretia wasn't paying attention. 'Dear gods, what's happening now?'

A masked man had galloped into the arena. His horse seemed to be trying to look in all directions at once. It was only the rider's skill which stopped the horse from spinning around or leaping into the lower seats to get away from the maniacs around it.

The two princes jumped into a standing position on their saddles and, as the horses began to career round the arena, tumbled while waving swords, somersaulting over each other, blades sparking.

The masked stranger leapt off his mount, hitched her to a post at the edge of the arena, and rushed to grapple with the gangly maiden. Meanwhile the princes landed on the table where they ran up and down slashing and stabbing at each other as the princess squirmed in her bonds and kicked out at both her captor and her rescuer.

'I'm not sure it's very sensible,' said Berenice.

'Sensible?' said Lucretia and Ieuan together.

'What they're doing. It looks a bit dangerous.'

Lucretia rolled her eyes.

Neither of the other men, still on the table-top, seemed to have noticed the three-way battle between the two women and the stranger, who finally wrestled the spurned maiden to the ground then bound her with the rope into a human skittle, bouncing about in fury and ready to topple at any moment.

Oblivious, the two princes paused their table-top fight to untie ropes looped round the corners of the framework. Now they swung from the wooden structure, still slashing at each other. As they dropped twisting back to the table they finally engaged, pushing and tangling as the chorus and orchestra grew louder, while the princess pulled against the ropes her captor was trying to untie and with a crash of cymbals, the good prince fell.

A great gush of red spurted forth and a head rolled from the table and across the arena floor.

'Ooh,' said the crowd and cheered.

'Isn't that the hero?' exclaimed Berenice. 'Why are they cheering because the *hero*'s dead?'

Lucretia shrugged. 'Everyone loves a villain. Do you suppose it's a *real* head?'

The evil prince jumped from the table in triumph, stopped the head with his foot, then held it up triumphant.

'Turnip,' grunted Lucretia. 'Disappointing.'

Throwing the turnip-head to the ground, the evil prince prepared to leap from the table. He swayed on the edge for a moment, apparently startled to see the spurned maiden hopping two-footed and the masked stranger in what would have been a passionate embrace with the princess if they weren't a foot apart.

A sudden blare from a bugle jolted the actors. The villain landed next to the princess, knocking the spurned maiden over, which loosened her bonds. With feigned regret, the princess unentangled herself from the stranger, touched his lips with her finger, then pulling a dagger from her bodice turned to face her enemy.

The audience held its breath.

As the gloating villain reached for her the princess stabbed him with fury. He squirmed, a tangle of red coils pouring from his tunic, then collapsed to writhe in the dust of the arena before falling still.

'Tsk,' said Lucretia, leaning forward. 'It's just dyed rope.'

The princess wiped her hands on her gown, picked up the hero's head, cradling it with as much affection as she might a rotten cabbage, and glanced to where the masked stranger waited with arms crossed. She dropped the head and gave him a little wave.

The spurned maiden, out of her bondage except for a few coils still binding her ankles, bounced up with a sword, plunged it deep into the princess's body and then into her own. The princess let out one last cry for help before falling to the ground.

The old queen staggered forth as the chorus cried:

> *Woe woe thou foolish queen!*
> *What tragedy thou wrought*
> *And now your daughter's blood*
> *Summonses the creature her sire created*
> *Behold!*
> *The dragophant!*

From behind the scenes came an enormous creature the length of a horse but with a neck, back and head swollen to grotesque proportions. It was covered in green leather with a long, leathery tail, eyelids like plates, enormous flapping ears and a trunk sticking up in the air.

The crowd rose to its feet and cheered, stamping their feet.

'For pity's sake,' snapped Lucretia, smacking the head of the man in front till he sat down and she could see properly.

Propelling himself along the ground in a sliding skid, the masked stranger reached the princess, picked her up and carried her out of range of the stamping dragophant to the edge, where he proceeded to revive her 'corpse' with another passionate kiss.

Sparks and smoke burst from the dragophant's trunk.

The audience cheered and clapped, drowning out the chorus.

The masked stranger's horse had had enough. She pulled herself free of her hitching post, reared, and collided with the disorientated dragophant which started to skitter sideways. The monster stumbled into the wooden structure with such force that it collapsed onto the old queen's head and knocked her flat. As a discordant screech from the orchestra almost drowned the audience's din, a proper flame shot from the dragophant's trunk and set fire to its eyelids. The bottom half of the creature neighed in terror and shot out from under its upper half. A man scrambled out just as the dracophant's green leather head caught fire, and flung it sideways onto the old queen as she staggered to her feet.

Her wig ignited. The remainder of the structure collapsed. And the audience danced on the terraces, cheering and whistling.

'Well,' said Lucretia, whacking the man in front again. 'I don't know what Contractes intended, but I suspect that was a vast improvement.'

9th October
Chapter 30: Tryssa

There had been no word from Amicus, but then why should there be?

He'd escorted her and Galyna to the performance then left, saying he had business to attend to with Olivarius. Afterwards, Tryssa had gone home with her sister-in-law, laughing at the spectacle they'd seen and wishing Corryx had been there to see it, before having a simple meal together by the fireside.

But for no reason she would admit to, all evening Tryssa wondered if Amicus would call - though there was no reason for him to do so. A memory of standing by a roundhouse door well after the family was asleep, looking out into the rain in case Rhys turned up, made her feel childish and old at the same time.

Why should he call round? The mystery about the ring was solved. Amicus had found his friend's body. Everything that could be done for Galen's soul was being done, and now life would settle back into normality. Amicus would manage as the justice in a small town with no serious crime until a second duovir was appointed, and that would most likely be Max after putting on such a spectacle - even one that probably hadn't turned out as it should have. And Tryssa - Tryssa could train up Sila, spend the winter with her brother's family, then go back to Pecunia in the spring. Yet there had been something in Amicus's face which worried her, and the fear that he didn't want to share it would hurt, if she let it.

When Sila came round the following morning to ask for help with the injured in the circus camp, Tryssa felt a little ashamed that other people's suffering would take her mind off feeling foolish.

Tryssa, Galyna and Sila found Contractes bouncing between Slab and Gravel, nearly beside himself with triumph. 'Yesterday's performance wasn't what I intended at all!' he said. 'It was even better!' He chewed his piece of stick, moving it from one side of his mouth to the other as he surveyed the charred wood, leather and horsehair wigs being piled up in front of him. 'Shame we can't do it all again tomorrow. But it'll take a week to build another structure and I'm not sure either half of the dragophant will do it again, so we'll need to train up another horse and rider.'

He punched Slab in the bicep in his excitement, winced and nursed his knuckles. 'I suppose I ought to let people's wounds heal first. What you got? Everything for cuts, bruises and burns? Capital! Off you go. There's not too many casualties, thank Thespis. Patch 'em up and get 'em back in the ring quick, that's what I say. Keeps them too busy to think they're in pain.' Deep in thought, he waved them towards one of the tents and wandered off to watch the uninjured in training.

There were, as he'd said, only a few injuries. Sila had said she was confident to do the work itself, but less confident among strangers. However, she quickly relaxed into the task at hand, her chatter cheering the gangling lad who'd played the old lady, and whose hair had caught fire, telling him folk-tales while the burn was cleaned. 'What lovely blue eyes you have!' she said. The boy swallowed, blinked back tears and gritted his jaw as the wound was packed with ointment and moss. With a little more experience, Sila would do very well for the town.

Blue, thought Tryssa. *That was the name of the beggar who died. The rich say his death is just one of those things. But according to Sila and Galyna, the slaves and poor are muttering. Whether they're right or wrong, it's inadvisable to ignore what the majority are saying. What's the name of the carpenter who'd shown us where to find Galen's hand? The one who said he'd met Blue on the road? Morgan, that was it..*

Leaving Galyna and Sila with the boy, Tryssa left the tent to find him.

It was no surprise to find him working. What was surprising was that Berenice was watching him, knees hunched under her skirts as she sat on a damp log. The girl barely acknowledged Tryssa as she joined them. Morgan himself lifted his eyebrows, then returning to his work, said, 'I'm not following why you're here, lass.' He ran his right thumb along the small object in his left hand, then reapplied the knife. 'You have wealthy connections.'

'I don't want them,' said Berenice.

'More fool you, then.'

Berenice swallowed. 'Why do you say that?'

'The world's a cruel place.'

'I know. That's why I'm here.'

Morgan snorted. 'You think running away to the circus then freezing your backside off in a field is less cruel than sitting in a warm house with slaves to run after you?'

Berenice sniffed.

'Did you hear about Blue?'

Berenice nodded.

'He must have half lost his mind from years on the road,' said Morgan, with half a glance at Tryssa. 'Dead of cold, they say, back of some houses in town.' He shook his head. 'Poor wretch, I heard some fool said he'd have preferred to pass away under the hedge where he usually slept, where he'd feel comfortable, rather than in some freezing alley. Pah! What kind of world is it where people think sleeping under a hedge is acceptable, let alone comfortable?'

193

Berenice turned to the older woman, her face wet with tears, and after a second's hesitation accepted an arm round her shoulders. Although the sky was clear and the air dry, every breath drew cold into Tryssa's lungs. She scanned the camp while waiting for the right moment to speak.

Two other carpenters were peering at a sketch in charcoal on bark, and a third was pacing the ground. A few yards away, performers were sitting with someone who was perhaps the stage director. There was a lot of arm-waving which looked as it if might turn into fisticuffs. A woman was putting flatbreads to cook on the hot stones at the fire's edge, while peering into the enormous pot as if willing its contents to be more appetising. In makeshift stables, someone sang to the animals. Children ran in and out of the tents which sagged in the shadows of the amphitheatre. The female dancers and chorus chattered, squabbled and fussed like a flock of sparrows outside the women's quarters.

At the edge of the camp she noticed Ieuan standing with a pony, looking irresolute.

'My home is like a prison,' mumbled Berenice. 'I have no money of my own and nothing to do. My fiancé's parents are worried about the dowry as if all I am is a prize cow. It's no better than slavery.'

'You really think so?' said Morgan, as indifferent as if he were contemplating a potential splinter.

After a few cold seconds Berenice's small voice said, 'No.'

'And you think joining the circus will help?'

'I just want some fun and for people to take me seriously.' Berenice lifted her head and stared at the troupe.

Morgan looked at her and then, glancing at Tryssa, raised his eyebrows again.

'Are you a runaway slave, Morgan?' Berenice sniffed. 'If you are, I promise I won't tell.'

Morgan shook his head. 'I'm sure you wouldn't, lass, but you can rest assured. I'm a freed-man.'

Berenice sobbed and swiped her arm across her eyes.

'Listen,' said Morgan, 'freedom isn't just doing what you want. Freedom is knowing you won't starve and you're safe and loved. That's what it is. Everything else is just loneliness.'

'No-one understands,' sniffed Berenice, shrugging Tryssa's arm away and rising to stomp out of the camp.

'Aren't you going to follow and see she's safe?' said Morgan.

'No,' said Tryssa. 'See the young man with the horse who's just stopped her? He's her betrothed. I think she needs to let off steam. Things at home are a bit peculiar.'

Morgan snorted. 'Least she's got a home.'

'True.' Tryssa watched in silence for a while. 'Thank you for your help the other day. It meant my … friend could lay someone to rest after many years.'

'That's good.' Morgan smoothed the object with his hand and satisfied, contemplated her properly. 'But it's not why you're here.'

'No,' Tryssa admitted. 'There's something nagging at me and I wonder if the beggar you met - Blue - knew more about the grove where the body was found.'

'No idea,' said Morgan. 'I met him on the road. He put me on to that bit of shelter and this job.' He paused. 'Although … he did remind me of something.'

'Something? Not someone?'

Morgan shrugged. 'Either, neither, both. I dunno. I've been on the road for two years. I'm getting old for a man in my situation. Forty-seven, give or take a year. Things merge.'

'Will you tell me your story?'

Morgan closed his left hand round the object. 'Born a slave, raised a slave. My master was a carpenter. He was kind.'

'What was his name?'

'Saer.'

Tryssa waited for more but none came. 'And Saer trained you and eventually freed you.'

Morgan shook his head. 'He trained me. His son freed me.'

'Where did you live?'

Morgan hesitated and shifted position to ease his lame leg. 'Sorviodunum's where we ended up,' he said. 'Where we started, I'm not sure. All I remember is you could run from one side to another in no time.' He sighed. 'My master had no children. I hoped he'd free me and adopt me. But when I was about six my mistress died, and my master insisted we move away.' A frown flickered across his face, and he looked past Tryssa to the country beyond the camp as if peering into his memory. 'I can recall being sad the day we moved.'

'Well, leaving everything behind -'

'That of course, but I -' He frowned again, shook his head and continued. 'After a year or so my master remarried and had a son. And then I grew up and me and another slave had a daughter together. Three years ago, there was a sickness in town. My wife died and then my master. His son…'

'Freed you.'

'Aye, he did,' Morgan rolled his shoulders. 'But it after his negligence lamed me and he turned me out as useless. Then I was free. Free of all obligations and free to starve.'

'But your daughter -'

196

'His possession. Sold her to a trader while I was away for a few days, trying to get work. No-one was sure where my girl had gone. Someone told me Durocornovium. She wasn't there. Someone told me Isca. I guessed Isca Silurum since it was nearest, but I was wrong. So I guess they meant Isca Dumnonorium. Stupid Roman names. The circus is going there next and I'll be with them. Maybe my luck's changed.'

Tryssa watched him. Morgan seemed a little more hopeful than he had when they'd met. A job, shelter and regular food had fed a hope that must have been fading.

'Sometimes I wonder why I'm bothering,' he said. 'Maybe she's got a warm bed and plenty to eat and kindness, and won't want to give it up for the open road and shelter in haunted groves.'

'Like the grove where you sheltered? You think it's haunted?'

'Not really.' Morgan shook his head. 'It's a place of sadness, not fear.'

Tryssa could see his mind whirring, his eyes flickering as if he tried to work something out. 'What is it?'

Morgan shrugged. 'Nothing.'

Tryssa stood and put her hand on Morgan's arm. 'You'll find your daughter.'

'Aye.' He nodded. For the first time, a real smile crossed his face. He opened his palm to reveal a carving. 'Have a look at this. What do you reckon?'

It was a wooden robin, delicate and simple but quite distinguishable. He pulled two more items out of the sack and handed them over - a dove and a sparrow. Tryssa could make out the character in each bird: one friendly, one coy and the other somehow cheeky. 'They're lovely.'

'I'm thinking of selling them in the forum. Reckon I could get away with it? I haven't got a licence for a pitch.'

'I'll speak to someone and make sure of it.' Tryssa tried to ignore the flush warming her face as she said it.

'I thought I'd try it here. I used to make these for my daughter because she liked to feed the birds,' said Morgan. 'Maybe when I get to Isca, if she's got a kind mistress, she might come over to my stall. Maybe I'll find her then - who knows? If I don't -' He sighed. 'But something tells me I will. Ever since I met Blue in that grove, even though it was cold and miserable, I've felt like I've come home, and I don't know why. It's like Nia's the south star and I've been facing north for two years, but all I had to do was turn the right way.'

'Nia's a pretty name,' said Tryssa.

Morgan smiled. 'It's common enough I suppose, but her mother and I liked it. Only -' His smile dropped.

'Only what?'

'The last day I saw her, I was only allowed as far as the kitchen door to speak to her. I was angry with my master's son but I took it out on her. I walked away with bitter words burning my mouth, her sobbing echoing in my ears. I never got the chance to talk, and maybe she won't want me now.'

'She will. I'm sure of it. But...if you remember what Blue reminded you of, will you find me and tell me?'

Morgan shrugged. '*If* I do. It's like a taste or a smell in a dream - it means something else entirely. Chances are my old mistress had something blue and it's just a connection in my head.'

'Blue's not an easy colour to come by.'

Morgan scratched his nose. 'That's true.' He pointed up into the cold bright sky. 'Maybe it's that. Maybe that's all it is. A fine day - a lovely sky. Like you feel the sun's on your face and you're eating something sweet. Only when I think of him and that sort of day, then somehow the taste is bitter after all.'

Chapter 31: Amicus

The Ordo meeting dragged, and Amicus wished he could have gone with Olivarius to Vademlutra. It was only a hunch that Dun and Gris's visit there had any relevance to anything. However, without a partner duovir, it was his sole responsibility to lead the assembly and deal with the judicial matters, even though there were few to consider.

The main business was a proposal that a series of fountains and a mosaic in the forum would bring prestige to the town. The man suggesting it was good at coming up with ideas, but any suggestion they might not be practical was met with cold indifference. They had people to sort things out, didn't they? Men like Olivarius?

Men like Olivarius, of course, could be blamed when things didn't work out, and it could be argued that the execution was at fault, not the idea. The Ordo was split between those who thought it worth the risk and those who thought it expensive folly.

In Amicus's view this was perhaps part of the reason why the theft of public money forty years ago had not been noticed for some time. Favorix's father had - it was said - constantly interfered with his own secretary's notes and accounts. And his secretary had been a slave, not someone who could argue. Amicus had expected poor records, but not the messy scrolls which Olivarius had finally unearthed and tried to decipher. There were notes down the margin indicating money going from one project to another, crossings through, and marks on the parchment as if the ink had been lifted with a blade. Olivarius had left him a report to read later, for what it was worth.

For now, he had to concentrate on the last item on the agenda.

'There are still only two candidates for the role of second duovir to work with Amicus,' said Rufus. 'Max and, erm … Gethin.' He looked sideways at the oldest decurion, fast asleep on his bench - a man who had somehow survived so long, despite various campaigns both as a British rebel and later a Roman auxiliary, that no-one was entirely sure how old he was.

Gethin jerked awake. 'When I wash in the legion…' he said, before subsiding.

Rufus glared. 'I'm surprised Max isn't here to tell us what he actually proposes to do if appointed, apart from put on preposterous shows.'

Ieuan's father Gwyn crossed his arms and scowled. 'At least he only wants to be duovir and not my fellow quaestor. We need to improve the pavements and keep the aqueduct clean, not waste it on extravagance. It's just as well it's his own money he's wasting and not Durnovaria's.'

'It was a *marvelloush* show!' Gethin declaimed through the gap where his front teeth had been. 'But more fool him to shpend money he ain't got.'

'He'd *better* have it,' growled Gwyn. 'For a start, the *town* isn't paying the circus.'

Amicus spoke. 'Who says he hasn't got it?'

There was a slight shuffling as the Ordo looked at each other and very deliberately not at Deryn, who glared into the middle distance, chewing on a thumbnail. There were a few frowns, but silence.

'My shenturion shaid never trusht a priesht,' whistled Gethin.

Amicus looked round at the Ordo. The priests were scowling at the old man. All were there bar Favorix. Someone had to be on duty at the temple these days.

'That,' added Gethin, 'was the day he was struck by lightning.' The priests looked smug. 'Although that might have been holding up his sword like that during a storm.' He fell into a snooze again.

'Well, the election will go ahead with those two candidates,' said Rufus. 'It's just as well there's so little to worry about, Amicus, and I suppose when - I mean *if* Max wins -' He rolled his eyes at Gethin, 'you'll be working alongside an old friend.'

Amicus nodded and rose. 'If there's no more business, gentlemen, I'll go and speak with him.'

Outside in the cold, damp air, Amicus wrapped his cloak more closely round him and scanned the forum. Dun and Gris were skirting the fringes, looking like they might slink down a drain but possibly heading to the baths. Tryssa and Galyna were crossing with the young wise-woman, heads down and chattering away. Or at least, Galyna and Sila were. Tryssa looked deep in thought and a little sad. Perhaps she was thinking over a hopeless medical case. He'd like to talk things over with her, but so far there hadn't been time and besides, from her point of view, the whole thing was over and there was nothing to discuss. He could perhaps ask if she'd found the Christian priest and asked for the necessary prayers, and maybe in doing so, just mention his uncertainty. No. That wasn't fair. She was here to get to know her brother again, not get involved in his probably fruitless quest based on nothing more than eavesdropping and disquiet.

'She's sharp, that one,' said Deryn, arriving at his side and following his gaze.

'Yes, she is. I suppose it goes with the job.'

'Perhaps she should put herself forward as a candidate for duovir!' Deryn chuckled. His face grew soft. 'Elli would have liked her.'

'I think you're right,' said Amicus without looking at him. 'Elli was generally a good judge of character.'

'Always,' said Deryn.

202

Tryssa had all but left the forum, pausing only to speak to Petros for a second. There was a brief moment of pointing, nodding, smiling and then she was gone.

Amicus started to walk in the opposite direction and found Deryn following. 'Looking for Max too?'

'The skeleton in the grove,' said Deryn. 'Do you really think it was Galen?'

'Yes.'

Deryn kicked a loose stone. 'I wouldn't have wished it on him.'

'Despite the fact that he snatched Lucretia's affections and you no longer thought of him as a friend?'

Was it like that? murmured the memory of Galen.

Deryn shook his head. 'It wasn't - it doesn't mean I'm glad he's dead. He ... it ... Lucretia and I weren't suited. Even if he hadn't been here to distract her, I doubt she'd have stayed. And besides, she flirted with Max and Favorix too. She wasn't as keen on Favorix as she seems to be now. He buzzed round her like a mosquito, like he did with us - always trying to get in on things. She was more attracted to Max, I think.'

'And despite the fact that Max was betrothed to Eira he flirted back, and that didn't bother you especially?'

Deryn clenched his cloak tighter and slowed his pace. 'Max has always said the occasional distraction keeps him cheerful. It never means anything.' His face was closed but his eyes flashed.

Amicus had often wondered why Max had married someone as indifferent as Eira, but then it had been a match made when they were children. He himself was glad not to have been subjected to an arranged marriage. There seemed far too much risk of misery attached. He sighed. 'Have you and Eira settled with Lucretia yet?'

'We nearly have. It's just that Max says the worth of the land has increased.' Deryn shook his head.

'Really?'

They stopped outside a small building. There were no windows of any description but from within the sounds of men's loud voices, clattering and the occasional cheer seeped through into the shadowed street. Something heavy hit the other side of the door.

'I don't suppose they serve wine in glass goblets,' said Amicus.

'They don't serve anything as sophisticated as wine and I suspect the beer is technically fermented soup. Look, let's go to Max's house. He's bound to be there.'

'I doubt it,' said Amicus.

Deryn caught his arm. 'Look, it's not like people think. Max knows when to stop. It's not like -'

The shade of Galen hovered in the air between them and said, *Is he talking about me?*

'Do you believe in ghosts?' asked Amicus.

Deryn scowled. 'No. The dead are dead. I don't even believe in gods and I don't care who knows it.'

'Then why so insistent about that grove?'

Deryn hesitated. Another bellow came from inside the house, more menacing this time. 'Tradition. And because Eira *does* believe, and after all it is - was - will be her land too.'

'And now that skeleton's been dug up?'

'What?' Deryn paled. 'I haven't told her. It'll make her feel worse. Look, why are we here? Max might not be inside and if he is - why shouldn't he be? Everyone misses Ordo meetings once in a while.'

Before Amicus could answer, the door was wrenched inward and Max was ejected onto the street.

Another man, sleeves pushed up and fists clenched, followed and snarled. 'No more money, no more bets, no matter who you are. I told you before, promises ain't currency.' He stepped into the house, pushing back the men peering into the street, and slammed the door.

Max winced a little as he heaved himself to his feet and brushed mud from his cloak. He forced a grin when he saw Amicus. 'It's not like you think.'

'Isn't it?'

'Everyone games. Well, most people do. *We* used to.' He put his shoulders back and strode towards the forum.

Amicus followed. 'I lost the taste for it when I heard about Galen.'

'I never had much taste for it even before,' said Deryn. His face was still dark, even in the shadows of the side-street. 'Come along, Max, we've business to discuss.'

'I know my limit,' insisted Max. 'That's the difference between me and Galen.' He jerked a thumb backwards. 'You can ignore all that - he's a sore loser.'

'Deryn says Eira believes in ghosts. Do you?' said Amicus.

Max stopped, swallowed and bent to brush more mud from his clothes. 'Do you mean Galen's? He ... I haven't thought of him for years.'

'Hadn't you?'

Max stood again and exchanged glances with Deryn. 'Amicus, I appreciate he was your friend - our friend. But he's long dead. Killed for his debt. It's why I'm not such a fool as to -'

'How do you know he's dead?'

Max's eyes flitted sideways to Deryn again. 'Well, I don't... But it's what I always assumed.'

'I told him about the skeleton,' said Deryn.

'Besides that, before that,' insisted Max.

'Ah,' said Amicus. 'The distinctive gambling stranger.'

Max paled then forced a smile, clapping Amicus on the shoulder. 'I wanted to ask you to dinner tonight,' he said. 'I left Lucretia in charge of ordering the meal, so it's bound to be wonderful. Favorix is coming, Deryn will be there of course. We'll raise a glass to the memory of Galen too, for the sake of what he meant to all of us.'

Out of the corner of his eye, Amicus saw Deryn scowl. 'I'd be delighted,' he said. 'I imagine you've invited Lucretia's friend Tryssa too?'

'Oh yes,' said Max. 'Of course, I'd forgotten. Yes, she'll definitely be there. I just hope it won't all be too boring for her.'

'I'm sure she won't mind,' said Amicus. 'I'll see you later. I have some paperwork to attend to.'

Chapter 32: Diggers

In the bathhouse stadia Dun and Gris huddled near a brazier. Feeling inadequate, they observed two young men with bulging muscles and taut buttocks lift weights and climb ropes. A third, equally godlike, was standing still while making various bits of himself ripple. Their naked bodies glistened with sweat and oil.

'Wears you out to watch them, don't it?' A stranger and two companions sat down, cradling hot drinks. One offered a dish of honeyed hazelnuts.

'Don't it just,' said Dun. 'Makes you feel cold, too.' He took a nut and contemplated the strangers. They were wiry and brown - either still somehow summer-tanned, or once from far-distant parts of the Empire. The speaker's accent wasn't local, his eyes blue and hair fair, and his skin was dry, burnt.

'It's all show,' said the stranger. 'It's like: "Look at my muscles!" That don't prove nothing. I could do that without all the fuss and oil. Bet you could, too.'

Dun was conscious of his own biceps, hard as rock under his tunic. It was true. He could lift stone, dig, and knock a man out cold, but he didn't bulge like the weight-lifters. Women didn't look at him twice even though he was a free man, but they'd flutter their eyelashes at the Adonises, despite the fact they were even lower down the pecking order than a grave-robber.

'You're right, I could,' he said after a moment. 'And they're slaves, all three of them. Maybe it is all show, but it's their masters ought to be taking notice. I hope they get treated right - know what I'm saying?'

The stranger chuckled. 'Yeah, I get you. All sorts in the bathhouse at this time of day. Bathing time for the poor, the disreputable and the slaves, ain't it?'

Gris scrunched up his eyes as he tried to work out which the strangers were. Or for that matter, who he was.

'We're not slaves,' said Dun, while he was still thinking.

'Nor us,' said the stranger cheerfully. 'Those of us that were got freed last summer. Our master gave us the choice to go or stay.'

'What did you do?'

'Stayed. I'm Vertus. This is Caesar and that's Frog. We're from the circus. So we're firmly in the poor and disreputable category.'

'I'm Dun, he's Gris,' said Dun. 'I guess we are too, though not for want of trying. Stopping being poor that is. Not sure I care about disreputable. It's not like the rich are all squeaky clean, even if they do get longer in the baths than us what actually work up a sweat. My mate here wants to be respectable though, don't you, Gris? You wanna little farm with your girl and grow chickens. Not that you know how.'

Gris grunted. 'All you gotta do is feed chickens grain and then you get more chickens.'

Dun rolled his eyes. 'Well if that's how you think it works, at least your girl's safe alone with you.'

Gris glared.

Vertus chuckled. 'So what is it you two do?'

'Trade in antiques.'

'Oh! You're burglars?' Vertus looked at Dun with something akin to respect. At any rate it was the most favourable look Dun had received for a while. He puffed out his chest a little.

'Maybe, maybe not,' he said, tapping his nose. 'Skilled workmen, that's what we is. Planning to move further afield to Isca. We just haven't the wherewithal to leave just yet.'

'Thought of joining the circus?' said Vertus. 'We're going that way after the gig. Always looking for extra hands - onstage, backstage, you name it. It's a place for all sorts.'

Dun and Gris exchanged glances.

'I can't leave my girl,' objected Gris.

'You can for a bit,' said Dun. '*She's* not going anywhere. You could make some money then come back for her. We just need to get safe to Isca.'

A gong sounded. 'Time's up,' said Vertus. 'They've got to swab our dirt away to make it nice for the nobs.'

Vertus rose and stretched. 'Give it some thought, Dun - could be the making of you. Anyway, best round the girls up and get back. Gotta keep an eye on them on the way through town.'

'Alluring, are they?' leered Dun.

Caesar's eyes widened. 'Depends on your tastes, mate. We got all sorts. But if we don't get them all back in one piece Contractes will turn us into a star attraction by feeding us to the dogs.'

'What do you think this boring town's gonna do to the girls?' asked Gris.

'Maybe we're more worried about what the girls'll do to the town.' Frog waggled his eyebrows.

The three strangers gave each other the nod and without another word somersaulted across the floor, forcing the weightlifters to stumble out of the way just as they were getting their leggings on. With a laugh, the circus men landed simultaneously and arm-in-arm burst out through the door into the street.

Dun and Gris followed them. The warmth of the bathhouse was replaced by chill air. A steady stream of bathers ranged onto the street, pooled in small groups to say their farewells, and then made their way home - or at any rate, to the homes of their masters. The circus men caught up with a small group of women coming from the other entrance.

'Any of them got three heads?' said Gris, as Dun sneaked a sideways look.

'I'm not sure one of them hasn't got three eyes.'

'Improvement on your last girlfriend, then.'

'And one of them might have a plaited beard down to her waist.'

'You're just jealous cos the only beard you can grow looks like mould.'

'Shurrup,' said Dun. 'There's a scrawny one with her face half-covered up. It must be horrible.'

'Like you can criticise on the face front,' said Gris.

Dun ignored him. 'And it looks like her hair was hacked off with an axe.'

'Yours looks like it was chewed off by a badger.'

'Stow it.'

'Anyway, she's arguing with that Vertus chap. He's not letting her get away, is he? She must be a wild one.'

'Never mind her - that one looks like the front of her dress is stuffed with squirrels.'

'Perhaps it is.'

'Or maybe it's just her...' Dun straightened his shoulders and smoothed his hair. Then he turned to Gris with a grin. 'You know, it might be worth thinking about joining the circus after all.'

****

The two men argued across the forum. It was lunch-time. Desperate shoppers - those with the least money - were bartering for what little damaged or stale produce the food sellers were trying to off-load before packing up. The stallholders trading dry goods and trinkets were settling down on stools to rest over a snack.

Masner, catching Dun's eye, gave a minuscule shake of his head.

'Like we got anything to sell him,' said Gris. 'What with people not letting us get on with things, we haven't had a haul for a week. How'm I gonna get rich at this rate?'

'Shoulda stuck it out to Isca, ghost or no ghost.'

'You was running faster than what I was.'

'Huh,' said Dun. 'Momentum. I'm heavier than you - made me faster going downhill. But I'm telling you we oughta try Isca. If we go with the circus we'd be in a crowd. Ghosts don't haunt crowds - I don't think. Anyway we don't have to stay with them forever, we could -'

'I gotta talk to her first.'

Dun waved his arms. 'I know. Not that it's the best time to try and talk to her. We oughta get some lunch first.'

'With what? We're skint.' In his agitation Gris tripped on a cobble, twisted his foot and collided with a well-built matron, bouncing backwards onto Dun. 'Pardon me, madam.'

'Oaf!' exclaimed the matron, curling her lip. She brushed herself down before continuing on her way, nose in the air.

Gris nursed his ankle, leaning on Dun's shoulder with his other hand. He cursed the woman's back as she waddled towards the temple with a scrawny slave-girl in tow.

The prime spot where Stump begged didn't seem to be doing him any good. He leered at the women and swore at the men. Right now, he was dribbling and waving a shattered hand. Gris, remembering the skeleton, shuddered.

'That's Blue's old cloak,' said Gris. 'I remember that bit of trim left on it.'

'Who cares? Look at the state of him,' said Dun. 'Beer all down his front.'

'That's not beer, it's too dark.' Gris frowned.

'Gravy, then.'

'Where's he gonna get gravy? *We* can't afford gravy.'

'What's his stains to us?' said Dun, shrugging Gris's hand off his shoulder. 'Come on, maybe your girl might have some nosh. Let's go.'

They walked past Stump, eyes averted, and turned into the main street. Almost all the old timber buildings had been replaced, the stone houses fine and sturdy, letting out onto pavements raised above the road. Narrow alleys ran between groups of them. Dun and Gris walked on until they reached another alley that led along the back of all the houses. A place where the hidden things happened: the removal of night-soil, the carrying of laundry, the coming and going of slaves.

It was cold and dark. The stones were still icy and slippery under their feet. They fell silent, keeping their wits about them for lurkers with no more business down there than they had. As they neared the back of the right house, Gris whispered, 'Why'd you tell Amicus we sold the bracelet?'

'What? Why you worrying about that?'

'He could check.'

Dun shrugged. 'Who with? I never said who I sold it to. And if he does, we'll say we've forgot cos it was worthless. Anyway, shh. Here we are.'

They slipped through a back gate to a rear courtyard. Three thin cats, waiting with varying degrees of nonchalance at the kitchen door, turned in unison to stare. *Know your place, humans,* their supercilious stares commanded. One aimed a swipe at Dun's leg as they approached.

Gris knocked, and after a pause the door was wrenched open. Fragrant steam poured out into the cold air.

212

'Oh, it's you again.' A sweating man holding a ladle rolled his eyes at Gris. 'I'll get her for you. She's got five minutes tops. We gotta get the family fed cos they're worn out from doing nothing. And if you're hoping for grub, you can forget it.' He slammed the door in their faces.

They stood stamping their feet, the cats slinking closer, smirks on their gaunt little faces which said as clear as words, *Bet there's grub for us because we're better than you*, until the door re-opened and Nia stepped out into the courtyard wrapped in a cloak. She gave Gris a small, shy kiss and with half a backward glance, sneaked two hot rolls and some cheese out from under her apron.

'Nia,' said Gris, 'we - '

'I thought you'd never come and I've been so worried,' Nia burst out. 'It's all my fault, cos look what happened! But the ratty old thing gave me the heebie-jeebies. I'm sorry, love, but it did. Weird symbols what weren't even *proper* weird symbols! They was all wrong. I didn't think you'd mind. Only-'

'Are you talking about the bracelet?' asked Dun.

Nia nodded. 'I knew it couldn't be worth much or you'd have sold it, and I know Gris meant it as a gift but it gave me the shivers and -'

'Slow down, slow down,' said Dun, exchanging glances with Gris. 'So you didn't like it. He forgives you. But - what exactly did you do with it?'

'I gave it to Blue. It must have been cursed and I gave it him and it's all my fault he's dead!'

'Why didn't you just sell it?' wailed Gris as quietly as he could. 'Another *as* or two for the savings! All we got to do is buy your freedom and then we can get a farm and -'

213

Nia gave him another kiss and a small hug. 'I know, but I don't have time what with Mistress Lucretia. When she's not slapping at me or -'

'She slapped you?'

'Or demanding a new hairstyle or another layer of paint or making me hike with her over to the mosaic maker or demanding snacks, I'm having to accompany her when she's being dragged to the temple by the old … I mean Eira, anyway I thought there's me going to the temple every five minutes which as you know, I'd rather not, following along with those two bickering old witch -*women* and then coming back to shelter and food, and there's poor old Blue freezing his bum off on the pavement and I thought, well I can't give him an *as* but I can give him something that's *worth* an *as* and maybe *he* won't get the heebie-jeebies and if he does he can sell it and get something to eat, but then look what happened? And that's not the *only* thing…'

'It'd have taken more than an *as* to stop Blue dying of cold and starvation, love,' said Gris.

'Yes, but he didn't, I don't think.'

'I heard he died in an alley like this. *I'll* die if I stay here much longer,' pointed out Dun.

'Yes, but what was he doing there?' said Nia. 'And after they'd taken him away there was blood in the dirt, I'm sure of it. The cats were licking something up anyway.' She looked down at the three cats, all of whom turned their heads in different directions. Dun could almost hear them whistling. 'And they say his cloak was gone and his bowl was empty. Maybe that bracelet cursed him. And it's all my fault.'

'Nonsense, love,' comforted Gris.

'And maybe I've cursed myself too,' sniffed Nia. 'Mistress Lucretia…' Nia gave a small sob. 'Mistress Lucretia wants to buy me and take me back with her to the wilds and I won't ever see you again. I can't lose anyone else!'

'No!' said Gris, pulling her into his arms. 'No! She can't.'

'And...' Nia's voice was muffled against his chest.

The door burst open. 'Time's up,' said the cook, hauling the girl out of Gris's arms. 'Stop canoodling. Mistress Lucretia's after you and I can't put up with her yelling. It's putting me off seasoning my soup.' He dragged Nia indoors and slammed the door.

Chapter 33: Lucretia

It was an exhausting day. Before breakfast, Eira's argument with Berenice in which the word 'dowry' seemed to figure highly, had been rather trying The girl's eyes were full of tears when she stormed into the hallway, causing Lucretia almost to fall into the room through the suddenly-open door.

'Oh no, is it my fault?' Berenice cried. 'I didn't mean to bump into you. I'm so clumsy - I'm so lumpy! I - I can't do anything right! No-one understands! It's all so unfair…' Her wails followed her to the back of the house.

'Good morning, Lucretia,' snarled Eira, stalking across the bedroom. 'I hope you didn't find the door too rough for your delicate ears, and I do so apologise for the thickness of the wood. You must have been barely able to hear a thing.' She slammed the door in Lucretia's face.

Now it was evening, and after several hours of talking, Lucretia had agreed a settlement in exchange for the grove. Max had squirmed like a louse on a hot-plate. Favorix might have wanted her to push for more, but Lucretia knew when a pimple was ripe for popping. Too soon, and the results are unsatisfactory. Too late, and poison gets in. Besides, she didn't want Favorix to overestimate her dependency. His attention was a little cloying but enjoyable. She could put up with it for another evening or two.

The house was lit with little lamps and warmed with braziers. Sitting in her room checking her reflection, Lucretia inhaled the scents of spice and richness wafting from the kitchen, and swayed a little to the trickle of music filtering from the dining room.

Nia had suggested softer make-up and dressing Lucretia's natural hair rather than using one of the wigs.

The result was wonderful. Pearls and beads woven in and out of her tresses made the streaks of silver seem part of an intricate design. In the lamplight, the lines round her eyes were all but invisible.

Lucretia, peering into the mirror, fell in love with herself one more time.

When the time was right, she walked into the dining room. She applied an elbow to Tryssa who looked plain and efficient, hair braided like a girl's, little curls frizzing out all round her head. There was a space next to Amicus. Lucretia bent her head and, looking through her lashes, reclined next to him, leaving Tryssa to recline next to Eira. Amicus blushed. It was very gratifying.

'We have a lovely menu tonight,' she murmured to Amicus as wine filled her goblet. 'One to make your blood pound and the sap rise.'

Amicus choked on his wine, recovered, and smiled. 'How goes the mosaic?'

'The design is now complete and the tesserae can be selected. I'll be leaving soon, and who knows when I'll be back.' Lucretia made a moue and glanced round the room. It was annoying that Favorix hadn't arrived, nor had Berenice appeared. Deryn was scowling at the floor. Quite absurd to be behaving like a sulky youth at his age, over a few acres of land.

'Where's Favorix?'

Max curled his lip. 'I expect his mother wouldn't let him out to play.' He raised his voice. 'We shall have dinner now.'

A door slammed and Berenice stamped into the room, followed closely by Olivarius.

'Mummy, you must speak to Daddy,' she shouted. Droplets glistened in her hair and she shivered, huddled in a cloak.

217

'Where have you been?' Eira half rose. 'I thought you were in your room. You shouldn't go out without a -' Her eyes flicked to Olivarius and scanned him from head to foot.

'I've been away all day and no-one noticed!' shouted Berenice.

'Daughter, remember our guests.'

Lucretia leaned over to Amicus. 'Every night an entertainment. There's usually smashing. It's more interesting than the musicians.'

'Where have you been?' repeated Eira.

'Daddy, you need to *do* something,' bawled Berenice. She whirled round, arms flailing, and a slave carrying a plate of oysters danced out of her way just in time. Nux, his mouth open in hope of falling food, growled and glared.

'It gets better by the second,' whispered Lucretia.

Berenice appealed to her. 'What sort of dowry did *you* give with your daughter? What did you demand for Marcellus's wife?'

Lucretia's smile was replaced by a frown. 'More than enough for Prisca and not enough for Poppaea. Ah, here are the oysters. Have some food. Men don't like scrawny women.'

'No-one will marry me because I'm too pooooor!' wailed Berenice. She flung off her cloak, tripping a slave with dishes of beans and chickpeas, to slump on an empty bench and swallow an oyster whole.

'Where have you been?' said Max more gently, rising to sit beside his daughter. He eyed Olivarius, who opened his mouth to speak but Berenice forestalled him.

'I ran away and no-one cared,' she sniffed.

'We thought you were in your room!' cried Eira.

Berenice wiped her eyes and surveyed the room. Lucretia approved. The girl knew how to work an audience. The musicians' tune had meandered into a minor key.

'This morning I packed my things and ran away.' Berenice rattled out her words. 'I found Ieuan in the -' glancing, it seemed, at Tryssa, she faltered before tossing her head. 'I met Ieuan and he said his parents are fussing about the dowry. I said "Let's elope" but he said "Don't be silly," and I was so cross. He escorted me home and -' She put on a face of utter woe, like a puppy in distress. 'Because everyone hated me I started to walk north on my own.'

'But…' Even Eira was startled. Her hand dropped and Nux took his opportunity to attack an oyster and chew on it, gagging on the vinegar.

'Darling!' said Max.

'I walked for *miles* and in the afternoon I met Olivarius. He was horrified.'

'I was,' said Olivarius.

'Should I tell them to bring on more food, sir?' murmured the steward, bending to top up Max's goblet.

'Yes, do,' Lucretia intervened. She leaned against Amicus and muttered, 'One can't watch a melodrama without nourishment, can one?'

Max ran his hand over his face. 'Olivarius - thank you - join us, please. Berry, how far had you got?'

Berenice squirmed a little and cleared her throat. 'Probably far enough to be in *terrible* danger.'

'Why didn't he bring you straight home?' said Eira.

'Oh, I said I wouldn't go home *ever*. He said "Let's go for a ride first and see how you feel".'

Everyone turned to Olivarius. 'I didn't quite -', he protested.

'The stars were trying to come out through the cloud,' sighed Berenice. 'It was *so* romantic.' She heaved a sigh and took two wine-cakes from a passing slave. 'He said I should go home to talk things over properly before making a rash decision.'

'I did say *that*,' Olivarius interposed.

Berenice's face fell. 'That was so *boring,* so I said, "First let's go and look at that old grove. I bet it wouldn't really be as hard to dig up as they say."'

'It's not just about effort,' said Eira. 'You don't mess with old places. The spirits, the *others*, don't like it.'

'That's nonsense,' retorted Berenice. 'Because someone has been messing there and no-one's died. I mean no-one that's not already dead. Apart from Blue.'

'What?' Eira frowned.

'Well, it looked as if they had,' amended Berenice. 'Clods of earth lying about and leaves piled up in the middle. Although it *was* getting dark.'

'Berenice!' exclaimed Eira. 'No-one should be by those stones when the wall between the worlds is thin.'

Lucretia tried to force a chuckle but the words 'All you need is some yew and a bit of iron' stuck in her throat. She thought of those brooding, waiting, watching stones and, despite herself, shivered.

Eira squeezed Nux so much he yelped. 'Who knows what disturbed that earth?'

'Me,' said Amicus.

'What?' Eira stared. 'It's our land! Deryn, did you know?'

'Technically,' pointed out Lucretia, 'until a few hours ago, it was *my* land.' No-one paid her any attention.

'I found a skeleton,' said Amicus.

'Well *of course* you found a skeleton. It's a sacred grove,' said Eira, echoing Deryn.

'This wasn't a sacrifice. It was Galen.'

'How can you know?' Eira paled. 'Surely one skeleton is the same as any other.' Nux pulled a rib-bone from her bowl and dropped to the floor with it, sucking and licking at the flesh and smearing gravy across the mosaic.

Eira pointed at Lucretia. 'I watched Galen head north fine and healthy. He was following you. You'd rejected him, but he wouldn't give up. What happened, Lucretia? What happened when he caught up with you?'

'Mummy,' said Berenice, 'can't you just -'

Into Lucretia's mind came Galen's face - those huge dark, black-lashed eyes, his soft mouth. She shook herself. 'He didn't, and I can't see how anyone could identify a skeleton.'

'Never mind,' interrupted Berenice. 'Look at what Olivarius gave me.'

The whole room turned to the young man again. His face went deep purple and he stared at Amicus as if begging for help.

'Oh *Mummy*!' Berenice stuck her bottom lip out. 'No-one was hurt, no-one's been haunted. Olivarius bought something perfect for a young woman who's intent on being independent.' She tossed her hair a little, the droplets of water sparkling in the lamplight. 'Perhaps a certain fiancé ought to pay a bit more attention. Can't you just let me show you?'

Eira subsided with a small, irritated nod. Olivarius opened his mouth and shut it again, and Berenice rummaged in her leather pouch.

Lucretia turned her attention to the bowls of food before her, and as she did, a thin stream of hot sauce poured over her forearm.

'Ouch!' exclaimed Lucretia, glaring up at Nia. 'What do you think you are doing?'

'Sorry, Mistress.' Nia had gone very pale. She wiped the gravy away with a trembling hand.

Berenice was holding up a bronze knife.

Lucretia felt her mouth drop open. With every ounce of her resolve she tried to avoid Eira's eyes, but couldn't. Eira was startled too, yet the glare she gave Lucretia was enough to melt diamonds.

'What?' demanded Berenice, glowering. 'Don't tell me this is another gift no-one approves of.'

'It's Lucretia's,' said Eira. 'She showed it off every chance she had forty years ago. Tryssa recognises it too.'

Tryssa caught Lucretia's eye and drew a deep breath. 'It does look like a present her brother Rhys gave her.'

Lucretia shrugged. 'I lost that long ago. This does look very similar.'

'Why can't I have things that people don't complain about? Why does it matter?' cried Berenice.

'Dear me, girl,' said Lucretia. 'I don't want it.'

Berenice rubbed her eyes, contemplated the knife with a sigh, and settled down to eat.

There was brief silence, filled only with soft music which had flowed into a calmer eddy. Max reclined next to his daughter and summoned more wine. Eira, her mouth curled at the sight of an old-fashioned, secondhand gift, was feeding Nux a mixture of rich meat and vinegared oysters directly from her platter. Lucretia hoped they'd all be able to leave the room before the dog threw up.

Amicus said, 'I'm sorry you found out about the discovery this way, Eira. I thought Max might have explained.'

Max picked up a piece of wild boar, considered it for a moment and put it back on his dish.

Berenice brandished the bronze knife again, watching the firelight catch on the gems.

There was a clatter as two of the slaves collided and a pewter jug fell to the floor. A thin trickle of honeyed

222

wine seeped across the mosaic and Nux jumped down to lick it up, growling as Nia reached down to retrieve the jug.

'Whenever I think of boars I think of Rhys,' muttered Eira. 'Did anyone ever catch the creature that killed him? Perhaps you ate it eventually, Lucretia, which in a way means you perhaps ate Rhys.'

'How can you speak so about my beloved brother? Even Tryssa cared for him, and nothing runs in her blood but herbal infusions.'

'Nothing runs in yours but money,' interposed Eira as Tryssa's mouth opened to retort. 'I think I shall retire. I can't eat with all this disagreeable talk of skeletons.' She glared at Amicus.

'I apologise, Eira,' said Amicus. 'I really came to say that Galen is surely at rest now and to toast his memory.'

Deryn motioned to Eira to settle back. 'I agree. Let's say our final farewell now. He was once our friend, regardless of what he did.' He glared at Lucretia.

Max nodded and raised his goblet. 'To Galen - may his shade rest.' He took a sip, then poured a splash of wine onto the mosaic. 'And for Lucretia's safe journey home in a few days - we call on Mercury to speed her way homeward.'

'Not too fast, I hope,' murmured Lucretia, recalling the bounce of the wagon.

Olivarius rose. 'Thank you for the meal, sir, I'll bid you goodnight.'

'Thank you, Olivarius,' said Max. 'I'll speak with Amicus about rewarding you.'

Amicus nodded and rose too. 'Certainly,' he said. 'I'm afraid I must leave now, too. I have things to discuss with Olivarius. Thank you, and I apologise again for upsetting you, Eira.'

He hesitated as if waiting for something else to happen, gave a warm smile to Lucretia, then an appraising glance at Tryssa. Tryssa raised her eyes from her dish, her face unbecomingly rosy with temper, and bit her lip. Goodness knew what was going through her mind. Perhaps it was her way of flirting. No wonder she'd never found anyone after Rhys. With a tiny nod, Amicus followed Olivarius out of the room. All the fine food was being wasted on the sullen moodiness in the room and now the only man worth talking to was leaving.

'Mistress -' Nia leaned over Lucretia. 'I need to say -'

'You needn't say anything, Nia!' shouted Lucretia. 'Get to my room and prepare my bed.'

'Nia or Mia?' said Tryssa, starting to rise as Nia left the room. How typical that she should notice a slave rather than Lucretia's feelings.

'Come now,' said Max. 'Let's forget old bones and celebrate the safe return of our lovely daughter. Don't let things get dull for Tryssa and Lucretia. Musicians, better music please! Steward, bring the sweetmeats and more wine! Tryssa, what did you think of the show Contractes put on for me? How did it compare with the one he put on at Pecunia? Berry, did you like the dragophant? I commanded it especially for you!'

Tryssa subsided, staring at the door. Lucretia considered her ridiculously contrary. The woman had no idea how to enjoy herself.

Chapter 34: Tryssa

Tryssa woke well before dawn to the sound of rain pattering and couldn't get back to sleep. She thought of the glances between Amicus and Olivarius as Berenice brandished the knife from Vademlutra. Not for one moment did she imagine Olivarius had meant the girl to take it as a gift. Vademlutra ... wasn't that where Dun and Gris had gone?

It's nothing to do with me, she told herself as she lay awake. *I'm interfering just like Lucretia always accuses me of doing. But it was Lucretia's knife, I'm sure of it. And I haven't seen it for forty years. But that means nothing in particular. She could have kept it locked up. She could have left it in Durnovaria, lost it, who knows. 'Knife? What knife? Oh, my eating knife.' That's what Dun said. They must have found Lucretia's knife and sold it despite everything they'd said about trading. And Olivarius went to Vademlutra and then bought it? Perhaps there was nothing in the records after all. Amicus seemed content to make a toast to Galen and have done with it. And then there's Nia. Is she Morgan's daughter? She's the right sort of age, but in the lamplight it's hard to make out features properly. And she was agitated. Being assigned to Lucretia is enough to annoy anyone, but... No - it's something else. It started the moment she saw the knife.*

Tryssa sat bolt upright in bed.
***

'The master's not back, madam. Nor Olivarius.' If Amicus's steward was surprised to see her on the doorstep, dripping with rainwater, he didn't show it. He let her into the vestibule, his face flickering in the light of the small lamp he carried. 'The master was hardly at home all yesterday. He went to the temple, then the

225

Ordo meeting, came home for a bite of lunch and a bit of work in his office, then went to the baths and straight from there to dine at Maximilian Hygarix Agricola's house. Haven't seen Olivarius since first thing yesterday when he took some bread and cheese from the kitchen.'

'They both left Max's house hours ago.'

The steward shrugged. 'The master did say he might go out to a tavern or something afterwards. It's what gentlemen do, you know.' There was a little pity in his voice.

Tryssa was glad the steward couldn't see her face burning as the meaning of his words sunk in. Of course. That's what men do. But then on the other hand she knew Olivarius well. He wouldn't chase after tavern wenches, and she hadn't thought Amicus the sort either.

'A few drinks, a game of *tabula* perhaps,' suggested the steward, as if reading her mind and trying to let her down gently. 'He'll be back soon.'

'Of course. Thank you.'

The steward considered. 'You could wait in his study.' He pointed at a door. 'He told us he'd banked up the fire himself so it wouldn't go out, and not to go in and tidy his desk up, so we haven't. But I don't suppose he'd mind if you sat there. There's a lamp just inside the door on a side-table. I can light it for you.'

'Don't worry,' said Tryssa. 'You go back to bed. I'll light it from the embers of the fire.'

The steward took something off a hook on the wall. 'It might not be very warm in there, madam. At least take off that wet cloak and have this spare one instead.'

She could just make him out shaking his head as she entered the study. She wondered what Amicus would say when he walked through the door and found her there, and her face burned again. But she needed to talk everything over with him. Tryssa pushed open the door and found, as she'd expected, a dark room lit only by the dying glow from the fireplace. She could smell a strange, unpleasant mixture of odours but she could find nothing on the side-table.

She stepped forward, feeling her way towards the chair. Her foot slipped on some viscous liquid. She took another step and her feet crunched on pieces of pottery. In the glow of the fire, she could just make out the lamp, shattered on the floor beside some a large awkward shape near the hearth. Before she could stop herself, she screamed.

'Tryssa! What's the matter? Who's hurt you?'

She spun to see Amicus in the doorway with Olivarius. He rushed forward and pulled her into his arms, his heart thudding against hers, his words mingling with the ringing in her ears. She couldn't let go of him, the rain on his cloak was soaking into her gown, but she couldn't let him go.

'Who's hurt you?' he said. 'What's happened?

'No - no-one. … I thought you were dead!'

'Me? What?'

Tryssa pointed at the indistinct shape on the floor.

'It's the rug that covered the chest,' said Olivarius, bending forward. 'And there's oil everywhere. And the chest itself… I'm going for the steward.' He dashed from the room.

Tryssa went to disentangle herself from Amicus's arms. 'I-I'm sorry. I couldn't see properly - the oil felt like - I thought - I thought -'

But he held her closer than ever and kissed her head, she could not have been more sure he was alive.

***

With lamps lit, the fire blazing and the beginnings of dawn light trickling through the window, it was hard to imagine she'd mistaken oil for blood or an old blanket for a man but Tryssa found herself wanting to scrub

227

blood from her fingers. As if reading her thoughts, he took her hand in hers. 'Why did you come?'

'Nia the slave knows something about the knife. And Morgan - do you remember? The carpenter Olivarius and I met? He knows something about something. I just can't work out what. Nor can he, for that matter. It's possible he and Nia are related. That's only relevant to them, but maybe, if Nia is his daughter and he needn't worry about her anymore, whatever it is he knows will come to mind. But somehow, I wanted to talk it over with you. I know you might think it doesn't matter anymore. But I - I couldn't sleep. I'm sorry - I didn't know you were going to the tavern with Olivarius.' She withdrew her fingers.

'I'd have taken you instead of him if it was a place for a decent woman.'

Tryssa raised her head. 'Would you? Why?'

'The men there know me too well to talk about others on the Ordo. And they know Olivarius works for me. Now you - perhaps they'd have been telling you about their aches and pains and asking for love potions and before you know it telling you all the gossip too. Or maybe not. I couldn't risk taking you.'

'Sir...' said Olivarius rummaging through the upturned chest.

'What is it?'

'The wax tablet with my report on it is missing, sir.'

'What?' Amicus stood and started looking through drawers. 'But it was there.'

Olivarius nodded, lifting a metal box from the floor. 'I know. And the documents I made it from - they're missing too.' He held up a clay disc engraved with abbreviations. 'This is all that's left. And as you know, this filing marker was misleading in itself. It says something about drains, but it was attached to the town accounts.' He sniffed the air. 'Talking of which...' He turned to the fireplace and reached down. 'I think they've been burned. Look. I told you they were all barely legible from mildew alone. Let alone the amendments. Am I imagining the smell of burnt rotten papyrus?'

Amicus shook his head. 'No. Look, Tryssa, I'm worried. I'm not sure who to protect most at the moment.'

Tryssa swallowed and thought of her dream. 'Yourself, surely. If someone got in here and destroyed those scrolls without your staff knowing…'

Amicus slammed his fist on the desk. 'Olivarius, can you recall the main points in your report?'

'Yes, sir.'

'Then find another wax tablet and write it up again. Do it in the guards' office. Tell Petros you're there on my orders.' He turned to Tryssa. 'Let's go to Max's. I'll get word sent to Morgan to meet us there. If we speak to Nia now, no-one can complain we're taking her from her duties.'

But when they arrived at Max's house the slaves were in uproar. Nia was dead.

***

'Of course it's inconvenient to answer questions,' said Lucretia, huddled in a chair. 'One is barely awake.' She tipped her head to one side in an attempt to look bashful as she batted her eyes up at Amicus, 'And I'm in my underwear. I wouldn't want to inflame anyone.'

'The only thing likely to be inflamed is your cloak,' said Tryssa. 'You're sitting too close to the fire.'

Lucretia glared. 'Some of us like to maintain our allure and mystery. But I don't know how people expect a lady to manage. Could *your* maid...' She scanned Tryssa from loose hair to sturdy boots. 'Perhaps not.'

'Can't you help us about Nia?' snapped Tryssa.

229

Lucretia shrugged and the black wig which she'd hastily put on herself slipped a little. 'It's no concern of mine, other than wanting to look presentable and having no-one to assist. I imagine Eira is probably *more* annoyed since she'll have to replace her. But of course she's indisposed as usual, and now Berenice is tending to her and wailing simultaneously which is probably making her worse. How is a woman supposed to sleep with all this fuss?' She readjusted her wig and pulled the cloak more firmly round herself while allowing a tiny gap to reveal a minute amount of cleavage. Amicus averted his gaze to focus on the blood-stained mosaic.

'I imagine that'll annoy Eira too,' said Lucretia, covering herself fully. 'I daresay it's soaked into the tiles, although I don't know a great deal about scrubbing floors. What do *you* think, Tryssa?'

Tryssa ignored the question. 'When did you last see her?'

'Eira? Before I retired to bed.'

'Nia.'

'*After* I'd retired to bed. She was very tiresome - kept dropping things and fidgeting to get away and yawning. She was more incoherent than usual and then, thankfully she went quiet. It was almost a relief when she'd finished mauling me about, although I did have to call her back to bring an extra blanket.'

Max entered the room and stared at Amicus. 'I'm surprised to see you here,' he said. 'Haven't you something important to do? At least they've cleared the mess away.'

'A murder should be of interest to anyone,' said Amicus, crossing his arms. 'I'd have thought you'd be more concerned.'

'I'm concerned because it's upsetting Eira. A slave is neither here nor there.'

230

'Aren't you at least worried for your family and guest? Have you checked to see if anything's missing?'

'Nothing's missing, although that's something of a wonder,' said Max. 'And I'm not worried because I've been interrogating the other slaves. It's quite obvious what happened, and it's nothing to do with my family or my guest. I'm just furious it took place inside my house - I can't think what Nia thought she was doing letting him in.'

'Letting who in?' asked Tryssa.

Max ignored her. 'I'm considering having my steward flogged for not keeping a better eye on things. I suppose you can sort it out, since you know him.'

'Your steward?' said Amicus.

Max scowled. 'Not him. The man who's been hanging around the place taking the girl away from her duties. The younger of the two grave-robbers you've been interrogating. You should have kept them locked up, or better still had them crucified.'

Amicus raised his eyebrows. 'If I crucified everyone who turned up with dodgy merchandise the forum would be almost empty. There's never been any evidence those men are burglars. And certainly none to suggest they're murderers. But I'll have them both arrested and questioned.'

'What evidence is there that it was Gris?' asked Tryssa.

'It's appalling how lax things have become,' said Max. 'My wife's upset and my daughter is hysterical. Her knife is missing and Nia was only a slave-girl. Now it's clear that low-life killed her and once I've punished the fool who left the door unsecured -'

'Does no-one pity poor Nia?' Tryssa's voice rose sufficiently for Max to stop talking.

He stared at her. 'She got what she deserved. She had no business letting men-friends into my home.'

231

'Quite right,' said Lucretia, rising and putting her hand on Max's arm. 'And if she had to get murdered she might at least have done it in the slave quarters. Poor Max. How you are suffering.'

'If you don't mind,' said Tryssa. 'I'd like to speak to the slaves before any of them are flogged.'

'Be my guest,' said Max, patting Lucretia's hand.

Amicus hesitated. 'Max. Where were you -'

There was a sudden bellow from the kitchen. 'Not my daughter! Not my girl!'

Tryssa blanched, her eyes filling with tears. She put her hand on Amicus's arm. 'Go,' she said. 'Arrest Gris before anyone else gets to him. I'll join you shortly.'

Chapter 35: Diggers

Gris shuddered with cold and fear. He had been wrenched from his sleep with such force he wasn't sure if this was a nightmare and he was yet to wake up. The warmth of what had passed for a bed was a memory fading from his bare arms, straw still caught in his hair and beard. Shackles dragged on his wrists, scratching and marking his skin with what he hoped was rust rather than blood. The expression of the man before him no longer held any suggestion of humour or offer of reprieve.

'I - I didn't do it!' Gris forced the words out through chattering teeth and a cut lip where the guard had hit him as he struggled out of slumber.

'I haven't even accused you of anything yet.' Amicus's voice was as cold as the floor under their feet. But Amicus wore sturdy boots. *His* toes weren't going blue on the tiles.

'Whatever it is. I didn't do nothing.'

'I just don't understand why.'

'We told you what we done. We said sorry. We shoulda told you about the skellington. We -'

'This is not about that.'

Gris felt his stomach lurch, and ran his mind back over the last few days. 'We didn't think it would matter.'

Amicus glared. 'Some people don't care about slaves, but I'm not one of them. At the very least it's a form of theft.'

'Wh - wha? I don't unnerstand,' Gris tried to think. The chill was seeping through to his bones, and his brain hurt from the earlier blow. The shackles dragged on his wrists as he implored. 'They said they wasn't slaves, that we'd stay free. We thought we'd get outta

233

your hair for a bit, come back when things had settled down.'

Amicus took a step back and appraised him. Gris, his heart thudding, took a deep breath and concentrated on telling his bowel and bladder to behave.

'Where's the knife?' said Amicus.

There was no point in prevaricating. 'Sold it.'

'Who to?'

'Dun's mother, Wena. She only give us a *denarius*. Bet she sold it for more.'

'I see...' Amicus circled him. 'You sold it and you think she's already sold it on? How? Where?'

'Over to Vadumlutra. Dunno how. Usual sorta way, I guess. You'd have to ask Wena.'

Perhaps it was just a nightmare. Perhaps his mind was churned up with everything like his stomach was after what passed for stew at the tavern. Amicus's cold anger was mixed with something else. His face was unreadable, but Gris sensed a touch of uncertainty.

'Take him to the cellar,' Amicus ordered.

'What? No! I never done it! Whatever you think I done, I never. That knife was lost, that's what it was. I didn't even steal it. Not the irons, please!'

'Not *that* cellar. Not yet. The other one. Let's go.'

Gris stumbled down the stairs, his elbow gripped by the guard, Amicus's sturdy boots clump-clumping behind him. *Where's Dun? Have they arrested Dun too? Is he already in the cellar with that ready tongue cut out? Will they arrest Wena? I shouldn't have named her, she's done nothing wrong except bear Dun. If this isn't the torturer's cellar what is it? Do they keep dogs down here?* Bits of grit on the steps dug into his soles, the air grew colder, and the light of the torch was crowded in by gloom.

'You're not gonna leave me in the dark? Don't leave me in the dark!'

234

'You should be used to the dark with all that digging in barrows,' snarled the guard. 'Thought it'd be your second home. Think of all them graves you robbed... They're all waiting for you, them dead kings.'

'Let's enjoy it for a moment, shall we?' said Amicus. 'You might as well get used to Hades.'

'Please, no...'

At the bottom of the steps Gris stumbled, slamming his head against the wall. He could feel dampness on his cheek. A hundred ancient warriors whispered from the shadows and the oily smoke. *Where's my treasure? Where's my sword?* He recalled a grave filled with an entire household of people, their bones crumbling as he and Dun sifted for precious things, digging out bronze trinkets from the skulls of a long-dead team of horses.

'Open the door!' commanded Amicus.

'Please sir, no sir...'

Gris was shoved into a bitterly-cold room and sensed Amicus step in after him. He tried to gauge its size but his mind was too crowded to think. There was a smell - blood? His bladder fought for release.

'Bring the light.'

The guard came in, the torch flickering and spitting. For a moment Gris struggled to adjust his vision. The room was low-ceilinged and just large enough for an old table on which lay a pile of rags ... no, clothes ... no... Gris ran his eyes along it. There was a small slippered foot, a strand of hair. A sleeping woman. She had to be asleep, but who would sleep down here?

'Who - who's that?'

'Did she try to stop you?'

'What?'

'Did she try to stop you thieving? Or was it a different kind of treasure you were after?'

'I don't -'

'I thought I was a good judge of character,' whispered Amicus. 'I didn't have you down as a killer. Look what you've done.' He grabbed the torch from the guard, held it over the table, and pulled back the cover. The slave girl was icy white, hands clasped against her bloodstained chest.

'Nia!' Gris lurched forward, his hands straining inside the shackles as he touched her barely-cold face. 'Who done this, Nia?' He spun round and shook his wrists at Amicus. 'Unlock them! Nia was my girl. Everything I done, I done for her. I'm gonna find the man who done this and tear him limb from limb, and *then* you'll see what a murderer looks like.'

Chapter 36: Tryssa

'I told Nia it'd end in tears,' said the cook, his arms folded as he watched a sniffing boy stir some sort of porridge with one hand while flipping honey cakes with the other. 'But she wouldn't listen. "He's going to buy my freedom," she said. "He's a bit rough round the edges but I'll make an honest man of him," she said. I told her it don't work like that. Once a waste of space, always a waste of space. But would she listen? "Everyone deserves a second chance," she said. I dunno how she thought he'd ever have enough money to buy her. He couldn't even make enough to get proper lodgings.' He reached over to cuff the boy at the stove without actually making contact, as if on principle. The boy ducked anyway. His face, just visible as he flinched, was wet with tears.

'We loved her, we did,' said the cook. 'I mean, she could talk the legs off a nest of spiders, but her heart was in the right place. She was like my own daughter.' He addressed Morgan who sat with his head down, stiff in Riona's embrace. 'I want you to know that. She's only been here a coupla years but I thought a lot of her. So help me, if they don't crucify that murdering scum, I'll do it myself.'

'Stupid Roman names,' muttered Morgan. 'People said she'd gone to Durocornovium. They must have meant Durnovaria. Or maybe I misheard. Two years wasted. And now it's too late.'

The boy gave a shuddering sob. The cook half-cuffed him again, but said, 'We'll get revenge lad, don't you worry. We'll make an offering to Nemesis.'

'Could you could see it coming?' said Tryssa. 'Criminals are often violent…'

Riona lifted her head from Morgan's shoulder, her eyes raw. 'Not Gris,' she snorted. 'He was so wet.

Dripping round her all the time. Bringing her things. Bits of rubbish he couldn't sell. Promising big. They was going to have a farm with chickens. He'd have been useless and it'd have been her doing everything - wringing their necks, plucking and drawing them. He couldn't step on a beetle without shouting about it. Why'd he have to kill her, eh?'

'I suppose Nia became tired of the promises, and if the gifts were things he couldn't sell, that could be a little offensive,' Tryssa suggested.

Riona rubbed her face. 'Nia was that soppy herself she *liked* all the tat he give her. Stay here, let me show you. They're not yelling yet, so we've got a moment...' She went out of the kitchen into the yard where the slaves' quarters were.

'Gris made her hide stuff and give him food,' sobbed the boy. 'I saw him. And all *she* got was kisses.'

The cook grunted. 'I knew she slipped him a bit of bread now and then. As long as that was all she was slipping him, I didn't mind. It's not like we haven't got enough food. But if I'd known what sort he really was, I'd never have let him see her yesterday.'

The boy dropped the spoon to put his face in his hands and the stench of burning filled the kitchen. Tryssa went over, rescued the honey cakes, and put her arm round the lad. 'You can't always tell...'

'No. Who could've realised?' said the cook. 'It was Nia what was agitated, not him. Cos of getting sold to *her*. But that must have been it. I suppose if Gris couldn't have her, he didn't want anyone else to. Although why not just follow her up there? I guess you've got graves to rob over your way too, haven't you?'

Tryssa stirred the porridge, pitying the person - presumably the lad - who had to clean the pot afterwards, since most of it was glued up.

Riona returned with a small box and with a little fiddling, opened it. Inside was a shabby leather money pouch with a few coins inside, a tiny carved wren and two corroded rings. 'Here you go,' she said. 'I suppose this belongs to you now.' She passed the box to Morgan who took it in silence, picking out the wooden bird and holding it tight.

Ondi burst in with Max's steward. 'I'm sorry, but the gentry say they're starving.'

'So what's new?' sneered the cook. 'The Master always builds up an appetite when he's out all night and the old bat eats like a horse no matter what's happening.'

Riona groaned. 'I wish they'd let us grieve,' she said. 'Can't they get their own breakfast for once? It's like Nia was an ant - here yesterday and gone today. Although she couldn't do anything right last night, could she? Dropping things, breaking things, worrying. Mistress Eira was more upset when the household cat died than she is about Nia. She said she wished everyone would stop making a fuss and clear things up. And I don't know how we're going to manage that old harridan - sorry … madam.' Riona's brief moment of fury subsided into worry as another thought crossed her face. 'She musta shook Nia something cruel - I saw the bruises on her wrists. What if they sell *me* to Mistress Lucretia instead? They won't, will they?' she implored the steward. 'I think I'd run away to the circus if they suggested that.'

'Was Nia thinking of running away to the circus?' asked Tryssa.

'I'm not sure.' Riona poked about in Nia's box. 'But that boyfriend of hers was. He came to tell her it was just to get to Isca, then make a fortune and come back. That's when he found out she was getting sold to the old - to Mistress Lucretia.'

239

'And that made him angry?'

'No,' said Riona. 'Just upset. He cried.'

'How do you know?' demanded the cook. He moved the pot of porridge off the heat and waved at the boy to dole it out.

'I was in the quarters. I wondered what he was going to give her this time.'

'Another present?' said Tryssa.

Riona shrugged. 'She used to hide things too - things he was gonna sell. A knife last time, I think. You know, when he was in all that trouble. But he was just there to tell her what he was thinking, and she was worried because she'd got rid of something he'd given her.'

'The knife?'

'No, not that,' said Riona. 'Although … it was funny. She asked me if she should talk to the mistress about a knife. Don't know which mistress. I can't think why - I mean, she'd get into trouble, wouldn't she? But I wouldn't listen cos we'd -' She started to sob again. 'We'd fallen out over a ribbon and I wasn't talking to her. And then she had to put up with old Lucretia - I mean Mistress Lucretia always shouting at her, and I laughed cos Mistress Eira just sighs and has headaches, and now I'll never get to argue with her again and it's not fair.'

Morgan gave a shuddering sob.

'No, it's not fair,' said Tryssa. She could hear Lucretia screeching. Ondi and the steward, in the absence of anyone else, started to take breakfast dishes through to the dining room.

'No,' said Riona. 'She was telling him about something else.' She rummaged in the box a bit more. 'It must have been the bangle, I can't see it in here. It was a funny-looking thing, I don't blame her for getting rid. But once she'd given whatever it was away, she

240

said she thought it was cursed, or she was cursed, or Blue was cursed. I didn't listen properly, cos like I said...' She sniffed and rubbed her eyes again.

'Blue? The beggar?'

'Yes'm. But she rattled on so I couldn't make head nor tail and now...'

'But you're all convinced Gris killed her?' said Tryssa.

The three slaves moved closer together and Morgan, raising his head, somehow seemed to side with them. Without looking at each other, four human beings whose existence mattered less than the dishes they filled, the wood they carved, the furniture they polished, the clothes they hung up, aligned against a woman who had the right to be heard and the right to have a slave's life ended without trial.

'Who else, Mistress?' said the cook after a pause. 'Gris was a grave-robber, he could get in anywhere he liked. Maybe he wanted Nia to show him where the master's money was. Or maybe he wanted her to run away with him, and she said no. Like I said, once a wrong'un, always a wrong'un. And if it's not him, who is it? Cos if it's someone else, none of us is safe.'

Morgan heaved himself to his feet, his face cold with fury. 'I want to see my girl and I want to see the man they say killed her. I'll know. I'll know as soon as I see him.'

Chapter 37: Amicus

Amicus ushered Tryssa and Morgan into the room where Nia's body lay.

'I want to see the murderer,' growled Morgan. 'Tell me you haven't let him go.'

'I thought you'd like to see your daughter first.'

Torchlight flickered over Nia's face, making it appear that at any moment she would open her eyes. Morgan went over to her, leaned his crutch against the table and leaned to stroke damp hair from her mouth. Then he stepped back and hefted his crutch again. He turned to Tryssa and Sila. 'You'll do right by her, won't you? Even though she's naught but a slave.'

'Of course we will,' said Sila, her voice choked.

'Don't fret, lass,' said Morgan. 'Just take care of her, so I can say goodbye properly when she's as beautiful as she should be.' He ran his hand round Nia's face and lifted her hand, frowning. Then he turned to follow Amicus.

***

Climbing the stairs with Morgan, Amicus murmured, 'I know you'll want to make your own judgment, but I think Gris is innocent.'

'Why?'

Amicus told him about the questioning up to the point when Gris fell sobbing over the body, holding Nia in his arms. 'We had to drag him away in the end,' he said.

'That doesn't make him innocent,' muttered Morgan. 'Just regretful.'

'Perhaps,' admitted Amicus. 'Mithras knows why, but I promised Gris I'd ensure she'd be taken off for burial. Was she Christian?'

Morgan's face was closed. 'So you think Gris is innocent because he's upset and wants her buried the way she'd have wanted?'

'I think he's innocent because things don't add up. And he's not the sort. Come and see for yourself.'

He opened the cell door and stepped inside. Gris was curled in a ball in the straw but sprang to his feet when the two men entered. He looked from Amicus to Morgan and then leapt forward. 'Is this the man what did it?'

The guard pushed him back.

'No,' said Amicus. 'This is her father.' He lifted the torch so that both men could see each other clearly. There was a long pause.

Gris swallowed. 'I never killed her,' he said. 'I ain't even gonna swear to it. It's just the truth. You can believe me or not. But I never. I wouldn't have hurt her for anything. I'd give my own life to bring hers back, but I ain't gonna till I've seen the man who done it get his just desserts.'

Morgan's jaw clenched, and then he gave a deep sigh. He put his hand on Gris's shoulder. 'You and me both, son. You and me both.'

***

Tryssa was sober when she returned to Amicus's office. 'Nia's in a side-room now.' Her eyes were sparkling with tears. 'Come and see her. She's as beautiful as she can be.'

Morgan peered out of the small window as they left the room. 'Who'd have known I'd have left this place happy and come back sad.'

Amicus frowned. 'I thought you were from Sorviodunum.'

'My master moved us there when I was five or so. Before that we were from somewhere else.'

'Here?' said Tryssa.

243

'The longer I've been here, the longer everything has felt familiar. The landscape, the hill-fort, the way the sky is. I think we might have lived in that direction.' Morgan pointed west. 'But when we left we must have gone north past Durnovaria.'

'How can you be so sure?'

'The town was different, I suppose, but I remember the sense of it looking down and I remember the grove. When I met Blue a week ago it was pitch dark and raining, but I could feel its mood. It wasn't till days later I went to look again and knew it.'

'There are other groves that look very similar.'

'True. But I knew it even after forty years. And after I talked to you yesterday…'

Tryssa touched Amicus's arm and mouthed '*Forty years.*'

'That's quite a memory,' said Amicus.

Morgan paused to shift his weight on the crutch. 'It's more like a dream. One I'd forgotten but is returning vivid.'

Amicus opened the door to the freezing side-room. Sila sat huddled in a cloak on a bench beside a low trestle, where Nia lay under a blanket.

Morgan sat beside Sila and reached for his daughter, but after a second dropped his hand.

'I know it might not seem important, but can you tell us about your dream?' asked Tryssa.

'It's nothing,' Morgan muttered. 'Nia's the only thing that mattered, and now it's too late.'

'It might be something,' Tryssa urged. 'I can't explain why I think so, but I do. Please - can you tell us?'

With a sigh, Morgan appeared to peer inward. 'In my dream I'm a child. It's very early in the morning, summertime and quite bright. The birds are making a racket. I'm tired of sitting in the wagon. No-one's looking, so I climb out and run into the grove. The wagon's not moving fast, I can catch up when I need to.'

'Why the grove? Isn't it a bit gloomy?' Amicus thought of how the grove they knew had appeared two days earlier - the uneven stones, the waiting trees, the leaves floating down, dead gold against the grey.

'There are flowers,' said Morgan, his eyes closed. 'I could pick some for my master and make him smile.' He chuckled a little. 'But it's warm in the grass. I'm small. I fall asleep. It seems like a happy place.'

'A happy place?' Amicus frowned.

'And then all of a sudden it isn't.' Morgan swallowed. 'There's a man and a woman embracing and falling to the ground. The woman's crying.'

'Shouting for help?' Amicus held his breath.

Morgan's voice choked. 'More like grief. And then she throws something. And a voice very close to me says, "Go. Forget you ever saw anything. Don't look back". So I crawl through the long grass and run along the hedge until I catch up with the wagon and get my ears boxed and then...'

'You forgot.'

'And then I forgot. Except the sadness. I felt it again that night I sheltered there.' He opened his eyes.

Tryssa bit her lip. 'You said you heard a voice. Are you sure you didn't *see* anyone?'

Morgan laid his crutch on the floor and screwed up his face in concentration. 'In my dreams there are blue eyes,' he said at last. 'The bluest I've ever seen.'

Tryssa started. 'Didn't they say that about Blue the beggar? Wasn't that how he got his name?'

Morgan frowned. 'So they did. But I never saw him in good light, and his face, you know - there was a scar, and one eye was half closed. And if it's not a dream then forty years is too long ago - I can't even recall what my old mistress looked like.' He glowered. 'None of it has anything to do with what happened to Nia.'

'It might,' said Amicus. 'I think you should stay here. Tryssa Doethion, you too. I -'

'We need to go back to Max's house.'

'*I* do.'

'*We* do. I can distract Lucretia if necessary. Sila will stay here with Nia and Morgan.'

'Are you always this argumentative?'

'Yes.'

The door opened and Petros entered. 'Sir, can you come? Half the Ordo are here. Well, three of them - Rufus Caelo, Deryn Durones, and Gwyn Silvestris. Favorix the priest has committed suicide.'

'How?'

'Stabbed himself. His mother found him but didn't raise the alarm for some time. She was just shouting at him to stop sleeping, and the slaves left her to it. There's a knife, but Favorix's old mum says she found it lying about and dropped it in the fire when she looked at it because it was slippery. I have to say, she's really not the full amphora.'

'What kind of knife? Bronze? Deeply patterned?'

Petros shook his head. 'Just a normal table knife. If that was what he used, it must have taken some effort. There's some sort of note on a wax tablet but he dropped it near the fire and it's pretty illegible. It's all a bit odd.'

'Is it now?' Amicus looked at Tryssa. 'Get someone to feed the Ordo and tell them I'll be with them in an hour.'

***

'The master and mistress are out,' said the steward.

'No matter,' said Amicus, 'I'm here with the guard. I can send someone to fetch your master but in the meantime, we need to come in.'

246

'I don't -'

'It's for Nia,' said Tryssa.

'But…' The steward paled and swallowed.

'Are you going to argue with me?' demanded Amicus.

'N - no.' He ushered them in. 'But will you speak for me if I get into trouble? They won't be happy. The Master's … doing business, and the Mistress - I mean all of the mistresses have gone to the temple to ask for - well I don't know, really. For the priest to come and cleanse the house, I suppose.' He pulled a face. 'Riona is taking a *denarius* - we all chipped in - to make a prayer to Nemesis. That's the right one, isn't it?'

'Revenge?'

'Yes.' The steward stood awkward in the hallway, the other slaves peeking out from doors. 'What do you want to do?'

'Search,' said Amicus. 'I won't let my men make a mess.'

They found the jewelled bronze knife in Lucretia's room, wedged blade-tip first into a joint under a tabletop. The engravings were stained dark, and dried brown dulled the bright stones. In her cosmetic box was a small glass vial and a box of dark, sweet-scented powder.

Tryssa sniffed very carefully and recoiled. Amicus watched her. She stood, looking somehow smaller than usual, hugging herself, not quite meeting his eyes.

He came closer. 'It's not a capital offence,' he said, as low as he could. 'Killing a slave is effectively theft. She can compensate Eira and all will be square.'

'I know,' said Tryssa, 'but…'

'She's your … well, maybe not friend. But you've known her all your life.'

'It's not that.' She said nothing more, biting her lip. 'Nia's injury wasn't deep enough to kill. It looked much worse than it was.'

Amicus turned the knife over in his hand. 'And they say Favorix stabbed himself. A man who was perhaps pursuing Lucretia again, and whom she perhaps rejected.'

'Was he the sort to take that course of action over rejection? At his age?'

'What has age to do with anything if the feelings are there?' said Amicus, avoiding her eyes. 'If anything it makes you feel more desperate.'

'That's true, but do you think he did?'

Amicus wrapped the knife in a strip of linen. 'Not really. I think someone killed him and I think that tablet is - was - Olivarius's report.'

Tryssa shook her head. 'Lucretia would never go out in the rain to kill someone. It would mess up her hair.'

'I'm being serious.'

'So am I. She could have lashed out at Nia, although to be honest if she was going to kill a slave just for annoying her, she'd have done it long ago. I'm not saying she couldn't murder if she was driven to it - but only in the heat of the moment, when everything is stripped away and all the pompousness and self-absorption is replaced by real emotion.'

'And you say you've seen her like that?'

'Only twice.'

'Then who's to say the third time didn't happen earlier that day? She's been seen visiting Favorix's house more than once.'

'And she somehow killed Nia, then him, with a knife that no-one has seen for forty years, which Dun and Gris dug up and sold in a town half a day's ride away, and then appeared with Berenice in Max's house *after* Favorix didn't turn up to dinner?'

248

'Then Favorix committed suicide and his mother really did throw the knife away.'

'I don't think so. Nor do you.'

Amicus nodded at the cosmetic box. 'No, I don't. What about the vial and powder? She could have brought those herbs from home.'

'I'm certain the vial holds belladonna. If you drop some in your eyes it can make them brighter. If you ingest it, it can induce delirium or more likely death.' Tryssa bit her lip. 'There's something not right about Nia. The stab wound really isn't deep enough to kill.'

'Poison?'

'If she was poisoned with that there would probably be evidence of other symptoms. Getting the dosage right to make it look accidental would be beyond Lucretia. She couldn't even season soup. She relies on other people to do that sort of thing. And then - why stab the girl?'

Amicus considered. 'If Nia stole from Lucretia's box and was trying to put drops in her eyes, could she have swallowed some accidentally? And would Lucretia stab her for theft? And if she killed Favorix, she must have slipped out of the house between dinner and going to bed and brought the knife back with her. She's been seen sneaking back and forth to his house, admittedly not in the dark. But then - '

Tryssa swallowed. 'Putting Nia and Favorix aside - forgetting the present - what if this was the knife that killed Galen forty years ago?' She said it so matter-of-factly, her eyes fixed on the smeared object in his hand.

He wished he knew the right words. Practical ones seemed inadequate. These two women had known each other from girlhood. And Tryssa was giving Lucretia away. 'Is it something she could have done?'

249

'I don't know,' said Tryssa. 'I really don't. But tell me -' She raised her head at last and met his eyes. 'If you think she did, will you arrest her?'

'I can't without a confession. The evidence is too weak,' said Amicus. 'But I'll arrest her for Favorix's death. If only to keep her under guard.'

'There's been too much blood.'

Amicus nodded. 'Too much blood by a long way. I have nowhere suitable to keep a lady before trial. I'd have to put her under house arrest.'

'Not here,' said Tryssa. 'Put her with me at Galyna's house.'

He caught his breath. 'That's not wise,' he said. 'If she's a murderess then you're not safe. I said I wanted you to stay with me.'

Tryssa gave him a small smile. 'I can take care of myself,' she said. 'I always have. I always will. But Lucretia deserves a fair trial and if you leave her here, she won't live to stand one.'

'Come back with me now. We'll send Petros to Galyna's house. I'd like you to sit with Morgan while Ondi finds Lucretia. I need to speak to the Ordo before they start to interfere.'

***

'Why have you kept us waiting?' demanded Rufus. 'This is no time to be wandering round town. You should be here deciding what to do about Favorix.'

'I don't see what you expect me to do,' said Amicus, sitting back in his chair. 'It's for the gods to choose a priest, isn't it? At least he didn't pollute the temple by killing himself there.'

'*She* drove him to it,' snapped Deryn. 'She teased him with her affections and -'

'Did she?' said Amicus. 'Who says so? I never saw any evidence of it.'

'His mother says she was constantly there, locked up with Favorix.'

'Constantly? Lucretia's only been in Durnovaria for a few days. And is this the same mother who is so addled she didn't realise he was dead? Where's the wax tablet with his note?'

'Here.' Gwyn handed it over. 'Much good it'll do you.'

The words had been smeared and flattened with the blunt end of a stylus, and the warmth of the fire had done the rest. Amicus could make out the odd word, but he recognised Olivarius's confident script. There was hardly enough left to make any sense of it. *I think, too many, distraction, misdirection, tracks, dishonour.*

'Odd words to use in a suicide note,' said Amicus. 'And surely this is far too long. By the time I'd written all that, I'd have reconsidered my actions.'

Deryn frowned. 'Where have you been?'

'Your sister's place. Her slave was found murdered today.'

'What has that to do with anything important?' snapped Rufus. 'The priests are saying Favorix killed himself due to bad omens. They believe Favorix read something in the signs that was too terrible to bear, and they say his message on the wax tablet would have told us what if his fool of a mother hadn't put it near the fire. We need another augur - or word to be sent to other temples. I hope you're not hoping for re-election next year, Amicus. I'm summoning the rest of the Ordo, as you seem disinclined to do so. We'll see you in the assembly room.'

Amicus ignored Rufus as he and Gwyn left. Deryn remained seated, staring at the tablet, his face pale.

'Did the priests send you here too, Deryn? I thought you didn't believe in gods.'

'Max met us near the temple and told us to come here.'

'Max did?'

Deryn's eyes lifted to Amicus's. 'He said you needed to stop wasting time and look into something critical.'

Amicus leant forward. 'I thought better of you and Max,' he said. 'I never thought you'd think the death of an innocent girl - no matter what her status - meant less than a man doing away with himself. Unless, of course, what you're saying is that he didn't. And if he didn't, then who exactly are you accusing?'

Deryn's chair toppled as he stood. His hands shook and his eyes remained fixed on the wax tablet. 'No-one. It's a mistake. I'll stop Rufus summoning the Ordo. Go back to the slave-girl.'

Chapter 38: Diggers

Dun was captured heading for Max's house to see if Gris was there. The rain was coming down in sheets and his worn shoes were sodden. He passed a neighbouring house where a short, stout matron with a furious face was being ushered through the door by a slave. With a shock he realised the slave was gripping the woman's arm and that Petros was behind the door, waiting to drag her inside. Things were getting bad when even the gentry were being bullied by the guard. Dun ducked into the shadows to watch.

'Unhand me, Ondi, you oaf!' the woman growled, trying to twist her arm out of her captor's grip. 'Do you think I'll make a fuss in the street like a hoyden? More than one slave could die today, you know.'

'Mistress Lucretia,' said Ondi. 'I'm not sure you understand. Amicus Sonticus said that if you wouldn't stay here under guard, he'd arrest you to be questioned in his place. No one will think it a social call then.'

The woman glared. 'Petros, arrest Ondi! I was dragged from the temple -'

'It wasn't like that,' said Ondi.

'That fool Tryssa has somehow influenced Amicus to make a ridiculous accusation. I should never have brought her. Anguis put me into Olivarius's care, and I don't know where he's been. Go and talk some sense into Amicus, and then get Olivarius to write a letter to Anguis and anyone of importance you can think of. And get Max. He will listen to -'

'Inside please, madam,' said Petros, his face grim, then shut the door.

Dun was unaware of a presence behind him until it was too late. He spun, hoping it was Gris, but it was one of the guard. 'Not you again.'

'I could say the same,' said the guard. 'Now, you coming quiet?'

'What am I supposed to have done this time?'

'Not for me to say, but I expect someone's getting the pincers nice and hot.'

***

Dun stood before Amicus, hands bound with leather thongs. His expression was cocky, but his shuffling feet belied his confident stance.

Amicus put the bronze knife on the table. It was very much less shiny than it had been when Dun had last seen it.

'If one more person tells me they're innocent today, I may have to have them executed out of sheer annoyance,' said Amicus. 'Tell me everything you know about this, and then tell me what you and Gris did from the moment you left the baths yesterday till now.'

'How d'you know we was at the baths?'

'You're clean.'

'What you done with Gris?'

'Never you mind. Just answer the question.'

At the back of the room, a burly guard as wide as he was tall cracked his knuckles. 'My fists are out of practice, sir,' he murmured. 'Want me to exercise them?'

Dun glanced at him and swallowed.

'Oh, and before I forget,' added Amicus, 'I take it back about you not having a mother, because she's being spoken to. So don't make anything up.'

'You leave her alone.'

Amicus settled back in his chair and gave a slow smile.

Dun puffed out his cheeks and then heaved a sigh. 'All right. So Gris finds a knife. We wants to sell it at

254

Vadumlutra but nothing doing, so my old mum buys it. End of story.'

'You want me to tell her you called her old?'

Dun went grey. 'You wouldn't. You might as well kill me horribly now and save her the bother.'

'Then tell me all the bits in between. Where did you find it? When? How long before you took it to Vadumlutra?'

'By the skellington.'

'It was with the skeleton?'

'By not with, I said. Down some sorta rabbit hole under the edge of the stones. By the two what's wonky.'

Amicus frowned. 'When?'

'A day or so after we found the skellington.'

'Why didn't you sell the knife to Masner?'

Dun shrugged. 'Thought we'd keep the profit for once. Gris wants to make more money.'

'Don't we all?'

'He's got something special he wants to do.'

'Which is...?'

'Buy his girl's freedom. She's a nice thing. Too good for him, but love's blind, ain't it. Not that he'll be able to buy her if you keep locking him up.'

Amicus exchanged glances with Olivarius, then looked back at Dun. 'Do you know why we've locked him up?'

'Same as usual,' said Dun. 'You're just picking on us.'

'So you found the knife and decided to sell it yourself. Straightaway? Remember your mum before you answer.'

'Yeah ... no ... yeah... Oh go on then, no. We stowed it.'

'Where?'

Dun fidgeted. 'Somewhere safe.'

'Where?'

255

'Here,' Dun sniffed. 'You know, doncher? I can tell.'

'So tell me.'

'I don't want to get anyone in trouble.'

'Honour among thieves, eh?'

'We're not thieves. And she's not one either.'

'She won't get into trouble, I promise.'

'Yeah?'

'Definitely.'

Dun sighed. 'Gris's girl hid it for us. Nia, she's called. Slave at Hagorix's house. Promise you won't get her in trouble, she's a nice kid.'

Amicus ran his hand over his face.

'Second part of the question, then. What did you do after you left the baths?'

'We went to see Nia. Told her we was thinking of joining the circus, getting out of town for a bit, then coming back when Gris'd saved enough. She's in a bit of a state cos some old battle-axe wants to take her north. Not sure we can do much. And she's a bit upset about Blue. Thinks she cursed him with that bangle.'

'What bangle?'

'One Gris give her. She give it to Blue. Blue musta followed her home one day and died in the alley behind the house. She thinks it's her fault cos the bangle had some weird symbols on.'

'And then?'

'And then we went and discussed about the circus and what to do about rescuing Nia, and borrowed some cash off of Masner against future hauls and got plastered at the tavern. Next thing I know, it's dawn. I've got a bit of a head and I'm out in the yard relieving myself and I hears boots on the cobbles. I can tell those boots a mile off.' He nodded sideways at the guard. 'I heard him go in the sleeping quarters and ducked in the shadows when they were dragging Gris out. I didn't know what we was supposed to have done this time but

256

I legged it. Ask the tavern-keeper, ask Masner, ask the butcher's lad, ask Nia. We dint do nothing except cadge stuff and drink the profits. We're innocent.'

The door behind him opened and the wise-woman Tryssa came in.

'It's what I suspected,' she said to Amicus. 'Come and see Nia. She's not dead.'

Chapter 39: Tryssa

A guard entered the room before Amicus could respond. 'I checked, sir, but neither of them have returned to the house. Just the daughter.'

'What about Deryn?'

'Last seen heading for one of the gambling houses. But if he's looking for Maximilian Hygarix Agricola, he's wasting his time. We've been through them all.'

'And has anyone looked at Favorix's body?'

'Not an expert, sir, but if I were going to stab myself, I wouldn't do it the way he did. His steward reckons there's money missing. His mother is screeching about wild women in hobnailed boots. It's not making things any easier.'

'Take someone and look for Maximillian Hygarix Agricola and his wife. They can't have gone far. If you find them, bring them back and put them under house arrest. I need to ask some questions here before I join you.' He waited till the guard had withdrawn, then went to Tryssa's side. 'Take me to her. What do you mean, she's not dead?'

'I thought she felt wrong. Rigor mortis should have started, but it hadn't. She was simply so cold and her heart so slow, she was fathoms deep and her breathing was imperceptible. She was left to die in a freezing room, then brought here and put in a freezing cellar. Washed and put under a blanket, she started to warm up.'

***

A brazier was now heating the room. Morgan sat cradling his daughter, the blanket wrapped round them both.

Amicus said, 'Nia, I'm sorry to ask but can you say what happened?'

'She's still very drowsy and barely making any sense,' said Tryssa.

'I was really upset,' whispered Nia. 'The old bat was really horrible. I just wanted to explain that Lady Berenice's knife must be cursed cos it came from the same place as the cursed bangle. It was my fault Blue followed us home. The bangle I give him must have wanted to be with the knife. I shouldn't have hid that knife. Should've told Gris to chuck it in the midden. And he wasn't sick before but then he died horrible. So I had to tell someone - get my conscience clear. But *she* wouldn't let me talk. There was a flask of wine in her room - like *she* deserved it. I thought of tipping it away but that'd have got someone else in trouble. So I drunk some of it and topped it up with water while she was still in the dining room. It was strong wine. I started seeing things and I couldn't really talk after that. Not properly. I thought if she was drunk, she'd be worse than normal, so I tipped the rest of that wine away and put some of the weak stuff in. Didn't do any good. The old bat was even horribler when I was helping her to bed.'

'That explains that,' whispered Tryssa. 'Lucretia would have drunk the lot.'

'I still felt sick when the house was quiet,' said Nia. 'But I needed to explain and I found the mistress wandering like she does sometimes. Then *she* done it. I tried to tell her sorry, but she wouldn't listen.'

'Which mistress?'

Nia started to cry. 'She's never lifted a finger to me before and I was confused. Said there was no room for beggars in the town. But then I said "you sent me with food and everything and it still didn't stop him from dying." It's all my fault. I offered to tell the guard and take my punishment, and then she done it. After that I heard someone say they'd put me on the midden, and I couldn't talk or move or do nothing about it and then everything went black.'

'There, there, lass,' said Morgan, tears streaming down his face. 'Hush now. Don't talk any more.'

Tryssa shook her head at Amicus and drew him out of the room. 'It's no good pushing now. And it's wasting time. We need to go and question them.'

'And I thought this was all to do with Galen.'

'It is,' said Tryssa. 'All of it.'

'Because those fools dug up the ring?'

'It's not really the ring or the knife or even the skeleton,' said Tryssa. 'It's the people coming together at the same time, raising shades that had been buried.'

'People? Lucretia, Morgan … and Blue. Of course.'

'Yes.'

'We need to move quickly. As long as they think Nia is dead and know nothing about Morgan, we've time.'

'I hope so.'

They rushed down to the stable yard, pulling cloaks over their heads. The rain was falling harder than ever, splashing on the cobbles, pooling in small hollows.

'Are you sure you want to come with me?' asked Amicus.

'Try stopping me.'

Amicus helped her onto the saddle and sat behind. His body warmed hers. 'When this is all over, will you come and eat with me at a tavern? Even if it makes people talk?'

'I'm all for being interesting,' said Tryssa.

His arms enclosed her a little closer. 'Why is Max so insistent I look into Favorix's suicide? It doesn't make sense.'

Tryssa leant back against him and dropped her voice. 'I think it's because if you're busy proving Lucretia killed a citizen, then no-one will notice that a slave-girl has been killed. What do *you* think?'

'I think I'll promise right now never to try to fool you,' he whispered, as the horse made its way through the streets.

'Did Olivarius remember everything in his report?'

'Pretty much. Names and dates altered, sums transposed. A clever man did it. A desperate man. It had been going on for months. But there's never enough for a gambler. Never enough.'

'Names altered.'

'Yes. On papyrus and in minds. Favorix's father was a fool. And so, it seems, was everyone else. Just believed what they wanted to. Misdirection all the way.'

Ondi opened Galyna's door, surprised. 'Lady Lucretia's not here, sir,' he said. 'The gentleman took her while Petros was talking to the guard out back. Said you'd asked him to.'

'Which gentleman?' said Amicus.

Chapter 40: Lucretia

Forty years earlier

Lucretia slips down the paved street, willing the horse's hooves to somehow muffle themselves on the cobbles.

'Steady on, love,' says a trader, heading towards the forum. 'He's long gone.'

'Who?'

'How many you got?' The trader sniggers and pretends to quail under Lucretia's glare.

'You want to watch yourself, lass,' says his companion. 'I don't know what your guardian's thinking of, letting you wander about unescorted.'

'What's it to do with either of you?' Lucretia straightens her back and leads the horse outside the ramparts. The road slopes down and then splits. Away to the south, away to the west, away towards the north, towards Pecunia - that stupid, dull little place no-one has ever heard of, with its dark roundhouses and village elders and wise-women, its secret druids and not-so secret grumbling, and everything you ever do gossiped over. The ancient decurion says he's a Roman, foisted on them, rotting out his last days in the back of beyond. He's her father's man somehow. It occurs to Lucretia, as she glances backwards into the ordered streets of Durnovaria, that Pecunia's decurion must have done something terrible to be marooned in such a hen coop. She must find out what it is and then see what she can do with the knowledge.

She mounts the horse and rides down the slope to head south a little way before climbing the ramparts' slope again and dismounting to sit, cradling her knees.

It will be a lovely day, the sun is already warm, the air fragrant with summer and there isn't a speck of dew on the grass. Below, a wagon is trundling along, heading north probably, piled high. It looks as if someone is moving their entire household. A child sits on the back of the wagon and kicks its legs.

She waits, sitting then standing then walking about, clenching and unclenching her hands. The horse senses her agitation and nuzzles into her shoulder to calm her, then flicks out his head over the world around them.

'I know,' says Lucretia. 'It's good land. It's good land.' Nothing at home can compare with these lush, fertile fields. At home there's the encroaching forest, clagging mud, bramble and stinking marsh. Every crop is a triumph and everyone has to help. So far there aren't enough slaves and servants to keep her from occasionally having to get her hands dirty with storing and drying and bottling in jars. That Tryssa sneers at her efforts to keep her hands soft. If she stays and marries Deryn they could put their brains to good use, and in no time this rich land would enable them to live like monarchs.

She glances at the southern sky to gauge the time, and thinks of that day when Max took leave from learning a quaestor's role with Favorix's father. They went riding to the sea. He's so good-looking that being seen with him is always gratifying, but it's hard to work out if the tangles in her hair and her exhausted horse

263

had been worth it. Max is effusive, but she has the impression it's just talk - the compliments spilling out like water over the edge of a fountain bowl feel too rehearsed to mean much. His gifts are as pretty as he is with the same doubtful veneer. He's flush with money one moment, borrowing from her the next. Besides, he's far too fond of staring in any reflective surface, and far too soft towards sulky Eira. Theirs'll be a miserable marriage. At least Deryn has a temper. Eira expresses nothing. She's well-named for snow. If Max has as much passion as he appears to have, it'll soon be quenched.

Lucretia doesn't want him. All those words. And far too interested in spending money rather than making it. For all the winks and whispers and attempted kisses, she feels his heart is no more interested in hers than hers is in his. She suspects all he wants to do is to make Eira jealous and set fire to the spark within her. Ridiculous boy. There's no spark in ice.

'Hello, my love.' Favorix makes her jump. Why must he always creep up from behind like that? His hands are on her waist and she elbows them away, twisting out of his grasp. She hasn't the patience for pretence today.

'Does mummy know you're out?' she snaps.

Favorix's smile falters. 'Stay, Lucretia. Mother's no match for you. She says she'll leave for my uncle's house if I marry you. So marry me. I'll let you do whatever you want.'

In his face she sees an expression of utter devotion. Funny how it appeals on some faces and irritates on others.

'I'll be an important man in this town one day,' he says, and he's probably right.

She stares up at Durnovaria. The forum will soon be busy with merchants and shoppers, men doing business, or plotting politics. She could have fine things from across the empire at a fraction of the cost of what bedraggled goods find their way to the market in Pecunia. She could be the wife of an important man in town. But towns come and go. It's easy to be important one day and the next discover there's nothing important about being dead. But land ... people always need land.

'I'm sure you will,' she says. 'But I'm still going home.'

'Then take me!'

She turns to him in surprise. His hands are twisting and there's a sob in his voice. The horse nudges her again and shakes his head.

'You can't leave your mother,' says Lucretia.

Favorix sags. 'I could speak with my uncle. Maybe he could help. You don't love me yet,' he says. 'Stay. Give me time.'

'I've just broken my betrothal to Deryn,' Lucretia points out. 'It wouldn't look well if I just went off with you. He's your friend; consider the scandal. I'm going home. I miss it.'

'Do you?' Favorix looks startled despite his tears. 'I thought you said it was a pig-hole.'

Lucretia shrugs. She wonders what it'll take to make him leave her alone.

She moves away, hoping Favorix will give up. Oh wonderful, now Deryn is riding out. Any moment now he'll see her with Favorix and say something. For a moment, she wonders whether if Deryn just once indicated that he desired her, rather than just endured her, she might be able to endure him and stay.

But it's not the same. Not the same. Endurance isn't love.

She watches, but Deryn doesn't turn. He doesn't see her. He just carries on down the slope and heads north along the road at speed. Presumably, if he doesn't come back before she leaves, they'll never meet again.

Lucretia brushes down her skirt and indicates to Favorix that he should help her mount the horse. She can manage well enough without him, but it will stop his endless pleas buzzing in her ears.

He's not coming. Galen isn't coming. He took her at her word and he's gone.

He's gone to find the world without her because she wouldn't go too. Because she wouldn't tell him that she loved him.

Well, it's all for the best. There's no wealth in wandering. It's time to go back to her own world without him. And if she can't find love again, she'll get rich on endurance instead.

***

'I need to decide which way to go,' said Deryn. 'We must get down from the wagon a moment.' He took the covers off Lucretia, helped her sit up, then lifted her

266

with a grunt. The wind, laced with rain, was getting up. Branches whipped about as if trying to lose shackles, their damp leaves flung into the air and down into the racing river. Lucretia, huddled under her cloak, tried to reconcile it with her memory of a trundling summer stream and failed. Yet this was the place, wasn't it, where she'd snuck out to talk with Deryn once?

'Do you remember...' They spoke simultaneously.

'After all this time...' Lucretia batted her eyelashes. 'You remembered one of our meeting places.'

'I only brought you here once,' said Deryn. He was still a fine figure of a man; the brooding face which had once bored her was now a challenge. It suggested hidden fires which wasted their time on poetry and art. If they'd married in their youth, she'd have distracted him good and proper from such nonsense.

The wind pulled against the cloak, dragging at the hood. Lucretia was already concerned about what the rain was doing to her make-up. Her wig was something else entirely.

'It's a pretty riverbank,' she said, ignoring the way the water poured and frothed in fury. 'But I wonder if you could take me somewhere with a roof and preferably walls, and maybe a fire, and definitely food.'

'Not yet. We need to plan.' The rain was making Deryn miserable too. When he'd sneaked her out of the back of Galyna's house his face had been bright with conspiracy, but now the spark had dimmed and he couldn't meet her eyes. Where was his backbone?

'Surely we can plan in a tavern?' said Lucretia. 'Or your farmstead. Who's going to question that? If asked, you can say you'd taken me to safety.'

'Hardly that, if the slaves at the farmstead think you killed Nia too.'

'I didn't kill her, and you can tell them so. But anyway, does it matter what they think?'

'It does when they're feeding you.' Deryn still seemed grim, and too close for her liking to the slippery edge of the river. He faced her again. 'I could get you to Lindinis and arrange for lodgings there, explain things to the magistrate. Give you time to get your son to support you.'

'I thought you would escort me all the way home,' she replied. 'Stay with me. See what you missed.'

Deryn shook his head, scanning the landscape. She followed his gaze, but no one could be seen bar some people ambling the other way, back to the town. The road ahead curved into a muddy lane obscured by trees.

'What are we waiting for?' demanded Lucretia. 'I don't see how I can be under arrest for Nia's murder. Even if I did it.'

'I think you're under arrest for Favorix's.'

'Favorix is dead?' She felt the world lurch. For a second the gangly, earnest, annoying youth and the thin, earnest, annoying middle-aged man merged - scheming with her, loving her. It had been nice to be loved. She had even been tempted to stay. How could he be dead? She pulled herself together. 'He was perfectly healthy when I saw him yesterday.'

'When was that?'

'Before closing negotiations with you and Max.'

Deryn turned to her and his face grew paler than ever, then reddened. 'Was he blackmailing Max?'

Lucretia had long since learned to hide any internal squirming. 'Had he anything to blackmail him about?'

Deryn shivered. 'We can't stay here. Perhaps we should go south. They won't be looking for you there.'

'Who? Amicus? The one who got me arrested? I can't abide that man's insolence a moment longer.'

'He should have protected you better.'

'Protected?' She bridled. Deryn was as stupid as Tryssa. 'The only person I need protection from is him.'

'No,' said Deryn, 'it isn't.'

'Just as well he didn't "protect" me otherwise you wouldn't have been able to rescue me.' Lucretia fidgeted. The rain was driving harder and starting to penetrate her cloak. If simpering wasn't going to work she could try ordering him about. It was less effort anyway. 'For which I'm grateful, but now could we get on? And then perhaps when we find lodgings we could pick up where we left off...' *By Morpheus,* she thought, *I'm really not in the mood. I hope he's too tired when we get to wherever he's taking me.* She tilted her head and smirked anyway.

He blinked hard. 'Where we left off?'

'Yes, back when we were barely more than children and I so foolishly rejected you.'

Deryn licked his lips. His breath, she noticed, was coming quickly and his face, despite the chill, was flushed. She stepped closer and put her hands on his chest. Yes, she could feel the racing of his heart through his clothes. *Is it passion or the risk of sudden death?* she thought.

She peered up at him, hoping the rain wasn't marring her face too much.

'Come, don't be so serious,' she murmured. 'Remember how much you once wanted me. Now that we are both very rich, I might even consider moving to Durnovaria after the dust has settled. It has potential.' Her feet were slipping in the mud, forcing her into his arms. 'Oh, Deryn,' she breathed. 'Perhaps we could finally...'

'We seem to be remembering different things,' he said. His voice was cold. 'I recall you running about with Max, tormenting me, teasing Favorix, but none of it meant anything to you. It was just a game. And you

269

never noticed whether any of us actually cared, did you? If someone was hurt, it made you laugh. If someone tried to ignore you, you made things up to lure them back. But all of us were eligible, weren't we? From me - the cousin you'd been sent to marry - to Max who was promised to Eira, to Favorix whose only restriction was his wretched mother and stupid father. It was all a game to you. Because all the time, the one man you wanted was the one you wouldn't let yourself have.'

Lucretia felt herself slip again and let go of her wig to grab Deryn's arms. 'What are you talking about? You met me here and begged me to stay in Durnovaria.'

'Yes,' said Deryn. 'I did. But not for myself.'

'You did it for Favorix?' Lucretia scoffed. 'He would never have been right for me. Any fool could see that.'

'No,' said Deryn. 'I did it for Galen. He was my friend. I never thought he'd settle down. Then he met you and fell in love. He'd have gone to the ends of the earth for you. And for all your pretence, you wanted him just as much.'

'What nonsense. I barely remember him.'

'Perhaps that's true. Whatever passed for a heart has long gone. But then -'

'It turned out he was a thief,' snapped Lucretia. Then Galen's face came into her mind and something made her anger subside. 'Although…'

'I know,' said Deryn. 'I know. That was what made me hate him. I could live with a broken heart - I think I knew it wasn't really broken. But I couldn't believe I'd been so wrong about someone. I never thought Galen could be a thief. Maybe if you'd just listened to me and married him as he was, he wouldn't have gambled and stolen just to be rich enough for a stuck-up little chieftain's daughter from the back of beyond. That's why I hate you. Not for what you did to me, but what you turned him into.'

Lucretia glared. Deryn's eyes stared into hers as they had all those years ago when he'd tried to convince her that he didn't mind losing her. As if that were possible. 'My father would never have countenanced me marrying him.'

'Since when did anyone else's opinion matter, Lucretia? It was just you. You wanted wealth and prestige more than anything, and when he pursued you, you killed him. You stabbed him with that knife and -'

The man was a fool. 'And how do you suggest I buried him?'

He hesitated, frowning. 'You had a wagon full of slaves with you; it wouldn't have been hard. And you killed Favorix because he wanted some of the money you got out of me for himself, and Nia because - do you talk in your sleep? Or was there blood on you?'

'Oh Deryn,' Lucretia tried to force tears but none came. Hopefully the rain would do. 'If you think I killed Galen and Favorix, why didn't you insist I face trial?'

'Because the shame would be too much for Eira, and I can't have that. She's always been delicate, and she's been worn down with misery ever since you came back. Be thankful I didn't leave you to the slaves.' He heaved a sigh and put his hands gently on her shoulders. 'Max suggested I bring you here and explain.' He pointed at the river. 'Max said you'd end yourself and save everyone from the dishonour.' The last word trembled on his tongue as if he were thinking of something else. 'Dishonour,' he muttered. 'Misdirection.' He frowned.

'But...' Lucretia swallowed. For a brief horrifying second she tried to imagine the world without her. It was unthinkable. 'I didn't murder anyone. I'm

271

innocent. Deryn, you must believe me, or you wouldn't have rescued me. Because that's what you've done really, isn't it? You just suggested taking me to Lindinis so I had the chance to go home.'

'If not you -' The rain was in Deryn's eyes. He swallowed. 'I'll tell Max you begged me to give you the chance to make your own amends.'

'Thank you. I'll make it worth your while.'

She stood on tiptoe to kiss him and their feet slithered. Deryn tried to hold her at arm's length and step away, but before he could someone rushed from behind the trees. All Lucretia could make out was a whirl of linen and light brown hair, and something glinting in the gloomy light.

'Leave him alone!' Eira shrieked. 'You can't break his heart again! You don't deserve anyone. I cursed you with misery when you ruined our lives. Yet you thrived, and came back to destroy me!' Her arm flailed, stabbing.

Deryn let go of Lucretia and reached for his sister. 'Eira! What are you doing?'

'Lucretia deserves to die. There must be blood. Nemesis demands it! I can't be cleansed without Lucretia's blood!' She wrenched her hand away from Deryn and lunged at Lucretia again. Over the sounds of rain and wind and rushing water came the sound of galloping.

'Nemesis? Cleansing?' cried Deryn. 'What are you talking about?'

'Eira!' It was Max. 'Stop! Enough! How did you get here?'

Eira stabbed at Lucretia and Deryn caught his sister from behind to restrain her. Max, running forward, slipped, crashed into Lucretia and fell to the mud with her.

'Why did no one want *me*?' cried Eira, flailing the knife at her husband. Deryn pulled her back.

'I do!' shouted Max, struggling to his feet. 'I always have.'

'You sneaked off with Lucretia then, and you've sneaked here to meet her now!'

'That's not what it was - is - you don't understand!'

Another horse galloped up and Lucretia looked into the face of Tryssa, sitting in front of Amicus.

'And him!' shrieked Eira. 'I told him she wasn't worth a forged *as*. I told him only *I* would make him happy...'

'Who?' Deryn struggled as Eira squirmed in his arms.

Her face was bright with fury, hair blowing into her eyes.

'Galen,' said Tryssa, slipping from the horse. 'You loved him.'

'And he was fond of me. He was! He was!'

'But you were betrothed to Max.'

Eira shook her head. 'I'd have left everything for Galen. I'd have gone barefoot. I'd have faced disgrace. He'd have loved me eventually, it was only a matter of time. But then Lucretia came. She was so busy flirting she didn't even notice I'd taken that knife. Or else she couldn't remember which pile of long grass she'd been rolling in with which boy when she lost it.'

'Excuse me,' said Lucretia, squirming in the mire, slipping every time she nearly managed to stand. 'Some of us weren't that stupid.'

Eira spat at Lucretia and twisted again.

'Isn't anyone going to help me?' muttered Lucretia, crawling towards the road.

'Eira,' said Tryssa. 'It's time to give up and come back to Durnovaria.'

'Galen *talked* to me, though,' Eira was oblivious, her words bitter. 'I was a little pet to confide in. When he came to talk I thought that finally he'd seen me properly, and then he said, "Lucretia loves me as much as I love her, but she's going home because her father won't approve."' She snorted. '"It's breaking her heart," he said. As if she had a heart to break.'

'And what happened then?' said Amicus.

'Then he said, "I've arranged to meet her the morning she goes, and I'll talk her round. Or cadge a lift north to see her father. She won't be able to say no."'

No-one spoke. The wind and rain battered them, and Eira stopped squirming. Amicus reached out and took the knife from her hands.

'But you suggested something different, didn't you?' said Tryssa. 'You told him to meet her earlier, in the grove. The day before Lucretia was due to leave.'

'What the...' Lucretia pushed herself up on her elbows.

Eira laughed. 'Oh Lucretia, if Galen could see you down in the mud like a pig. Not so alluring now, are you?'

'Eira,' said Amicus. 'Come back to town with us. Let's talk in the dry.'

'Hush.' Deryn murmured. 'Don't say anything more just now. Let's-'

Eira sneered. 'It's too late. I don't know how she's worked it out, but it's true. Yes Tryssa. I told Galen exactly that. I sneaked out early dressed in Deryn's clothes, I took a horse and met him at the grove.'

'But that's not what you said at the time, or since,' said Deryn. 'Is it, Max? Max?'

'Stop it,' said Max, slipping as he reached forward. 'Stop it, Eira. Shh. I promise I'll look after you, just

274

like I always have, but you need to stop talking.' He smoothed his wife's hair away from her face.

Eira twisted out of Deryn's arms. Her rain-sodden cloak flapped and her hair draggled out of its pins. Even fury couldn't bring her long-dead eyes to life, but all the same she stared unfocussed into another day and another place, and the rain and her tears mingled. She screamed into the heavens, 'Nemesis! Why is it me you're punishing?'

'The only one punishing you is yourself,' said Tryssa. 'Because you killed the one person who mattered, and you never meant to.'

'What?' cried Deryn. 'Not Eira! No!'

Eira sobbed and put her chin up. 'It wasn't my fault. It was Lucretia's.'

'You killed him,' said Tryssa. 'You tried to tell him that Lucretia was nothing, that you were the one he needed. What happened next? Did he look on you with pity?'

'He laughed.' Eira fell silent.

Deryn hesitated. '*You* couldn't have killed him, Eira. I don't understand why you're saying all this, but it's not true. Whoever killed him buried him. You couldn't have done that. Not on your own.'

Eira stared past him, still focused on a long-past summer's morning. 'I had Lucretia's knife. I didn't mean to use it on *him*. I meant to threaten killing myself if he didn't listen.'

Tryssa put a hand on Eira's arm. 'But you did use it on him and then you threw it away and tried to save his life, didn't you? Because you had never, ever meant to kill him.'

Eira wrenched away. 'I didn't know what to do… We fell to the ground and he died in my arms. It was the only real embrace we ever had. I would have killed myself but the knife… The knife had disappeared, and

275

then Max arrived -' She focussed on her husband as if she had only just realised he was there. 'Why didn't you just help me finish myself then? Why didn't you realise that was the only way you could really help?'

'I did what I could, Eira. And I love you. You've never realised that. I did it all for you.'

She shook her head. 'You? You were useless. The man in the grass who saw it all - you couldn't even kill him properly. You told me after, that you'd dumped his corpse on a ship. You said he was dead but he wasn't, was he? And somehow he came back. All these years later he came back as a stinking beggar.'

'I -' muttered Max, his face grey, 'I didn't -'

'And because you didn't kill him properly he turned up all these years later and followed me back from the temple telling me I owed him, sneaking round the back of the house with his wretched begging bowl. So I had to send Nia out with poisoned food myself. And then she started fussing about a curse and telling the guard how she'd caused his death.' A flicker of doubt crossed her face. She focussed on Max with a frown. 'Now I think of it, why was he there all those years ago in the first place?'

'He was following Galen,' breathed Max. 'Galen owed him all that money and -'

'Enough!' said Amicus. 'It's time to give up, Max. *You* were the one Blue was after. Perhaps he followed Eira to put pressure on you. Or perhaps he just followed you following her. Or more likely, you arranged to meet him there not knowing what Eira was doing. Come away from the river bank. Come back to town. I'll see you're both treated fairly.'

'Max?' Eira shook off Tryssa's gentle hand.

'No.' Max breathed, imploring. 'Amicus has it wrong. He was following Galen. He was -'

'No,' said Tryssa. 'He wasn't. Two young men were being trained to work with the quaestor. Only one was in serious debt.'

Eira's face flamed. 'Max? *You* were the thief? You traitor!' Tears flowed from eyes which had come to life at last. 'It's true isn't it? And I never realised. All those years Galen's been blamed for that missing money, and who made us believe it? The rich boy - you! Even Deryn believed the lies you fed into our minds. Even Amicus. Even Lucretia.' Her voice dropped to a whisper. 'Even me. So much for loving him.' She lifted her face to the skies again and shouted, 'Nemesis, you were right. *I'm* the one who should be punished.'

Before anyone could move, she turned round and leapt into the swollen river.

'No!' Deryn and Max both rushed forward. Deryn slipped and fell on the bank but Max flung himself into the water after his wife, his arms flailing as he tried to reach her, until tangled together they sank below the churning surface.

'Eira never did have a grip on things,' said Lucretia, as the last of her things were packed away. 'Any sensible woman would have kept her mouth shut. There was no proof the skeleton was Galen. No-one of importance cared about the beggar. And as for Max, what a fool. Most people thought Favorix had committed suicide. No-one would ever have convicted me of anything. He always did indulge Eira. Can't imagine Porcius fussing over me like that.'

'Hardly,' said Tryssa. 'But I'm surprised you're sorry about Max. He was the one trying to get people to think you killed Favorix.'

'As if I'd go out in the rain and stab someone. I don't like being messy. Someone like you wouldn't understand that.'

Tryssa laughed. 'You never did explain why you wanted "someone like me" to come down here with you.'

Lucretia fidgeted. 'I don't have to explain myself.'

'I wonder if you thought you might need me on your side.'

'It's the second year I've been nearly murdered or arrested. I'm not sure if you're saving me or causing it.'

Tryssa shrugged, then gave a soft smile. 'At least, after all this time, you know Galen is decently at rest.'

Lucretia put out her bottom lip. The jewelled knife, clean and polished, lay on the table before her. She reached out her hand but didn't quite touch it. 'I can barely remember him.'

'So you say.'

'And no-one would ever have paid Blue the beggar any attention. Whatever Max did while trying to kill

278

him had sent him mad. I doubt Blue even knew why he went to the house.'

'You're probably right. In a way Max *had* killed him; his mind, not his body.'

'They weren't good at killing people, were they? Look at Nia. She wasn't dead at all. And me - Eira tried to poison me at least twice, and she only managed to poison herself.'

'You're right. They weren't.'

Lucretia stared down at her hand. Galen's ring fitted her finger better than Berenice's, and the girl couldn't stomach it anymore. She thought of the grove. Storms had wrenched most of the leaves from the trees and now it was, somehow, empty.

'The skeleton,' she said, 'you saw it. Could you tell if he was properly dead before they buried him?'

Tryssa hesitated and Lucretia inwardly cursed. Why couldn't the woman lie if she wasn't sure?

'No. But I imagine Eira tried everything to save him, Lucretia, so I suspect you needn't worry.'

'I wasn't worrying.'

Lucretia cleared her throat and diverted her thoughts to her ruined wig. The mud had finally been removed, but the tresses had had to be unbraided, and there was no telling what it would look like if anyone tried to reconstruct it. 'Do you think I could suit long flowing hair?'

'You're not fifteen,' said Tryssa. 'You could give it to Contractes, though. He could use it for one of his actors when they need to play a girl. If he doesn't hire a girl, of course.'

'Ridiculous man.' Lucretia shook her head and handed the wig over. 'Olivarius is refusing to escort me home.'

'Amicus has offered him a job,' said Tryssa. 'You'll be fine with Petros. He'll bring Camilla back to join

279

Olivarius. Berenice will be glad to meet her. She needs a friend.'

'How will Camilla ever afford a mosaic and fine clothes as the wife of a secretary?'

Tryssa rolled her eyes. 'There's more to life than mosaics and fine clothes.'

'I can't think what. And Camilla never used to think so.'

'People change.'

'I never have.'

The other woman's scrutiny unnerved Lucretia.

'I think you changed that summer,' Tryssa said, at last. 'You left Pecunia expecting to fall in love with Deryn, and then you came home and eventually married Porcius. In between, you fell in love but turned your back on it. The girl who went away and the girl who came back were subtly different.'

'I could never have married Deryn. We'd have made each other utterly miserable.'

'I'm talking about Galen.'

Lucretia looked at the old ring again. 'I'm not Camilla. We'd have been miserable after a while too.'

'You and Porcius weren't exactly love-birds.'

Lucretia lifted her chin and contemplated herself in the mirror. 'He left me to my own devices and didn't interfere in the running of things. Galen wanted…' She shuddered a little.

'He wanted a soulmate?' suggested Tryssa.

Lucretia pulled another face. 'Something ridiculous like that.'

'Some people prefer a soulmate to a mosaic. Some people will risk everything for the one they love. All it takes is a little courage to step into the unknown.'

Lucretia put the mirror down and glanced once more at the jewelled knife. 'More fool them,' she said.

'Passion fades and then, if you're poor, what have you got left?'

'Possibilities,' said Tryssa.

'Changing the subject,' said Lucretia, 'I hope your stuff won't take up too much space in the wagon. I'll be bringing back Riona, remember.'

'I'm not returning to Pecunia,' said Tryssa.

Lucretia boggled. 'Why? If you're not there and Camilla's not there, who's going to look after everyone?'

'Lys is fully capable. I'm still training Sila, remember, and I always intended to stay through the winter anyway. I like it here. I want to do some exploring - maybe have a meal in a tavern in Vademlutra.'

'Has everyone gone mad?' said Lucretia.

Riona entered with Lucretia's cloak. It had taken a day of laundering and three of drying but the mud was gone. The girl had a skip in her step and a wide smile.

Lucretia's eyes narrowed. 'Have you got wind? I hope you're not going to grin like that all the way to Pecunia.'

'No, Mistress,' said Riona. 'I'm not coming to Pecunia with you. Mistress Berenice says she won't sell me after all. She says I'm to stay with her at Master Deryn's house and then go with her when she marries Master Ieuan.'

'That's ridiculous,' said Lucretia. 'Why does no-one think of me? What am I supposed to do? Am I supposed to take Nia even though she stole wine meant for me and drank it?'

'And thereby saved your life,' said Tryssa.

Lucretia frowned. 'Well I suppose I should thank her in a way, but I do hope she's learned not to be so clumsy. I wonder what Berenice will want for her. I presume I can knock a bit off the price in the circumstances.'

'Ah,' said Tryssa. 'Now there might be a small problem with that.'

***

'Going where?' said Dun. 'You can't leave me.'

Gris was grinning and bouncing. 'Lady Berenice has freed Nia and given us a bit of land. She says it's only right.'

'Yeah but you can't leave *me*.'

'So lodge with us. Her dad's coming too. We'll be a kind of family. Who knows, maybe you and me could start our own business selling stuff off the side of ponies.'

'Off the side of ponies?'

'You know what I mean. Take it on ponies to the forum instead of lugging it ourselves.'

Dun grunted. 'I might go back to Mum's.' He thought for a bit. 'Or maybe not. Where's this bit of land, then?'

'Well,' Gris sucked his teeth a little. 'Thing is, I could do with your help really. We'll need to clear it before building.'

'Clear it?'

'Few stones, a coupla trees…'

'You gotta be joking. Not the grove?'

'That'll be part of the land, but we won't live in the grove itself,' clarified Gris. 'Just next to it. I'll feel sorta protected. It sorta feels like home, we've spent so much time there.'

'You reckon?'

'Yeah,' said Gris. 'Cos just think, if we hadn't found that skellington, I wouldn't have Nia, would I? So it all sorta worked out in the end.'

Dun scratched his chin. 'No-one will mind us digging there if it's yours, will they?' he said.

Gris pondered. 'I suppose not. It'll be mine.'

'And all them sacrifices, like I said, just deeper down. Princes, not slaves… Bronze torcs, amber, lapis-wotsit, gold, maybe…'

Gris brightened. 'I like your thinking Dun. I like your thinking.'

Dun clapped him on the shoulder. 'So what's keeping us? We got work to do. Where's them shovels?'

Acknowledgements, historical note and bibliography

With many thanks to Liz Hedgecock for her wonderful editing and honest input, and to my lovely beta readers Christine Downes, Val Portelli, Paul Savile and Gosia Thornton; to Liz and Val for encouraging me throughout the drafting process and to my mother and mother-in-law who kept asking when the sequel to Murder Britannica was coming out.

This is not a historical text book but Durnovaria was a real place which became Dorchester where you can see wonderful relics of Roman Dorset in the County Museum, visit a Roman Town House and also Maumbury Rings where the amphitheatre was. I hope the shades of ancient citizens are not too put out by my use of artistic license. The stone circle was inspired by The Nine Stones near Winterbourne Abbas. From the story's point of view it's in the completely the wrong place, which is very inconsiderate of Deryn and Eira's ancestors.

I recommend the following books and if I've misinterpreted any information it's entirely my fault.

Legends and Folklore of Dorset by Robert Hesketh

Suburban Life in Roman Durnovaria by Mike Trevarthen

The Roman Cookery Book by Apicus, Barbara Flower and Elisabeth Rosenbaum

The Romans by Bill Putnam

About Paula Harmon

Paula Harmon was born in North London but her father relocated the family every two years until they settled in South Wales when Paula was eight. She graduated from Chichester University before making her home in Gloucestershire and then Dorset where she has lived since 2005. She is a civil servant, married with two children at university.

https://paulaharmondownes.wordpress.com
https://twitter.com/Paula_S_Harmon
https://www.facebook.com/pg/paulaharmonwrites

Books available from: http://viewauthor.at/ PHAuthorpage

Murder Britannica
It's AD 190 in Southern Britain. Lucretia won't let her get-rich-quick scheme be undermined by minor things like her husband's death. But a gruesome discovery leads wise-woman Tryssa to start asking awkward questions.

The Cluttering Discombobulator
The story of one man's battle against common sense and the family caught up in the chaos around him.

Kindling
Secrets and mysteries, strangers and friends. Stories as varied and changing as British skies.

The Advent Calendar
Christmas without the hype - stories for midwinter.

The Case of the Black Tulips (first in the 'Caster & Fleet Mysteries) (with Liz Hedgecock)

When Katherine Demeray opens a letter, little does she imagine it will lead her to join forces with socialite Connie Swift, racing against time to solve mysteries and right wrongs.

Weird and Peculiar Tales (with Val Portelli)

Short stories from this world and beyond.

The Quest

In a parallel universe, dragons are used for fuel and the people who understand them are feared as spies and traitors.

The Seaside Dragon (a book for children)

Laura and Jane expect a weekend break without wifi. They don't expect to have to rescue their parents from terrible danger.

Printed in Great Britain
by Amazon

34184778R00173